THE HEALER'S MANTLE

WRAK-AYYA: THE AGE OF SHADOWS
BOOK TWO

LEIGH ROBERTS

DRAGON WINGS PRESS

CONTENTS

Editing by Joy Sephton http://www.justemagine.biz
Cover design by Cherie Fox http://www.cheriefox.com

Sexual activities or events in this book are intended for adults.

ISBN: 978-1-951528-07-2 (ebook)
ISBN: 978-1-951528-10-2 (paperback)

Dedication

For my readers, who haven't lost the ability to wonder...

What If?

CHAPTER 1

Icy winds blew across the High Rocks. In warmer months, the People mostly spent their days outside; planting, harvesting, hunting, and playing with offspring. But now winter had descended, and many of the People's activities had moved inside. The cold months provided more time for socializing while the People worked in pleasant companionship on the tasks for which they did not have time during spring planting and late summer harvest. Most of these activities took place in the Great Chamber, the largest region of the cave system they called Kthama. It was here that shared events took place—meals, meetings, celebrations, rituals.

From his usual solitary table Khon'Tor, Leader of the People of the High Rocks, glanced across at the High

Protector, Acaraho, who instead of sitting with his watchers and guards had been invited by Khon'Tor to join him.

The two had finished eating and were discussing the distribution of tasks for the next few days. As their conversation wound down, Khon'Tor broached the subject of Whitespeak with Acaraho.

"You have connections. If there is anyone who can help me with this task, it is you.

"Adia believes the Waschini offspring should learn Whitespeak, and I have promised to provide for whatever training he needs. But I admit I have no idea how to provide a Whitespeak teacher."

When he invoked the sacred Rah-hora with Adia, the People's Healer, Khon'Tor had promised to provide a way for Oh'Dar to learn Whitespeak, and she had agreed because she was firmly convinced that learning the language of his people was somehow critical to Oh'Dar's future. As her repayment for this, Khon'Tor had demanded that Adia keep her silence about his brutal mating of her Without Her Consent.

Therefore, Khon'Tor's power, his reputation, his place as Leader of the People of the High Rocks—all the things that mattered to him—lay in Adia's hands and therefore hung on his ability to find a Whitespeak teacher for the Waschini offspring.

"I believe I know of someone," said Acaraho. "I would be glad to make inquiries for you. However, I imagine this person would need to have considerable access to the offspring for some time. Arrangements would have to be made to compensate her and her people for taking her away from her normal day-to-day responsibilities."

It was Acaraho who had encouraged Adia to approach Khon'Tor with her request. He would not have done so without being confident he could meet this need for her, though, unaware of the extent of Khon'Tor's act against Adia, the High Protector had no idea how distorted the response to her request had been.

"Whatever it takes. Whatever you need to provide for this to happen, I will ensure it. You have my word," replied Khon'Tor.

Acaraho, not letting on that he already knew of Adia's request, asked, "Have you spoken to the Healer about this? The teacher's presence will most likely affect her daily activities as well as that of her Helper Nadiwani."

"I have not. But I know she will accept the offer. You may approach her once you have a better idea of the arrangements. Thank you, Commander."

If Acaraho had not believed that Khon'Tor was responsible in some way for Adia's injuries, he might have allowed himself to trust the Leader—this Alpha alongside whom he had served for many years.

Khon'Tor frowned as he left the Great Chamber. Acaraho seemed to have no care in the world, which reminded Khon'Tor that he had even more to worry about than just finding a teacher.

His mate, Hakani was with offspring by another male. He could not put her aside for fear she would broadcast that emasculating news, but neither could he endure her having the upper hand—and precisely because he could say nothing, her offspring would be his heir one day.

He shook his head to clear it. One thing at a time. He was a driven Leader who thought nothing of taking advantage. Having dealt with Adia, he would be free to turn his mind to his troublesome mate. With the Healer encumbered by the Rah-hora, he would find a way to control Hakani, too.

The night Khon'Tor had announced that his mate was with offspring, Nadiwani and Adia had stayed awake, too wound up to sleep. They discussed Nadiwani's ideas for Oh'Dar's education. Now, knowing Khon'Tor was supporting whatever the offspring needed, the females added more to their list. At the top was the matter of teaching the offspring Whitespeak.

The next morning, Acaraho sent word to Adia that he wished to speak with her. Traditionally, no one was allowed in the Healer's Quarters except with the Healer's permission. Before Oh'Dar's rescue, this had never been an issue but since then had become a fairly frequent occurrence.

Acaraho was happy at the excuse to see her again; he knew she would be pleased about the Whitespeak teacher and smiled at the thought of her eyes lighting up at the news.

Because Khon'Tor had removed Acaraho from her daily protection, he'd had to resort to over-hearing pieces of news about her and Oh'Dar during the evening mealtime.

The older females who enjoyed preparing food for others had an appreciative following made mostly of unpaired bachelors, paired males who did not live with their mates, and an occasional guard or watcher coming off duty. Acaraho now joined this group for its gossip if he was not sitting with Khon'Tor or First Guard, Awan.

Now, at last, he would be able to see her face-to-face. Although no longer in his temporary capacity as her personal guard, in his role of High Protector, it was not a breach of protocol to address her directly.

Adia sent a return message that he should come to the Healer's Quarters. She felt her heartbeat flare at the thought of Acaraho's visit. He had been a daily part of her life for some time, and she missed his comforting presence. Now she would be seeing him without the constraints of his assignment, which had kept him silent and removed. Now, they would be able to converse freely.

And she had no idea what to say.

A web of tunnels spread out from Kthama's Great Chamber, leading to living spaces and other smaller working and gathering areas. Some of the tunnels led to the lower levels where there were still more quarters of varying sizes. Living quarters were private, and many had a stone slab blocking the entrance, with a rock placed near the doorway that others could slam against it to request entry. Some simply had an open doorway. It was rude to enter another's living quarters without an invitation, or even to glance inside while passing.

Filled with anticipation, Acaraho approached Adia's quarters. He squared his shoulders, took a deep breath, and cracked the announcement rock on the stone door. In a moment, she was standing before him. He looked down at her, and her beautiful smiling eyes met his. It hit him again how attractive she was. "Hello, Adia," he said softly. "It is good to see you again."

Their eyes locked together for a moment. Then he let his eyes trace the outline of her face, the curve of the dark hair flowing over her shoulders, her dark eyelashes.

Seconds ticked by. Finally, Acaraho found the presence of mind to break the spell, "May I come in?" he asked, nodding toward the interior.

"Of course. Of course, please," said Adia, stepping out of the way so he could move past her into the room.

Nadiwani was playing with Oh'Dar in the middle of the floor, and she looked up as Adia showed Acaraho in.

"Hello," she said warmly. "Today, we are working on Oh'Dar's Handspeak vocabulary. He is learning the signs for some of the main plants we use in our medicines and healing powders. Ginseng, Goldenseal, Lavender, Willow Tree Bark—"

Acaraho squinted at Nadiwani, "He is learning all that already?" he asked a bit incredulously.

Nadiwani laughed, "No, not really. He understands *Mama* and *eat*, though. We are just having fun," she chuckled.

Acaraho smiled at Nadiwani then said to Adia, "I have been sent by Khon'Tor to make arrangements with you regarding a Whitespeak teacher for the offspring."

"Khon'Tor has found one?" she asked.

Acaraho could not help himself. At seeing how happy she was, he had to let her know he was the source. "I know of someone at the Brothers' village," he continued.

"But before I make the arrangements, I need to speak to you about what those might be. I am assuming that this teacher would have to spend a fair amount of time with Oh'Dar every day. This will impact your day-to-day activities."

"Is the person a male or a female?" asked Nadiwani, looking up from where Oh'Dar was busily making a mess of all the plants.

"It is a female. She would have separate living arrangements, but she would be at your disposal otherwise for as much time as you need her. Again, I have not yet gone ahead because I wanted to speak with you first," he reiterated.

Finally, Adia recovered her senses.

"Thank you, Acaraho," she managed to get out, her voice almost stumbling at his name. "Whatever arrangements you have to make, please do so. Nadiwani and I will adapt; just let us know."

"Great news, yes?" Nadiwani was trying to break Adia out of her trance.

"Yes. Absolutely," replied Adia. She had heard brief mention that there might be a woman in the Brothers' village who had recently returned from being raised among the Waschini, but she did not know much more. It made sense that such a person would know Whitespeak. She walked with Acaraho back to the doorway and reluctantly closed the stone door behind him.

Not much escaped Acaraho; he was astute at collecting information from his surroundings. He had noticed Adia's discomfort and was secretly pleased. Her eyes had widened when she saw him. Her lips had parted ever so slightly. He knew her heart rate was elevated—he could see her nervousness in how she held herself. He was pleased that his presence appeared to have the same effect on her as hers did on him. But Acaraho admonished himself the minute the thought surfaced.

She is the Healer. She can never be paired. You are going down a path that promises only disappointment and heartache at the end of it. Get ahold of yourself. His brows knitted tightly together.

The best I can hope for is a lifetime of unfulfilled daydreams and restless nights. But it's too late. Even though I can never be with Adia as I want, I must find a way to get back into her life.

Both stood there for a moment—Acaraho on one side of the closed door and Adia on the other, each lost in their own thoughts—each registering but not wanting to admit how deeply the other affected them.

Nadiwani had not missed a thing either.

This promises disaster no matter how you look at it, she thought to herself. *Perhaps it is best that Acaraho is no longer charged with her protection. They would do best to avoid contact with each other as much as possible.*

She shook her head. *It is probably already too late. They have allowed a connection to develop between them.*

Acaraho immediately sent word to Is'Taqa, Second Chief of the Brothers, that he wished to speak with him and the next day the High Protector was on his way.

Is'Taqa was concerned about the news that Acaraho wanted to meet. He had plenty of time to think as he walked to the meeting place, approximately halfway between the two settlements.

I wonder if this has anything to do with Khon'Tor's attack on Adia. I wish I had never seen it. I respected Khon'Tor, and I had no idea he was capable of such an abomination.

Is'Taqa had kept his silence other than confiding in his sister, the Brothers' Medicine Woman, Ithua. The nature of Khon'Tor's crimes, if known, would split the People and destroy any peace for generations to come. And to bring such charges against the greatest Leader of the largest community of Sasquatch in existence was to bring an end to the generations of goodwill between his people and theirs. They did not interfere in the affairs of each other's tribes.

"I have heard nothing to indicate that Adia has

come forward about what Khon'Tor did to her," Is'Taqa confided to Ithua. "I know she was conscious for the first blow; after that, I am not sure. Maybe she has no memory of it, or maybe she is keeping it secret for the same reasons I cannot come forward. Perhaps she is no more willing than I am to sacrifice so much, despite how despicable his crimes. A matter of this significance would be for the High Council to decide."

"In a war between our two people, there is no doubt who would be the victor. We are more agile, more dexterous. But they have a distinct advantage in size, strength, and numbers. If a conflict ensued, we would pay a high price," she replied.

Is'Taqa let out a deep sigh. "If and when Adia ever comes forward, I will speak up and bear witness to what I saw. But their culture is built on the predictable, the repeatable. They are many things, but adaptable is not one of them. Change comes slowly and hard for the Sasquatch."

He arrived at the appointed place in time for Acaraho's arrival and heard him as the high brush and saplings were parted noisily down the incline.

"Greetings," called Is'Taqa across the distance.

Acaraho raised his hand in acknowledgment.

Though not exactly on a friend-to-friend basis, they were counterparts in their own tribes. They shared an understanding of the importance of order and structure and shared mutual respect and trust. Neither saw much benefit in altercation and believed the deterrents of a strong defense and good relations to be a better approach.

Closing the distance between them, Acaraho found a place to sit.

Is'Taqa imagined that because of his size, Acaraho sat to avoid any appearance of presenting an unfair advantage or creating an atmosphere of coercion. *It is what I would do in his place.*

Acaraho began, "I know you are aware of the presence among the People of the Waschini offspring who was brought to us by the Healer, Adia. Khon'Tor has ordered that the offspring should learn Whitespeak and has sent me to ask your assistance."

Is'Taqa knew immediately of whom Acaraho was speaking.

Despite what the High Council had heard, and what Khon'Tor asserted, not every Waschini was evil. Long ago, a group of them had passed through the Brothers' land. They wanted only to make passage and were gentle, wishing no one any harm. When one of the Brothers' warrior scouts came across them, they were in terrible shape. Their supplies were depleted, and they were miles from their destination with little idea of how to make it the rest of the way. Many of them were sick from exhaustion and covered in cuts and rashes.

The Brothers took all the Waschini under their

care. Though not all of them survived, once the health of those who did had returned, the Brothers replenished the supplies and materials the travelers would need for the rest of their trip. But they had a long journey ahead and were ignorant of the difficult terrain they had yet to cross.

Recognizing that without help they would most likely not survive, the Brothers sent one of their maidens with them as a guide, along with one of the braves for her protection. She was an exceptional scout and knew well the path they needed to take. As fate would have it, over the long hard journey, she and one of the Waschini fell in love. The maiden was torn as she loved her life among her people, but as ways of the heart go, she found she could not leave him. They soon married and produced a daughter. The brave returned with the news of what had happened.

For many years, the couple lived together in the White Man's village amid great controversy. Finally, no longer able to bear the animosity and the threats leveled against them, the mother and daughter had recently returned to the Brothers. Not long after, the mother passed, and Ithua had taken on the daughter, who showed promise as an apprentice. It was this young woman's assistance that Acaraho had come to secure. Having been raised among the Waschini for many years, she was fluent in Whitespeak.

"You are speaking of Honovi."

"Yes," replied Acaraho. "I realize it would be a

hardship for her to leave home. And we do not know how long she would need to stay with us. Khon'Tor is willing to meet whatever compensation you and she wish in return for this great favor."

"I will speak to her, and Ogima Adoeete," said Is'Taqa, referring to the High Chief of the Brothers. Is'Taqa knew of Honovi. She had often caught his eye, but he felt it was too soon since her mother's death to make his interest known. He now wondered how long it would be before he might see her again.

"Honovi has a helping heart; I know she will be glad to assist the People's Healer in this matter."

With that, the two spoke a bit longer about logistics and then parted, making arrangements to meet again in a few days. Unless something went wrong, the next time they met, Honovi would be present and Acaraho would be bringing her back to live among the People for some time.

Acaraho returned and informed Khon'Tor that he would shortly know whether the Whitespeak teacher would be coming, and then sent word to Adia to the same effect. As much as he wanted to deliver the news to her in person—to seize any chance to see her again—he had much to do in arranging quarters for the teacher.

Acaraho had never met Honovi, but he knew that coming to live here, for however long it was, would

be a significant change for her and no doubt stress-
ful. The People did not always realize their larger
size. For a Brother to be around one of the People
could be intimidating in itself. To face a roomful,
often with most line of sight obliterated, could be
disconcerting even to a warrior such as Is'Taqa.

Honovi looked up as Is'Taqa called her name, and
trotted over to speak with him, hiding a smile.

"Honovi. I have a request for you. It comes from
the People. Their Healer, Adia, needs help. I am sure
you have heard of her through my sister. Adia
rescued an abandoned Waschini child a while ago
and is raising it among them."

"Yes, I saw the infant when she brought him here
on the day she found him. A Waschini child, being
raised with the Sasquatch."

"The Healer is requesting your help."

"*My* help?" she asked.

"Yes. The Healer wants the child to learn Whitespeak. They do not anticipate him ever leaving their
community but feel it is his right. You are the only
one I know of who could help out. But it would mean
you would have to go and live there for a while. They
said they would trade whatever you wanted if you
would help them."

Honovi thought for a moment. *The poor child, he
has no idea of how different he will be and the challenges*

ahead. I can certainly relate to the difficulties that will face him.

"I would be honored to help. But what of Ithua? I am her apprentice. And when would I have to leave?"

"Thank you, Honovi. I have already spoken to my sister, and she is prepared to do this if it is what you want. You will, no doubt, make trips back here from time to time. And I am sure you will find it an—interesting—experience. We have lived together in harmony for many generations. You may find their size a little intimidating at first. But please, above all, remember they are peaceful."

He paused. "Are you afraid?"

"Well I was not until you said that!" and they both laughed.

The appointed day came soon enough. Acaraho had made the arrangements for Honovi's quarters and her care. He left Kthama and made his way to the meeting spot while Khon'Tor, having such a huge stake in the matter, waited anxiously for news of Acaraho's return.

Honovi packed a few things to take with her for her personal care. She placed her cleansing items, changes of clothing, and a comb for her long black hair into a woven carrying satchel. The comb was one she had brought back with her from her childhood. It was beautiful—carved from a variegated piece of wood and polished to a high shine. It was her most prized possession. She also packed some special dried food items that she was not sure the People would have.

Honovi sighed. She did not know how long she would be there but knew it would be a while. The child would not learn Whitespeak overnight, so she had prepared for a lengthy stay, though, as Is'Taqa had pointed out, she anticipated some going back and forth.

Is'Taqa and Honovi stood waiting for Acaraho to appear. Holding her satchel tightly, Honovi assured herself she was reasonably prepared. What she was not prepared for, however, was the magnificent sight of Acaraho coming down the hillside toward them.

Honovi stood frozen as she watched this giant easily part the branches and saplings in his way. He was muscular, broad-chested, and transported on legs that rippled with strength. He was mesmerizing —she had underestimated how big he would be. Had she not known who it was, she might have hidden behind Is'Taqa, overwhelmed. Acaraho was far larger than she expected and a little frightening in motion, though at the same time eerily attractive.

The young woman had heard stories about other Sasquatch in the farthest reaches of the land. They were said to be even taller than the People. Bulkier and thicker featured, their hands lacked delicacy. And their language was said to be more guttural than the People's. But they were still all considered Sasquatch.

She did not find this hard to understand. The variation in the birds that inhabited the region was a perfect example—differences in size, color, type of feathers, even habitats, and song. That the Sasquatch should have differences among their kind was not too hard to grasp.

Is'Taqa waved at Acaraho, then turned to her and said, "Relax Honovi. Neither Chief Ogima Adoeete nor I would put you in a position of danger. Remember. You are as safe with Acaraho as you are back in our village—indeed, you are safer."

Honovi took a deep breath and dropped her shoulders. After all, this was the renowned High Protector Acaraho of the People of the High Rocks. She had heard stories of him told around their fires at night.

Acaraho came to a stop about four feet from Honovi. He greeted Is'Taqa first, and then the young woman. Is'Taqa then made the formal introductions, trying to make it as normal as possible for Honovi to be standing here speaking with one of the People.

Acaraho then spoke. "Honovi—forgive my informality—I am not sure how else to address you other than Teacher. I have made arrangements for your living quarters, and I will take you there if you are ready. Once you are settled, I will introduce you to the Healer and her Helper. I realize this will be a big adjustment for you."

He is so open and recognizes that this might be hard for me. I can see why Is'Taqa and Chief Ogima trust him.

Having this kind of frank conversation with someone in his position of authority was a great comfort to Honovi, who felt that she, in turn, could be candid with Acaraho.

"I am ready to join you, High Protector of the People," she replied. I am pleased to be of service to your people, our friends and neighbors." She then leaned down and picked up her bag as a signal that she was ready whenever he was.

Is'Taqa and Acaraho took leave of each other.

"Tell me when you decide what we must provide in return for this great service," said Acaraho before they parted ways.

"Ogima Adoeete has asked that she might be taught in the ways of the People's Healer, to whatever extent Adia feels comfortable and has time. Honovi is Ithua's apprentice, so this would be a help to the Brothers, but she has asked nothing for herself," answered Is'Taqa.

Acaraho nodded and replied, "I will pass this information on to Khon'Tor and Adia."

With that, he relieved Honovi of her bag, and they made their way upward over the rough terrain. Acaraho cleared the way, decreasing his speed to match Honovi's much slower pace. Had it not been improper, he could easily have carried her, saving a great deal of time. But he would never suggest something so informal nor as intimate as to touch one of the Brothers, and especially a female.

It was nearly twilight by the time Acaraho and Honovi reached Kthama. Word had spread of her impending arrival, and Acaraho had asked that the Great Chamber be cleared of everyone except the minimal company of guards. Also at his request, they notified Khon'Tor when the watchers spotted the two approaching, so he could be present when they arrived.

As they entered, Honovi looked around at the height and breadth of the People's home. In the background, she could glimpse a number of tunnels connecting to the vast cavern. *How big is this place?*

Kthama was indeed intimidating. And because it was cold weather, the majority of the People were inside.

Had Acaraho not cleared the Great Chamber, it would ordinarily have been filled with females entertaining themselves with their interests. Some would be working on weaving baskets from the leaves and vines they had prepared earlier, trying to improve the tightness of the weave, changing designs to make the patterns more interesting. Others would be experimenting with new tools for cooking, new playthings for the offspring, or sewing new wraps.

Mothers with young offspring would be happily chatting while watching their offspring frolic together in the large open area of the Great Chamber.

Many of the males would also have been scattered about, occupying themselves with their interests, whether it be honing sharp edges onto rocks for use as hunting and cutting tools, planning their next hunting expedition, or exchanging noteworthy or humorous stories of the past.

Acaraho introduced Honovi to Khon'Tor. Honovi was exhausted, dusty, and hungry. Standing there with not one, but two massive Sasquatch males in front of her, was almost all she could bear. She was overwrought, and she almost started to cry but squeezed her eyes to fight back the stinging tears.

"Welcome to Kthama," said Khon'Tor. "Once you get settled, if there is anything you need above what we have provided, all you need do is mention it to anyone here, and it will be taken care of. I told my people that you were coming."

Acaraho noticed that Khon'Tor was speaking more gently than usual, abandoning his curt, to-the-point, and sometimes sharp rendition of the language.

It was unlike Khon'Tor to be so courteous, but a great deal was riding on the teacher's success in teaching Whitespeak to the Waschini offspring.

"Thank you for your kindness," said Honovi,

then looking at Acaraho, hoping she could soon go to her quarters to recover.

Acaraho had taken great care in selecting a place for Honovi to stay. He did not want it too far away from the Healer's Quarters, or too close to the other general living arrangements. He wanted her to have privacy, yet not feel excluded. It had taken him some time, but in the end, he was satisfied with his selection.

He tried to anticipate everything necessary to make Honovi's stay more comfortable. He had visited with the females who cooked for the general visitors and discussed a more subtle presentation of the raw meats that were part of their diet. These might offend Honovi if displayed openly, as the Brothers tended to cook meats before eating. Acaraho made sure each of the guards and watchers knew she was in their care, and that they knew where her quarters were in case she got lost in the many tunnels and various rooms. They all looked much alike at first, other than the location markings on the tunnel walls.

The markings were indeed directional, and in time he would explain them to Honovi. The People's offspring also had to learn their way through the tunnel system and the marks were there to teach them how to find their way—just as they would help Honovi.

Finally, they arrived at her quarters. Acaraho signaled for Honovi to open the door herself. He'd had the stone door replaced with a wooden version, lashed together with dried vines and sinew. Everything was more extensive in scale from anything she was used to, and he wanted her to know she would be able to operate the door as she wished.

Honovi tugged the wooden door open and stepped into the room. Acaraho knew she would find it large, which was to be expected considering everything at Kthama was oversized—even by the People's standards.

He had solicited the help of the older females of the community to prepare the room. He made sure it had the usual appointments but knew that for it to be pleasing to a female, it needed a female's touch. They had not disappointed him. Despite being essentially a rock chamber that was buried underground, it was surprisingly welcoming. Baskets of dried flowers lined the floors up against the walls and hung from the ceiling above. Small baskets holding nuts and dried foods sat on a small stone table over by the far wall. The females had used a chalk wash to lighten the wall behind the table, giving an appearance of separation as well as brightening the overall area. They had placed small, decorative rocks to add color.

Not being able to see as well in the dark as the

People, Acaraho knew nighttime would present a problem for Honovi. As a solution, just as they always did if one of the Brothers had reason to stop over at Kthama, he had a collection of phosphorus rocks of different sizes brought in and placed around the perimeter. It meant the room would never be in total darkness unless she chose to cover them while she slept.

A small basket of the same calcite and fluorite rocks sat next to the sleeping mat to serve as a type of portable light for her to carry around as need be. They could be placed under the overhead shaft on the worktable and recharged in the sunlight, to be replaced at dusk. There were other larger woven baskets set around for her to store her personal belongings.

Honovi scanned the area and then turned to look up at Acaraho. "Thank you, High Protector of the People. You have gone to great trouble to make me feel welcome. It is beautiful, and I deeply appreciate it."

"It is later than I expected. Perhaps you would like to rest and meet the others in the morning? I will arrange to have a selection of food sent to you. I will also be placing a guard at the end of the corridor here for your convenience should you need something. Please do not let this alarm you. You are free to wander and go anywhere you wish here, Honovi. And please call me Acaraho."

"Thank you again, Acaraho. For everything," she answered.

Adia and Nadiwani were waiting, still expecting the Teacher's arrival. Acaraho made his way to their quarters to let them know she would instead be coming in the morning. He was pleased he would have another excuse to revisit them so soon when he brought Honovi to meet them.

He announced his arrival and Nadiwani called out to him to come on in, fully expecting the Teacher to be with him.

Seeing she was not there, Adia frowned slightly.

"Our return trip took longer than expected. The Teacher is tired. She is resting and looks forward to meeting you in the morning," he explained. "I hope you will take the advantage to get some additional rest as well. Even though I know you have both looked forward to this, no doubt the days ahead will be taxing for all of you," he added.

On his way back to his quarters, Acaraho asked First Guard Awan to station someone outside Honovi's rooms as he had promised.

Acaraho enjoyed being in the females' company again. In a way, it felt like coming home. He had forgotten how much he enjoyed watching the Healer and her Helper together. They were very close; they had more than a working relationship.

He remembered an unguarded moment when Adia's control had wavered. He had seen the look of tenderness in her eyes when she looked at him, and he memorized it to savor later when his attention was not divided and the night was his alone.

The next morning, Acaraho collected Honovi and brought her to meet Adia and Nadiwani, who were anxiously awaiting her arrival. The two had discussed the night before how overwhelming this would be for the young woman, not only leaving her own kind but making the transition to such a large and intimidating world as the People lived in. How much things had changed since the times when no one ever entered the Healer's Quarters.

Acaraho brought Honovi into the room and introduced them. Adia and Nadiwani had decided to remain seated for fear of overwhelming Honovi, and the three sat together for a while, exchanging chit-chat until Honovi was more at ease. Mapiya was watching Oh'Dar in her quarters so they could talk without distraction.

Adia looked at Honovi while Nadiwani was talking to her. *I can see her mother was one of the Brothers, and her father was Waschini. Her skin color is lighter and her eyes more golden than any of the Brothers'. With her background, she will no doubt understand the difficulties awaiting Oh'Dar as an Outsider.*

The conversation moved on to the subject of Oh'Dar's training. They discussed the times Honovi would be there with them, determining a schedule that would not exhaust her physical reserves. They talked about what Oh'Dar was like and answered her questions.

"Thank you again for coming. So tomorrow you will meet Oh'Dar and start his training?" asked Adia.

"Yes, that will be fine. I am happy to help you, and I will appreciate anything you can teach me about your practices," Honovi answered.

Adia smiled at her. "Ithua and I often compare practices and new ideas; we enjoy learning from each other. I will be glad to answer your questions about anything the People might do differently, and show you whatever you are interested in."

The next morning, Acaraho brought Honovi back to the Healer's Quarters, this time to meet Oh'Dar. Honovi had a natural love for children and was looking forward to meeting the little boy.

Adia and Nadiwani were sitting on the floor playing with Oh'Dar when Honovi arrived. Adia picked him up and turned him around, pointing him in the direction of his new teacher, who was coming over to meet him.

Oh'Dar looked up at Honovi and started screaming hysterically, then turned back to Adia and buried his face against her, wailing.

They all instinctively reached out to comfort Oh'Dar, including Honovi, which only scared him all the more and made him cry even harder.

"Oh, I was not thinking!" exclaimed Adia. "Oh'Dar has never seen one of the Brothers, and he has no memory of his parents. He has only been around the People. He has no idea he looks far more like you than he does us!"

I may look as foreign to him as Acaraho looked to me when I first saw him bursting down the hill a few days ago, thought Honovi.

"We are going to have to take this more slowly," said Adia.

Oh'Dar would need more time to adjust to Honovi's frightening appearance.

❖

While Adia was feeling greatly relieved now that Acaraho had found a teacher for Oh'Dar, Khon'Tor's mate, Hakani, was not in so pleasant a state of mind.

CHAPTER 2

K hon'Tor could not put it out of his mind that one of the males—males he trusted and believed in—had lain with his mate and seeded her. Someone who was not Khon'Tor's offspring would, therefore, be heir to the People's leadership. But the Leader had to let everyone think it was his own. He hated it, but he hated, even more, the idea of his people knowing that Hakani had betrayed him, so he could not evict his mate from his quarters as he wished. Going back there to her presence was agonizing. And now that more eyes were on them both, he could no longer overnight in the meeting room he had taken over before, without creating talk and inciting her anger.

Hakani knew that, as Khon'Tor's mate, she was living on borrowed time. Her mind was working feverishly, trying to figure out how to gain leverage over him once she 'lost' the offspring she was pretending to be carrying.

She had been enjoying the attention showered on her by the other females since Khon'Tor's announcement that she was with offspring. Not too long before that, she had felt shunned by the community—powerless and invisible—but time had softened their attitudes toward her. The advent of any new life was always an occasion of great joy, and rumors she and Khon'Tor were estranged, that he had evicted her from their shared bed, faded away.

At least, she thought, *everyone assumes it is his. Khon'Tor never stated it* was *his offspring. But I am not going to be able to keep this up much longer.*

She was going to have to fake a miscarriage. *It may get me some sympathy for a while, but after it wears off, there will not be anything keeping Khon'Tor from going to the High Council and replacing me with another mate—someone to give him his precious offspring. Oh, it might be a while before he can, but in time, that is precisely what he will do. If I do not produce an heir for him, he will find a way to get rid of me.*

For Hakani, her greatest pleasure had become getting back at Khon'Tor for the slight of not being his First Choice, followed closely by making trouble for Adia.

She knew it would be driving Khon'Tor mad

trying to figure out who the father of the pretend offspring was. *It will eat at him for the rest of our lives. Until I can think of another way to make him pay, I will have to be satisfied with that.*

Hakani had heard that Khon'Tor had found someone to teach Whitespeak to the Waschini offspring. She still resented that Khon'Tor had welcomed it into their community and asked for everyone's support at the same time he had announced she was with offspring. She was sick of hearing about the Waschini and the Healer everywhere she went. *Somehow, despite my efforts, the Healer has won back the favor of our people.*

Eventually, Oh'Dar got over his fear of Honovi. When he crawled up onto her lap, he would stare at her, fascinated by her long straight coal-black hair. She used his curiosity about everything to tell him the Whitespeak words for each object he picked up, dropped, or turned over. Coupling the Handspeak words he knew with the corresponding Whitespeak words made it that much clearer. Though he could not yet form the Whitespeak words, she knew his mind was taking it all in and storing it for later.

She found Oh'Dar to be incredibly bright. He was also a naturally happy offspring, as Adia and Nadiwani had said. Oh'Dar used the same sign for *Mama* for both Adia and Nadiwani. Honovi taught him a different word to use for Nadiwani, something akin to *Auntie Mama*. She knew Nadiwani would not mind, much as she loved Oh'Dar, because it was she who had suggested Adia deserved the title of *Mama*. It was Adia who had taken the risk and suffered for it in saving his life.

So far, Honovi had spent her time in either the Healer's Quarters or her own, but word quickly spread that Acaraho had found a teacher for Oh'Dar. The People kept watch, hoping to learn something about her. There were mixed feelings about his learning the Waschini language, though, if he were going to learn Whitespeak, the mothers understood better that the time was while he was young and absorbing everything easily.

Adia lay on her sleeping mat in the early hours before dawn, reflecting on the past few months. *I would do it all over again for Oh'Dar, but I am also glad it is behind me; I need some peace and predictability. I do not even remember how long it's been since Khon'Tor attacked me. I should have marked it on my Keeping Stone, but that would have made it all the more real. There are two things it is best I not dwell on. One is what Khon'Tor did to me, and the other is Acaraho.*

Adia sighed and rolled over, wanting very much to go back to sleep.

Though she did not know the exact date it

happened, Adia knew it had been a while, and she thought she should be feeling better as time went on, not worse. She was tired most mornings, even when she'd had a long rest, which was not like her. She knew Nadiwani had also noticed.

A few hours later, as Honovi was working with Oh'Dar, Nadiwani and Adia were standing at the worktable when a wave of dizziness hit Adia. She caught herself on the edge of the rock slab.

"Are you alright?" asked Nadiwani, clearly seeing she was not.

"Yes, just a little dizzy, that's all, and I have a headache," she answered, holding her palm up to her forehead. Then all of a sudden, Adia rushed over to one of the empty baskets by the wall and threw up violently.

Nadiwani did not think much of it until it happened again the next day. Once was understandable, but two days in a row?

Tiredness, headaches, nausea, Nadiwani checked Adia's symptoms off in her mind.

Suddenly, her mouth hung open. *Oh no*, she thought to herself. *No, no, it's not possible*, she told herself again. *The symptoms are all there; only it is truly not possible. Adia is the Healer, a maiden. There is no one more dedicated to being a Healer. Adia has even been called the Healer's Healer. Her reputation is renowned.*

She is above reproach. There is no way she could be, would ever let herself become—seeded?

It was if Adia's seventh sense had heard the exact words Nadiwani was thinking. Adia looked up directly into Nadiwani's eyes, then looked away.

The Healer took some fresh water, and after cleaning up, finally looked back at Nadiwani who was still staring at her, wide-eyed in disbelief.

By now, Honovi had noticed what was going on. Realizing that the teacher was watching them, Nadiwani took the Healer's arm and led her a little way off.

"Adia. It cannot be— But everything you have told me— There's no way, you cannot possibly be—" stammered Nadiwani.

The look in Adia's eyes confirmed Nadiwani's fears. Nadiwani's hands flew up to cover her mouth as if she could keep it from being true by holding back the words.

Adia finally had to face what had been lingering in the back of her mind. She had not wanted to consider it either. She wanted peace, and she needed things to get back to normal. Listening to Nadiwani struggling with the thought of it herself, Adia finally had to admit it. Yes, she absolutely could be—and was—with offspring.

She closed her eyes. *I do not want to face this. I do*

not want to talk about it. I know Nadiwani's first question is going to be who and how. I've never had any secrets from her until now. This is one I cannot reveal, but oh how I need her friendship to help me through this.

Adia braced herself for the next question—the question she could never and would never answer. She turned, held her hand up to Nadiwani, and said, "Do not ask. Do not ask, Nadiwani, I am begging you. I cannot tell. I cannot nor will I ever tell you or anyone."

Nadiwani lowered her eyes, then in the next moment they flew wide open. She turned back to Adia and signed, "*Acaraho.*"

"Acaraho? How could you possibly think *Acaraho*—"

Adia knew Acaraho had never treated her or any female with anything but the utmost respect. *Nadiwani thinks this was a consensual mistake I made. So, no wonder, it makes sense she would think of Acaraho. Perhaps she has caught me looking at him when I thought no one was watching? And maybe the other way round, too.*

"No Nadiwani. Stop. Please stop. No, why would you think of Acaraho?"

"I have seen how you look at each other, Adia. It is not so much of a jump to a conclusion, is it, considering when you were so ill he lay with you and held you against his body to keep you warm," she continued

"What?" asked Adia. "*What are you talking about?*"

She quickly stepped forward to get Nadiwani's attention, "What are you *talking about?*"

"After you were brought in—after Is'Taqa found you—you were so sick. You were sick, and your body temperature was too low. It was the only way to bring your core temperature up. I needed body heat, and Acaraho is the largest, most muscular male. It was the only way to save you. And he was already assigned to protect you— It is a proven clinical approach—*you know that yourself*" she stammered.

Adia thought she was going to pass out—this time not from the dizziness, but from the thought that she and Acaraho had shared a sleeping place. That she had lain, propped up against him while he warmed her with his natural heat. He had saved her life, and she had never known it. Then she remembered the feeling of comfort and safety that had come with her when she woke from the fog. She had thought it was from when Acaraho had carried her back to the cave. She realized now it was probably some vapor of a memory she had retained of feeling safe, warm, and secure lying up against him for that time. Oh, how she wondered what Acaraho had thought of that experience.

Is Nadiwani insinuating that Acaraho took advantage of me sometime during that period? No, not Acaraho. Anyone but Acaraho; he has too much honor. He has too much respect for females; he would never take advantage of anyone. Nadiwani should know he is not capable of such a thing!

But at least this tells me it was Ithua who tended to my intimate injuries, as I thought. If it had been Nadiwani, she would have known I was brought in already violated.

"Nadiwani. This is the last thing I am going to say on the topic. Do not ask me anything else. But hear me very clearly. Acaraho had nothing to do with this. *Nothing.* And I will not tolerate his reputation being tainted with any insinuation to that effect either. You will put the thought out of your mind completely. I have never lied to you, and I am telling you the truth now. *Acaraho did not seed this offspring,*" she said sternly and slowly. Her eyes were fixed on Nadiwani.

"Alright," said her friend. Silence took its place between the two females for some time. Now that Adia was confident she had made it clear there could be no thought of Acaraho's involvement here, her thoughts turned to her predicament.

As they stood there in silence, everything began hitting Adia at once. It was all so overwhelming. Suddenly, she needed to be alone, where she could have some privacy with her thoughts. But where to go when Nadiwani and Honovi were here with Oh'Dar? She desperately needed to get away, so she excused herself, left the Healer's Quarters, and started walking.

The array of tunnels in their underground home was extensive. If you needed to walk, you could do so mindlessly for some time without having to give a thought to where you were going. Adia had not grown up at Kthama as the others had, but she had learned much, and she knew how to read the markings on the intersections, so she was at no risk of getting lost.

As she was walking, Adia realized she was heading toward a special place about which she had forgotten. So many years had passed since she first discovered it. Tucked far away in the back tunnels, through a small opening that most would never notice, was a charming little cave enclosing a small, shallow pool. Adia had found it when she first arrived to become the Healer for the People of the High Rocks; when she was grieving the loss of the People of the Deep Valley—her community and the life she had known there growing up.

This pool was not like the Gnoaii, the shallow underground pool formed by the Mother Stream. The Gnoaii was always stocked with fish before the first snow, providing an easy source of protein for the winter months if the hunting groups came up short. However, this was a place which possibly no one other than she even knew existed.

It had not been in her mind to come here when she started walking, but now she realized it was exactly what she needed. She negotiated the opening and sat down by the clear little pool, leaning back against the cool smooth rock wall. She put her feet in the cool water, and as she had done years ago, she let the tears fall and sobbed out all the pain and despair locked inside her. She had never felt so alone in her life, and she had no one to turn to for help.

Adia stayed there for a very long time. Finally, she was ready to return to her quarters, expecting that by now Honovi would have returned to hers and Nadiwani would have put Oh'Dar to bed.

She tried to enter as quietly as possible, carefully slipping onto her sleeping mat, beside Nadiwani's. The Helper had taken to staying with her more often since Oh'Dar's arrival and the work it entailed. Adia curled up on her side and tucked her hands under her chin. As she tried to drift off into sleep, silent tears streamed down her face and disappeared into the soft bedding, their brief existence witnessed only by her and the Great Mother.

The next morning, Nadiwani was as quiet as she could be. She knew her friend was hurting. After Adia had left the previous evening, Nadiwani realized her own insensitivity. So stunned by this turn of events and so obsessed with who the father might be, and how this could even have happened, she had not stopped to think of the position Adia was in. Nadiwani felt ashamed she had focused on the drama of the situation and had questioned Acaraho's honor rather than consoling her friend. The High Protector was above reproach, and that was precisely why she had pressed him into service to help warm Adia. *What was I thinking? Besides, I, or someone else, was in the room the whole time.*

And Nadiwani had plenty of time to think about Adia during the rest of the evening. She could not fully grasp what her friend was going through, but she did know this was pretty much the worst possible situation a Healer could be in. Not allowed to mate because of the dangers of carrying and delivering an offspring; now, she was facing all those risks.

Not to mention the reaction of the community. *Regardless of Adia's dedication to her vocation, she has crossed a line sacred to the Healer's calling. People will demand to know who the father is; they will not be able to let it go. It all boils down to a terrible situation for Adia and one with no solution other than to bear up under it and try to survive. Well, almost—*

Adia woke, realizing Nadiwani was already up. Even though she could not confide in her Helper, Nadiwani was still her closest friend, and her presence alone was comforting.

Eventually, she joined Nadiwani at the work table. They often leaned over the table while talking or drinking brewed herbs. Nadiwani did not say a word, only putting her arm across her friend's back and drawing her over in a hug.

"I am so sorry," she said. Adia just closed her eyes and nodded.

Nadiwani knew Adia had been crying. In all the years she had known her, she had only known her to cry twice before—the first was when she first joined the People and was grieving the loss of her own family and community. The second was when her father returned to the Great Spirit. She could only imagine the loneliness Adia had felt during those times and knew she must be feeling very lonely now.

A few more moments of silence passed between them, this time not uncomfortable silence, just a natural and respectful quiet shared between close friends.

"Adia," said Nadiwani softly. "There are ways. You know there are ways," she offered quietly.

Adia looked over at her friend with tears welling in her eyes. *Yes, there are ways.*

There were ways to end a pregnancy using any number of herbs. Parsley, Cotton Root Bark, Blue Cohosh, Black Cohosh. The People's Healers knew about these methods and would choose whatever was available in their location—but they had to be used early, within the first season, before the little life inside had taken hold firmly.

In her solace in the little cave next to the pond, Adia's thoughts had also turned to that solution.

Oh, how I wish I could avoid this path. I do not want to face the long road ahead of me: the judgment, the talk, the sideways glances. And Khon'Tor—I do not want to think about him yet. I cannot fathom what he will do to me when he finds out I am carrying his offspring. How easy it would be to make it all go away. A few days of some carefully prepared brews and my body would expel the little life growing within me. No one but Nadiwani and I would ever know of its tiny, brief existence.

In the same way, Adia had stood over the pitiful little White offspring, Oh'Dar, struggling with the choices and the consequences and finally knowing she could not abandon him, and no matter what the cost, she knew she could not abandon this life either. No matter that it had been formed by an act of violence and hatred. Khon'Tor had not known he was speaking to his situation when he had declared to the People that "All offspring are innocent." Little did he know that even as he made his grand speech, his offspring was silently taking form within the very maiden he had violated.

Adia took Nadiwani's hand in hers and held it, shaking her head ever-so-slightly. Nadiwani nodded her understanding and squeezed Adia's hand in acknowledgment.

The Healer spoke up. "I cannot remember a time when I did not know what to do—what the next step should be. I have accepted what life has handed me as bravely as I could, but at this moment, all my confidence is gone. I wish my father were here."

She needed someone stronger than herself to turn to, someone she could lean on—a place to rest where for once she did not need to have all the answers.

While the two were still leaning on the table, lost in thought, Acaraho arrived with Honovi. Adia and Nadiwani looked quickly at each other; they had not noticed the time passing.

Nadiwani hurried over to greet them, buying Adia some time to collect herself. Adia quickly dried her tears and prayed that Acaraho—who seemed to miss nothing—might by some chance not notice she had been crying.

Adia's prayers were not answered. As usual, Acaraho had seen everything.

He felt the sadness in the room the moment he entered. He could sense Nadiwani's solemn mood. He could see Adia had been crying; everything about her denoted vulnerability. He wanted to put his arms around her and comfort her but knew he could not. And he also wanted to know what had happened to upset her so.

Instead, he just looked at her, his eyes soft.

Adia met his gaze and could feel his concern. She had to turn away lest his kindness break the last remaining self-control she had and start her tears again.

Acaraho. Adia admitted to herself that her feelings and her attraction to him were inappropriate.

She knew she could never tell him how she felt, but hoped he understood. That if there were any way she could be with him, she would be. There was no one in her heart but him.

And then it hit her.

I am going to have to tell Acaraho I am with offspring. Now he would believe she had broken trust with the People. But worse than that, he was going to think she had mated with someone; that she had chosen to be with another male. *Not him.*

If she could tell him that Khon'Tor had taken her Without Her Consent—then he would know this was not of her choosing. But she could tell him none of that, either. *Of everything I am facing, this is the most unbearable part of it all. What will he think of me? Does he know me well enough to realize I would never choose this voluntarily? And if I had, it would have been with him and him alone? I must tell him right away before anyone else notices and the rumors start.*

Suddenly, a feeling of protection and safety and comfort came back to her, and she remembered lying against Acaraho when she was ill. It was a memory of what Nadiwani had told her, how she had pressed Acaraho's muscular body into service to raise Adia's body temperature. And in that brief recall, Adia could feel his tenderness toward her.

Her heart was breaking. She would rather disappear than have to see the look on Acaraho's face when the time came to tell him. She knew it would not be long before she had to do so. It devastated her to realize that when the time came, it would be both the longest and the most painful conversation she had ever had with him.

Acaraho was standing there, watching her. He had seen the anguish play over her face, and he knew she was struggling with something huge. He wished she would turn to him for help; he could not bear to see her so unhappy.

What could be weighing her down like this? She was so glad Honovi came here to teach Oh'Dar Whitespeak. But all of a sudden, something is seriously wrong. Whatever has happened, I cannot depend on snippets and rumors any longer. I have to find a way to be close to her again. But Acaraho knew that to avoid suspicion something like that would have to come from Khon'Tor himself.

If something was to be Khon'Tor's idea, it meant there had to be something in it for Khon'Tor. Acaraho knew everyone had something they valued above everything else, and the one thing the Leader valued above all else was his position of power. Which, to his detriment, he gauged based on what the People thought of him.

The outside Waschini threat is no longer at the forefront of his mind. It has been replaced by Hakani's seeding and the Waschini offspring. In the past, I was Khon'Tor's source of information about what went on in the Healer's Quarters. If I could reignite Khon'Tor's interest, he might reinstate my contact with the Healer and Oh'Dar.

Khon'Tor was sitting in the meeting room waiting for their regular update. Acaraho was not late. Acaraho was seldom late. The Leader had arrived early to have some time alone to reflect on the situation at hand. Khon'Tor was confident Adia was under his control and would never reveal he had attacked her. He was satisfied that she felt compelled by the Rah-hora to keep it secret.

But he had other worries on his mind, the first being his mate Hakani and a lifetime of pretending the offspring she was carrying was his. The second was his obsession with who the father of the offspring might be. The third was his ongoing concern over Akule, the watcher who had told him Adia was leaving Kthama against his orders. Of these three, the only one he could actively do anything about was the situation with Akule. Khon'Tor still did not know if Akule suspected he had something to do with Adia's *incident*.

If he approached Akule to ask him anything further about that evening, if Akule did *not* already suspect Khon'Tor, then the Leader risked raising his suspicions by bringing it up.

Khon'Tor was lost in his thoughts when Acaraho arrived. After the standard updates, which reflected great process on essential repairs and the recent success of the hunting parties, Khon'Tor turned the conversation to one of his usual interests, to the state of community in general.

Acaraho reported there was still overwhelming goodwill toward both the Leader and Hakani over her expected offspring. He said there was a good amount of interest in Honovi, Oh'Dar's Whitespeak teacher, and the offspring's progress. After all, compared to usual day-to-day living, these were exciting times for the People.

"How is the Waschini offspring progressing?" asked Khon'Tor.

"I do not know. I am not around them as I used to be, Khon'Tor. I do suspect though that Ogima Adoeete would appreciate an update on Honovi's progress and how she is adapting to living here among the People. I imagine people in her village are wondering how she is doing," he added.

Khon'Tor considered what Acaraho was saying. *Good relations between the People and the Brothers are essential to all of us. And Honovi set aside her responsibilities in her community to provide this service to me. I also want to know what is happening with that offspring. Perhaps pulling Acaraho away from the situation with the Healer was a mistake. But I need Acaraho to run the cold weather activities. How can he be in both worlds? He would have to do it in his free time, and it is not appropriate for me to order that.*

CHAPTER 3

Days trickled by. Adia knew her time was running short. Before long, someone would notice her changing body. She had already put on more weight than she would have imagined should happen this early. The older females were the most likely to notice and raise an eyebrow at her changing figure.

She was overwhelmed. The worst of it was that she had to tell Acaraho. Then she had to face Khon'-Tor. She had not decided whether that would be best done alone or quietly in a public place. She knew he would have to control his reaction if there were others around.

On the one hand, he was the father of her offspring, and Adia thought perhaps she owed it to him to tell him one-on-one. Then she argued with herself that it had not been consensual and whatever rights he had would be those she bestowed on him.

And those would be if, and only if, she thought it was for the good of the offspring.

Adia felt sick when she thought about the offspring's future. *No father, no one to mentor him or her other than myself and Nadiwani. Three females, if I count Honovi's presence. Regardless of whether it is a male or female, the offspring will need a male figure in its life to provide balance.* She knew Khon'Tor would not be providing that as he could never claim the offspring without the details of its conception coming out. So he or she would never have a father; he or she would have the shadow hanging over it that it had been born of a Healer—a Healer who had selfishly abdicated her responsibility to the People to produce an offspring.

Without the truth being told, Adia would bear judgment against herself, as would her offspring. *But there is no way to redeem me other than revealing that Khon'Tor took me Without My Consent. And I have already accepted that the devastation to the community would be far worse than living with the personal injustice.*

But that was before there was an offspring involved, thought Adia. Did that fact affect her decision? She thought long and hard about it. She tried to envision which would be harder for the offspring.

What would be worse? To live knowing its mother had failed in her calling as a Healer? And never to know who its father was? Or to know who its father was and bear the burden that it was conceived by force, without its mother's consent? It would carry the stigma of either all its life.

Adia paced the room. No matter how it came out, it would be a difficult life for the offspring.

Even if I could convince Khon'Tor to come forward and claim the offspring, to let it be raised as the heir to his leadership, there would still be the resounding damage to the community because of his crimes.

Perhaps it would be best if she gave the offspring up—let it go to another community to be raised. But what effect would that have? Would it scar her offspring forever? Would he or she feel rejected, thrown away, not loveable enough? Perhaps it would be better not to know. To grow up unaware with two loving parents not related to it by blood would surely be better than having a shamed Healer for a mother and a disgraced rapist for a father.

Offspring are so fragile, thought Adia. *They need stability to flourish. In the best of all worlds, they receive love from both a mother and a father who conceived them in love and awaited their birth anxiously and with excited hearts. But mine will never have that. And I know I cannot send my offspring away. Only if there were a grave threat of danger, could I bring myself to make that decision.*

As Adia was considering all angles, it dawned on her that she and Nadiwani had discussed that Oh'Dar would need a male mentor. He was being raised entirely by females because his other caretakers were females too—Mapiya, Haiwee. Where was Oh'Dar going to learn about being a man? Yes, he was never going to have the influence of a Waschini father, but males had a common thread across all tribes. She knew enough of the People and the Brothers to be aware that males filled the same roles of responsibility, protection, leadership, and providing for their families. How would Oh'Dar learn the way a male demonstrated values of honesty and kindness and honor? If he had any chance of finding a mate, he would have to be able to function as a male and fulfill a male's responsibilities.

There is time to decide, thought Adia. *Oh'Dar is just a small offspring. He will not truly need that influence until he is six or seven years old.*

And then Adia thought again about what would happen once she told Khon'Tor she was with offspring. He would not take it well, to say the least. Despite all the goodwill he had shown in the assembly—the intention for Oh'Dar to have what he needed, and the call on the community to help with his upbringing—there was a genuine possibility it would all disappear once she told him about this.

Adia decided that though it was not necessary yet, she would ask Khon'Tor if she could select a mentor to be a male role model for Oh'Dar. *Perhaps if he agrees and it is put in motion now, the promise will hold up through the terrible storm that is coming once he learns of my condition.*

Another person might have gone to Khon'Tor and demanded what she wanted, threatening to reveal his crimes if she did not get what she asked. Another person might have used the fact of her pregnancy to blackmail him through the rest of his leadership. None of these thoughts, which would have come easily to someone like Hakani, even occurred to Adia.

Adia did not know who to tell first. She dreaded both confrontations, though it would not strictly be a confrontation with Acaraho. She would rather face Khon'Tor's wrath a hundred times than have to tell Acaraho and risk seeing hurt cross his face.

Even though she knew she could never be with Acaraho, she still had the dream of being with him. And now she was about to lose even that fragment of imaginary happiness.

Adia decided she would tell Acaraho first. It was the more difficult of the two, and she did not want to take a chance he might figure it out before she could tell him. He must hear it from her. He deserved to hear it from her. The question was where to tell him. The only place she could think of was in one of the small meeting rooms, much like Khon'Tor used, but one far away from observing eyes.

Adia spent the morning in meditation and preparation. She prayed to the Great Mother for help—for the right words, for strength, for wisdom. She prayed for Acaraho, that this would not hurt him as much as she thought it would, and that in time he would come to know that it could not have been of her choice. Even though that would raise more questions, she needed him to know there was no one in her heart but him.

It was time. Adia sent word for Acaraho to meet her in the room she had selected. She had picked one as far away as possible from the others. She felt as if her heart was about to explode in her chest, and it was all she could do to still her mind, to keep the tears from falling. She was so afraid, so afraid, to see the look of hurt on his face when she told him.

Acaraho arrived, and Adia turned and motioned him to come in.

"Acaraho," she started, speaking slowly. "Thank you for coming. I am sure you have no idea why I want to meet with you. I know it is unusual, out of convention. We have hardly exchanged any words, though we have spent a great deal of time together. I wish there were words to explain how desperately sorry I am that in the first real conversation we have together, I have to tell you what I am about to." And then she had to pause to collect herself. Tears were welling up in her eyes, ready to fall at any moment.

"Before I tell you what I must, please try to remember who I am. Please try to remember who you know me to be." Then she broke down. The tears fell, and she could not get herself back under control.

Before he could stop himself, Acaraho had his arms around her, pulling her into his chest. Adia leaned against him and sobbed. He could tell by how she was responding to him, melting into him, that she cared for him too. *So what could be so terrible, what matters so much?*

He had been alarmed when she sent word she wanted to see him. He had no context for the meeting—why it was being held there and not in the Healer's Quarters. The nature of it was clandestine and secretive, and it put him on edge. *Did she know he cared for her and was going to rebuke him?* He was worried, and if he admitted it, he was afraid too. But now that was behind him, and he was about to find out.

He did not want to, but still holding her with both hands, he pulled her away enough to look into her eyes and said to her softly, "Adia. Just tell me. It will be alright. Just tell me," he whispered. His kindness broke her last reserves, and she broke down, sobbing. "Acaraho. Acaraho. I am seeded with an offspring."

Acaraho could not have heard that correctly. He frowned and blinked as if clearing his eyes would clear his mind.

"You're with offspring," he said, as if saying it himself would make it sink in.

"Yes. Please do not ask. Please. I am so sorry. I am so sorry," was all Adia could say, more tears falling.

A million feelings and thoughts burned through Acaraho simultaneously. *It is not possible. She is the Healer. She would never— Who? How? I thought she cared for me. I know she cares for me. How can this be? It cannot be,*" one after the other, almost faster than he could process them.

And then, amid the pain and confusion and anguish, a small opening cleared, and a rational thought poked its way through to his consciousness; it was the only explanation that made any sense. *Khon'Tor.*

Acaraho stepped away from Adia and roared in anguish. He picked up the rock slab table and threw it against the wall, snapping it in two. He knocked over the seating boulders, sending them rolling across the floor. He destroyed everything he could get his hands on, trying to dispel the rage. Then he pressed his hands to his forehead and stormed about.

Adia backed up against the wall, and she watched him tear the room apart piece by piece, rocks and boulders flying, shattering—until there was nothing left to destroy.

Some of his anger dispelled, Acaraho came back to himself. He turned to see her terrified, pressed up against the far wall. He looked at her as she stood there staring back at him, frozen.

"I knew Khon'Tor hurt you, Adia," he yelled, "I *knew* it was not an accident. But that? Never that he would do *that*!"

"Acaraho please," she said, "No one is sorrier about this than I. But I cannot. I cannot—" and her voice trailed off.

Acaraho remembered the Rah-hora. Now he understood—though how Khon'Tor had extracted this silence from Adia, he did not know. Whatever she had received as her part of the deal, and he was sure it was the Whitespeak teacher for Oh'Dar, it was not enough. It was brutally unfair and beyond the pale.

The female I love was attacked and violated by the so-called honored and respected Leader of the People, Khon'Tor. And she is left to bear the shame alone, shame which should not be hers at all. She is innocent but unable to defend herself with the truth. I do not know what is going to happen, but I know one thing for certain. At some point, I will have Khon'Tor to myself, at my mercy, pinned on the floor in front of me, with his throat between my bare hands. And at that point, there will be no mercy for him whatsoever.

"I can say no more, Acaraho. Please. There is so much I want to say to you—you are the only—" she said, reaching out toward him.

Acaraho had gained sufficient control over himself now to where his anger was manageable.

"I understand enough, Adia. I hope he will be held accountable, but I will follow your lead. However, do not expect me to be less than who I am. Make no mistake. Someday it will be him and me alone, and nothing you or anyone else can say will stop me from extracting payment for what he has done to you."

She did not doubt for one second that he meant what he said, or that he was capable of carrying it out.

There was nothing else for Adia to say. She started to leave, but as she passed him, Acaraho took her arm and pulled her close. He towered over her, and she looked up into his eyes. Her breath caught as she felt his gaze pierce directly into her soul. Despite the anguish of the situation, the desire to reach up and press her lips to his was excruciating.

"Thank you for telling me yourself," he said. Adia nodded, and he released her.

As she was almost through the door, he said, "Adia. Does he know?"

Without turning back, Adia answered, "Not yet."

Acaraho stayed in the room after she left. Everything was in shambles. He spent a few moments putting it back together as best he could. The rock slab of the table had split in two when it slammed against the wall; there was no repairing that. He could not think of an explanation and had to let it go. Hopefully, no one would know it was they who had used the room, and the mystery of how the table had been broken would just become more fat to be chewed. Chewed in the mandibles of speculation and gossip that were about to start grinding at a level never before seen in Kthama.

Very slowly, Adia walked back to her quarters. She needed time to process what had just happened. Somehow Acaraho had figured out the truth. But how? Had she spoken in her fevered state? Had she mumbled something? How did he know? How long had he known?

She had wanted to tell him he was right. *More than anything, I wanted Acaraho to hear from me he was right—that Khon'Tor did this terrible thing, that it was not of my choosing, that he did it Without My Consent.*

But she could not. As much as she wanted Acaraho to know for certain, she could not say it, and she had almost said too much as it was.

For now, she was still committed to keeping secret what Khon'Tor had done. It was not just the Rah-hora—she had not thought about that for some time. It was about the destruction to the community that would happen in a war over this with Khon'Tor. She knew he would never admit to it. It would be her word against his, and the result would destroy the peace and harmony among her people for the foreseeable future and perhaps beyond.

As if it was not enough that to spare the People she had to bear in silence what Khon'Tor had done to her, now she had to endure the public shame of being with offspring, unable to offer any defense. And at the moment, she saw Khon'Tor for what he was—not a great Leader, but a callous, self-centered despot. Someone who could do such things to her, leave her to die, and then when she did not, leave her to bear the shame of his wrongdoing. He was not the great Leader she had thought him to be. And she grieved the loss of her belief in him as much as anything else.

Her earlier thoughts solidified. *All offspring need a positive male role model. I will talk to Khon'Tor tomorrow about a mentor for Oh'Dar.*

Things had changed and the fact that had made her sad before—that her offspring would never know who his father was—now comforted her.

When Adia made it back to her quarters, she was glad for the distraction of Nadiwani, Honovi, and Oh'Dar. Honovi was occupied with Oh'Dar, so Adia joined Nadiwani in sorting the baskets of harvest they had not gotten to as yet. She was glad for the relatively mindless work. She was emotionally drained and did not want to think anymore. Tonight, when she could have quiet time with her thoughts, she would let herself think about the day's events, and just this once, let her thoughts dwell on Acaraho.

Acaraho did not know what to do with himself. With the feelings still raging inside him, he could not go back to his quarters—not yet. He made his way back down the maze of tunnels and out through the Great Entrance into the wintry cold. The stinging icy wind felt good on his face. He followed the path away from the entrance and down to the forest floor. He was still seething inside. He had to find some release before he could go back to Kthama. And he could not risk running into Khon'Tor tonight before regaining control of himself.

Picking up the nearest fallen log, Acaraho hurled it against the trees standing nearby, watching it splinter into a thousand pieces with a satisfying series of *cracks*. He uprooted a young tree and easily tossed it into a nearby cliff wall, causing a landslide of loosened stones and rocks. Boulders, more trees, whatever he could find to take the brunt of his anger. He was sick at heart over what Khon'Tor had done to Adia, what the Leader had taken from her. Without Her Consent. It was despicable. He could not let himself think of it in any detail because it enraged him so. What would drive Khon'Tor to do it? What would drive any male to do that?

Acaraho pictured the setting in which they had

found Adia. As they approached, he had taken the time to memorize every detail. He remembered the copious amounts of blood everywhere.

There were aspects of the scene that were not natural—the position she was lying in for one. The locket curled up in her open palm. If someone fell and hit their head, even if they remained conscious for a while, they would not naturally continue to clasp an object. And if by some bizarre chance that had happened, the fact that it was lying neatly in the center of her open hand—as if to ensure it would be found—was in no way a natural occurrence.

He remembered giving the locket to Is'Taqa when he lifted Adia to carry her back to Kthama. He also remembered how Adia had grasped it with relief when Is'Taqa returned it to her.

Acaraho went over the events of the night. Awan coming to tell him they did not know where Adia was. Arriving at the Great Chamber to see Khon'Tor and Akule talking. Is'Taqa showing up, agitated and frantic, telling them she had fallen and hit her head.

Akule.

I am in charge of all the guards and watchers. Akule was not posted in the Great Chamber that night. In fact, Akule is not a guard at all; he is a watcher. I had assigned Kajika to that post. Only Khon'Tor, the First Guard, and I have the authority to change duty assignments. Perhaps I should talk to both Kajika and Akule, very cautiously.

Without involving Adia, Acaraho wanted to find out as much as he could about what had happened. *I respect her right to handle this as she wishes, but I am not going to stand by forever and let Khon'Tor get away with this. At some point, justice will be served if I have to deliver it myself.*

As Acaraho finally made his way back up the hill to Kthama, he reaffirmed that he had to get back into her life. He had planted the seed with Khon'Tor, and now he must wait for the opportunity to present itself. He knew that tomorrow he would no doubt see Khon'Tor. He had the rest of the night to get himself under control so he could conceal his bitter disgust from the Leader.

Finally.

Nighttime and the peace of the dark had arrived. Alone on her sleeping mat, Adia let her thoughts return to the events of earlier. She replayed each moment, each feeling. How Acaraho had figured out what had happened, she did not know. She knew he was astute; she knew there was very little that escaped his attention.

Then she remembered his violent reaction. It had frightened her at first, thinking he was angry with her. An angry Sasquatch presents a terrifying spectacle, even to another. And Acaraho was capable of tremendous strength. *He tossed the table slab across the room against the far wall as if it were nothing.*

If he had not caught her so unawares, she would

have been in awe of the impressive display of raw power.

She remembered Acaraho's statement that at some point, Khon'Tor would be held accountable. She shuddered to think of that day. There was nothing she could do to stop Acaraho. He and Khon'Tor were almost identically matched in size and strength, but she had no doubt Acaraho would be the victor. She knew the rage Acaraho felt over what Khon'Tor had done would give him the full advantage. She did not enjoy the thought of the two powerful males engaged in battle but did feel oddly pleased that Acaraho was so protective of her.

Mostly she was relieved that the conversation was done, and deeply grateful that he did not hate her. It would have been unbearable if he had turned against her, as she had feared. The hurt look she envisioned in his eyes had never appeared. That told her there was not even a moment when he thought she had chosen another. She was so happy that he knew her well enough to realize it.

So many things I want to tell him, so much in my heart that I will never be able to say. If I were not the Healer, he would be the one, the only one I would ever choose. I am trapped now in this nowhere place of longing forever. Unable to claim him and unable to let him go.

She still had not decided how to tell Khon'Tor that he had seeded her, but she *had* decided to approach him about a mentor for Oh'Dar. With luck, with the Mother's help, she would get that settled before the fruit of his attack on her showed.

Adia busied herself with Nadiwani over the next few days. But finally, it was time. Nadiwani had a full day of work planned, for which she said she did not need Adia's help. Since Nadiwani did not need her, she decided she would approach Khon'Tor about Oh'Dar that morning. After they shared their morning tea and Honovi arrived to take over Oh'Dar, Adia went to find him.

It took her a while to locate Khon'Tor, and she finally asked one of the guards where he might be this early. She doubted he would still be in his quarters; however, there was no way she was going to look. She did not want to be alone with him there, and if there was anyone she did not want to see, it was Hakani. She still did not know why Hakani hated her so. Perhaps she would never know, but she had tired of trying to figure it out.

Instead of being in the meeting room he had recently appropriated, Khon'Tor was in the Great Chamber. As she entered, she could see him at the far end, talking with several of the other males. The closer she got, she could make out Awan who was First Guard, and—Acaraho. It was too late to turn back; they had seen her, and it was clear she was coming toward them—to change her trajectory now would be too obvious.

It felt as if it took her forever to cross the floor to get to them. She made sure she kept her eyes off Acaraho. She wondered what he was thinking, how he was handling having to talk to Khon'Tor as if he did not know what the Leader had done.

The males opened their circle as she approached. She nodded at them in greeting and said, "Khon'Tor, when you have a moment, I would like to speak with you."

"We are in the middle of discussing assignments and some related problems. Can we not speak here, in this place?" asked Khon'Tor. Adia decided that might go in her favor, so she agreed, and he motioned her over to a sitting area.

To Adia's consternation, Acaraho and Awan walked with them. She wondered if anyone else could tell how tightly under control Acaraho was holding himself.

She started with the customary niceties. "Thank you for your time, Khon'Tor. And thank you for your commitment to helping Oh'Dar become part of the People. I am also very appreciative that you brought Honovi of the Brothers here to teach him Whitespeak."

Khon'Tor stared at her.

Receiving no reaction from him, she continued.

"I know there are limits to how much I can expect Oh'Dar to fit into our community. I do not have unreasonable expectations of that. He will always be Waschini, and he will always be an Outsider. He is making good progress, though, under Honovi's instruction," she added, to keep herself talking.

"I realized the other day, however, that Oh'Dar is being raised entirely in the company of females. And even though he will never be one of the People, there are some common threads among all of us—the People, the Brothers, and the Waschini. We all seem to share a similar division of roles between males and females," she continued.

"In a normal situation, Oh'Dar would have contact with another man. Usually, there is a male in the family unit, whether it be the father or even an uncle, to provide a male role model.

"Someone is going to have to teach Oh'Dar, show him what it means to be a man, Waschini or otherwise. I have no family here to provide this, no brothers; I left everyone I knew when I came here. So I am asking for a mentor for him. Someone who is of good character, patient, who can teach him skills, values, the laws. I know it is a lot to ask of anyone."

She finally got it out, much to Khon'Tor's relief.

"Are you asking me to assign someone to this, Healer, or are you looking for volunteers?" he asked. Before he could say anything else and before Adia could answer, Acaraho stepped forward just the slightest bit.

"I volunteer, Khon'Tor. I would be willing to take the Waschini boy under my tutelage," he said.

Khon'Tor was always on edge whenever Adia was around—even more so since *the incident*, as he preferred to think of it. *Is that all she wants?* he wondered. *Someone to mentor the White PetaQ?*

He turned to Acaraho and raised his eyebrows. He did not have to think twice about this. He wanted to find a way to insert Acaraho back into Adia's day-to-day activities, and this was the perfect opportunity. Khon'Tor did not know how Acaraho was going to balance this with his other responsibilities, but he did not particularly care, either. After all, the other males found the time. It suited his purposes, and he could not have been happier at that moment.

"I have no problem with that, Acaraho; Adia?" He looked at the Healer. Then, to increase the pressure, he added, "You will not find a better choice than Acaraho. And no other male here has the skills or possesses the character of the High Protector," he threw in just for good measure.

A feather could have knocked Adia over. This she had not expected; this she had never anticipated. She knew she could not refuse Acaraho. There would be absolutely no reasonable excuse for it. Khon'Tor was right; there was no better role model than Acaraho. The seconds were ticking by, and Adia did not have time to figure this out right now. They were waiting for an answer. The obvious answer was yes, and the longer she took to get the words out, the stranger it would look. *Any female would jump at the chance to have Acaraho as a role model for their son—or anything else,* she thought.

"That would be fine," said Adia lamely. *Oh, far too lukewarm a response.* So she shook her head and added, "That would be great. Thank you both so much. We can work out the details later. Acaraho, I know you also have many other responsibilities. —I will be grateful for any time you can give," she added.

Rising, she nodded to them all, being very careful not to let her gaze linger on Acaraho, and took her leave.

Adia did not know who she had in mind when thinking of finding a mentor for Oh'Dar, but she had thought there would be time to identify some suitable candidates. She had thought it would take a while to find someone because it would be a draw on whoever's time and was a lot to ask. Also, Oh'Dar was still only a very young offspring. She had been trying to gain Khon'Tor's promise for later down the road, and she had certainly not expected to walk away with a commitment.

Acaraho. He is not paired. He is precisely what

Khon'Tor said he is—there could be no better choice. She knew he was capable of great kindness and great wisdom. It was a joy and a heartache every time she saw him. She was already having trouble reigning in her thoughts of him. And now he would be even further entrenched in her life. She would have to be around him on an ongoing basis except now he would not be standing against the wall as a Protector, never participating. Now he would be spending time with Oh'Dar, talking to her about what to teach him as he grew, perhaps the two of them would even laugh together over the funny things the offspring did or said.

Something was going on outside of Adia's volition, and she was doing her best to keep up and hang on. *I feel as if I am being swept down a path, and the feeling only grows stronger as time passes.*

For the next few days, Adia buried herself in her work as Healer. She focused on cleaning and sorting the leaves, roots, stems, and other parts of the plants collected during the harvest. She kept herself busy—so busy that at night she fell asleep exhausted, with no time to think of anything else. It was as if she were running through the days—but to where? Or to what?

CHAPTER 4

Time was running out.

Adia needed to tell Khon'Tor. *All the cleaning, sorting, and categorizing is not going to change anything. The longer I let it go, the harder it gets,* she thought.

She returned to the little secluded cave with the shallows as often as she could. There she could think, ponder, and allow her feelings to flow.

The role of the Healer was central to all the communities of the People, just as it was to the Brothers. It was not only the important nature of the Healer's work. It was also the influence exerted by her position of Second Rank. The Healer's role was meant to bring balance to the more authoritarian position of the Leader of the community. Whereas issues could appear more black and white to the Leader, who held the primary responsibility, the

Healer's view was counted on to soften that perspective so that a more holistic, well-rounded solution might be found to issues and—in the worst case—alterations with those not of the People. The problem must be solved but the repercussions of the solution had also to be considered.

This was one of Adia's great gifts—the ability to keep the broader perspective in mind. Just as she had given up the need for personal revenge against Khon'Tor to spare damaging the peace and cohesiveness of the community, so she embodied the first of the First Laws, that the needs of the community come before the needs of the individual.

The position of Healer was not passed down through a bloodline. The Healer was critical to the wellbeing of the People on many levels; the possible death of a Healer through complications in carrying and delivering an offspring was never worth the risk. Anyone chosen as Healer accepted that she would never mate and never produce offspring. The requirements of the position also made it difficult to balance dedication to the community with the demands of personal life and family; the Healer was meant to keep the needs and welfare of the People foremost in her heart and mind.

The Leader was required to mate and have a family, one reason being that this would soften a potentially heavy hand. Conversely, the Healer was forbidden to for the opposite reason. It was all designed to provide balance, point and counterpoint, and had proven effective through the generations.

Alone in the small, secret little cave, Adia had realized that the impact on the community of her being with offspring was more important than how it impacted her personally. She could not make this all about her any more than her decision to turn Khon'Tor in was about her alone. She was with offspring, and as a result of that, her life and role as Healer were at risk.

Adia sighed. She admitted to herself the truth she had been trying to push out of her mind. *I have to tell the High Council that I am with offspring. It cannot be handled within the community. It is not something that our own Leaders can decide. My mother died giving birth. What if the same happens to me? The People need a Healer.*

The burden of this was almost more than Adia could bear.

Under extreme circumstances, the High Council *could* be called by any individual, whether a Leader or not. However, it was a risky move, and most community members would never dare chance it. When a matter involved only one community, as Adia's pregnancy did, usually a smaller number of the High Council members would come to hear the matter. Weighty cases affecting both the People and the Brothers, such as the threat of the Waschini, would be resolved with a meeting of the full High Council.

Bringing an internal matter to the High Council is not a decision to be made lightly. It will remove the issue from Khon'Tor's control, which will be uncomfortable for everyone involved. As angry as Khon'Tor is going to be over my carrying an offspring, bringing it to the High Council will inflame him to an unimaginable level.

And she would have to deal with that, live with that, and bear up under that for the rest of her life.

Adia never shied away from difficulty. She had learned from her Father that problems usually only became more complicated the longer they were ignored. *No matter how hard it is, it is as easy as it will ever get*, she told herself.

The Council would most likely be made up of Ogima Adoeete, High Chief of the Brothers; Is'Taqa, Second Chief of the Brothers; Lesharo'Mok, Leader of the People of the Deep Valley, which was Adia's birthplace; Harak'Sar, Leader of People of the Far High Hills, and Kurak'Kahn, the High Council Overseer. The High Council Overseer and Lesharo'Mok were involved in all matters, to provide continuity in how problems were viewed and handled. They always heard issues of this nature in private.

Adia knew Khon'Tor would also sit in on the small group since he was not only a High Council member but also the Leader of the affected community. That meant he would hear about her being with offspring at the same time they did. How this would affect his handling of the news, she could not tell.

Will the fact that this is his offspring—that I will be the Mother Of His Offspring—soften his anger toward me at all? A rational male would not blame a female for being seeded by a mating forced on her, but in violating me, Khon'Tor has proven he is not a rational male. He is a strong Leader, and in many ways, he has the best interests of the People at heart—but when his ambitions and goals conflict with the interests of the community, he is unable to set them aside. His own needs and desires will take precedence.

Adia did not know if anyone else of rank would be involved in the meeting. It was not unheard of to have other influential members of a community participating in a hearing. She realized it might include Hakani. She shuddered to think of Hakani's reaction should she ever find out that Adia was carrying Khon'Tor's offspring.

Adia had to get her request to the High Council. Ordinarily, this would be sent by the community Leader, in this case, Khon'Tor. But Adia felt it best if Khon'Tor did not know any more ahead of time than he did already. She preferred he find out the details when the hearing began.

Because Acaraho was the High Protector, it would be appropriate for her to send the request to the High Council through him. She considered sending it through Is'Taqa of the Brothers but realized Acaraho would have to know ahead of time, regardless. There would be the matter of overnight arrangements and other logistics to put in place before the High Council members arrived.

Adia was certain that Acaraho would immediately know what it was about, once he knew it was she who had requested the meeting. On the day she had told him about her condition the last words he had spoken to her, just as she was leaving, were, "Does he know?" to which she had replied, "Not yet."

Khon'Tor walked down one of Kthama's paths to the valley. For a change, he was having a better morning.

Finally, I have Adia under control. The incident is now a thing of the past. Everyone in the community has accepted it was an accident, that she tripped and hit her head on the rocks. I worried they would question why she was outside after I expressly forbade it, but it has not been an issue. They have probably assumed that in her delirium, she was not thinking clearly.

And Akule. He seems to keep to himself, but he has never brought up that evening. The few times I have seen him, it seemed it was not even on his mind.

And so Khon'Tor put the matter of Akule out of his mind as well.

Khon'Tor's main problem now was his mate, Hakani, and the offspring she was carrying. The offspring of another male. Hakani was right; Khon'Tor could not stop trying to figure out which of the males had betrayed him. The other matter he could not put out of his mind was how Hakani had tried to incite him that evening into breaking the First Law: Never Without Consent—luring him, enticing him, inflaming him, leading him on—and then rejecting him at the last moment. Hoping he would not be able to stop himself and so mate her without permission. Khon'Tor felt smugly that Hakani was not as smart as she thought—even if he had not stopped himself, it would be his word against hers.

Our union has been unsatisfactory from the very beginning. She has carried ill will toward me almost from the day of our pairing. And I still do not know why.

He tolerated her because he had to, but if the opportunity were ever presented to free himself of Hakani once and for all, he would not let it slip by.

Khon'Tor calculated that her offspring was still in the first third of development, which meant she would deliver near the end of the warm days. He also knew she was enjoying the attention of the other females in the community.

Offspring were always a cause for celebration, and even more so because they were raised with everyone's help. As uncomfortable as Khon'Tor's life was, it was going to be far worse when he had to raise another male's offspring as his own. *And if it is a male, that PetaQ—not of my blood, not of my making—will inherit my leadership. Hakani will have the last laugh after all. She will have fulfilled her role to produce an heir, and only she and I will know the truth.*

A chilling thought shot through Khon'Tor's mind. *Did the other male know he had seeded her with his offspring? Would she go so far as to include him in the deception?* Khon'Tor did not know. It would depend on what Hakani felt she could use against him more —he was sure of that.

But Khon'Tor had underestimated Hakani. Getting him to mate her against her will was not her end game. She had counted on inciting him to hurt her. A *he said, she said* situation was nothing in comparison with real, verifiable physical wounds with which to discredit him. Her gamble was that she had not enraged him to the point where he would kill her. But the watcher who came to their quarters had foiled her elaborate plan.

Hakani was worried. *Time is running out. I will not be able to keep up this lie of being with offspring much longer. But once I lose the offspring and have no more leverage over him, Khon'Tor will only ride out the public sympathy before he disposes of me.*

Try as she might, Hakani could not figure out how to regain leverage over Khon'Tor. She knew he would not fall for the *Never Without Consent* seduction scene again. She doubted she would be able to incense him back to a level where he might hurt her. He had made it clear he no longer trusted her, and that her only purpose was to produce an heir. And if she would not or could not provide an heir for him, he would find a way to set her aside.

The only way I could gain power back over him would be to bear his offspring. But giving him that satisfaction is the last thing I want to do. What is worse? Submitting to him, or having him take another mate? I would rather one of us be dead than go through either!

Hakani had given a lot of thought to how she would fake a miscarriage. Her primary problem was that females in her condition would ordinarily be enlisting the aid of the Healer. Seeing that she hated Adia and that she was not actually carrying an offspring, this was an impossibility.

She knew she did not have to convince everyone she had miscarried; convincing one was enough, as long as that one would make sure everyone else knew. And it would have to be someone who would not know a real miscarriage from a pretend one. Who better to achieve both those purposes than Khon'Tor? No one would be happier about this miscarriage than he. No one would be quicker than he to make sure the word spread like wildfire. And no one probably knew less than he what the results of a miscarriage would look like.

Hakani and Adia were running against very similar deadlines. Hakani was running out of time to end her pregnancy; Adia was running out of time to announce hers.

Adia again sent word that she needed to speak with Acaraho.

Acaraho was in his quarters, lost in thought when Awan brought him the message. He assumed she wanted to talk to him about mentoring Oh'Dar.

Acaraho's quarters were orderly and peaceful. They were his place of respite and the only place where he felt able to drop his guard. Here, he could think about Adia; here, he would replay their few conversations, or remember the times they had spent together when he was assigned to be her Protector. He was looking forward to being inserted back into her life. He knew that as Oh'Dar's mentor, their interactions would be far more personal than before, when he had observed her only from his post against the wall.

He was also happy at the thought of being back in the company of both females. In a way, being around them felt like coming home. He had forgotten how much he enjoyed watching the Healer and her Helper together. They were very close, with a friendship far deeper than a working relationship.

But seeing Adia, meeting with her, talking to her, will all test limits of my self-control. From how she fell into my arms, I believe it will also test hers.

Adia had arranged for Nadiwani, Honovi, and Oh'Dar to be elsewhere. She did not want to be seen too often speaking with Acaraho on a prolonged basis. Once it became known that Acaraho was going to be Oh'Dar's mentor, it would not seem so out of the ordinary for them to interact frequently.

Acaraho arrived, and Adia invited him in. She asked him to pull the stone door closed—another affront to protocol and another signal that whatever they were about to discuss was either very personal or very important, or both.

"Acaraho," she began. "I will not take long with this because of the unusual nature of our meeting here alone.

"The matter of my condition is greater than the personal problems it presents me with. Because of my role as Healer, because of my position in authority here, it warrants consideration at a higher level than within our community. I am asking to convene a session of the High Council to inform them that I am with offspring. Considering certain aspects, I do not feel it prudent to send such a request through the normal channel, which would be Khon'Tor. Also, because there will be logistics to arrange, I know you will ultimately be involved in this matter anyway," and she finally paused for a moment.

"I am asking, Acaraho, if you would convey my

request to the High Council without Khon'Tor's knowledge. If this puts you in an untenable position, please let me know, and I will find another means to ask for their intervention."

Adia assumed Acaraho would realize she was speaking formally to add a sense of propriety to their meeting here in private. She was addressing him in an official capacity in her role as Second Rank. She was trying to keep her personal feelings out of this, and she trusted he would honor her intention.

"I will take care of that for you, Healer," Acaraho said, replying in the same tone she had used. "I will let you know as soon as I receive word of their proposed arrival date. I will also take care of any other arrangements you may need," he added.

"Thank you. I appreciate your assistance, and your discretion."

"Will that be all for now?" asked Acaraho.

"Yes. Thank you for coming," and Adia rose as Acaraho turned to leave. When he made it to the door, he turned back to look at her. And when their eyes met, all the words unspoken between them were said.

The People did not have a written language as such, but they did utilize symbols to represent significant events or commonly recognized terms. Each family had a marking of its own through the father's line.

And the markings on the tunnel indicated the junction, and which branch led where. They also used symbols to transmit high-level messages between their communities, with the Brothers, and in this case, with the High Council.

Acaraho went back to his quarters, took out a large piece of treated hide, and drew the message out with the same clay ochre pigment used for the tunnel markings. He made the symbol for the High Council, a collection of three ovals representing people, which hovered above a smaller group of circles that represented a general assembly, then underneath he made a representation of an outstretched palm signifying the request for help. The symbols had been in use by the communities for ages past, so there was no mistaking the meaning of a message when sent.

Acaraho rolled up the skin and secured it with a binding of treated sinew. He gave the scroll to his fastest and most reliable messenger, with instructions as to whom it should be delivered. He also told the messenger to wait to hear who would be coming, and when they could be expected, even if that meant it might be days before he could bring the answers back. Acaraho was sure to select an unpaired male so as not to create family hardship through such an extended absence.

Once the message was on its way, Acaraho went about deciding where the meeting would be held, where the High Council members would be lodged, and the other hundred details that he had to work out ahead of time.

In the meantime, Hakani had assembled what she needed to fake her miscarriage.

Most of the living quarters were designed to include a general open area, separate sleeping area, food storage and preparation areas, and one for personal care. They differed in size and location. Once allocated, most were occupied by the same family for generations, though sometimes the older members would move to separate quarters or those on the higher levels so they could access the outdoors more easily and were closer to the community areas. Community members who preferred a quieter environment often chose quarters in the lower levels. Most of the quarters were of similar size, with only a few being larger and more elaborate. The Healer's Quarters were an example of a more spacious combined living and working area, which reflected the need for privacy for both the personal and professional aspects of her calling.

The Leader's Quarters were among the largest, though still not large enough to make living with Khon'Tor bearable. Fortunately, he stayed away a great deal of the time, which gave Hakani the privacy she needed to hide the monthly evidence she was not with offspring, as well as to stage her miscarriage.

I do not need an elaborate performance to fool Khon'-Tor; it is the other females in the community I need to convince. I doubt anyone suspects I am lying about being with offspring, so I do not expect a great deal of scrutiny, but it is still best to be prepared. Khon'Tor is not going to question something he will welcome so much, as long as there is reasonable proof.

She knew what items she wanted to collect; however, Hakani had to wait until she was ready to present the evidence and deliver her performance. She also needed Khon'Tor to be around as her witness, and with his extended absences, the timing was a challenge.

Hakani prepared the way by complaining of cramps and discomfort to a few of the other females. She had to be careful not to overdo it, or she would trigger pressure from the others to see the Healer, but it had to be just enough for them to remember it later. Hakani was quite the master planner. Had she not been consumed by her hatred of Khon'Tor and Adia, she could have been a great asset to the People.

Acaraho's messenger returned and informed him that the High Council members, five of them, would arrive within a week. This left Acaraho just enough time to complete preparations. Now that it was official, he would have to tell Khon'Tor—but not until he had spoken with Adia.

Honovi and Oh'Dar were involved in some kind of conversation when Acaraho arrived. Whether Honovi knew what he was trying to say or not, she played along as if she did, encouraging his babbling.

Nadiwani and Adia were at the worktable sorting their medicines. Acaraho entered, this time without knocking, which surprised Adia. She interpreted this to mean he had something important on his mind.

"Adia, may I speak with you a moment?" he asked, nodding to the others.

Adia stepped outside with him. Acaraho motioned away from the entrance, and they began walking. He turned to talk to her about halfway down the tunnel that led to her quarters.

"I have heard back from the High Council. They will be here within about six days. I need to tell Khon'Tor that a request has been made for their attendance to an issue. He knows he is not supposed to ask what it is, and I doubt he will, but I would expect him to be on edge in the meantime," said Acaraho.

I am also going to be on edge, Adia thought. "I want to tell Nadiwani. She is my friend. I trust her."

"I am sure you need a friend to go through this with you right now," Acaraho replied. "I must continue to make preparations, so I will speak with Khon'Tor tonight. I cannot put it off any longer, nor would it be appropriate to keep it from him now I know they are coming," he added.

Adia nodded. "Thank you. I know you will keep

me informed. Do you know who is coming?" she added anxiously.

"Ogima Adoeete, High Chief of the Brothers; Is'Taqa, Second Chief of the Brothers; Lesharo'Mok, Leader of the People of the Deep Valley; Harak'Sar, Leader of the People of the Far High Hills, and Kurak'Kahn the High Council Overseer. And of course, Khon'Tor will be in attendance as a High Council member, and as Leader of the High Rocks," he answered.

"Will you be there?" there she asked. She wanted Acaraho to be present because he understood how difficult this would be for her. It did not occur to Adia that she might need him for protection; she knew Khon'Tor would be upset, but she doubted he would do anything to her with witnesses around.

"It would be appropriate for me to be, considering my role as High Protector," said Acaraho.

Adia looked up at him with gentle eyes and said quietly, "Please."

Acaraho gave one slow, brief nod, his eyes never leaving hers. Adia did not let herself think about how she would deal with their relationship as he became more actively involved in Oh'Dar's life.

And then it hit her. The offspring she was carrying would also need a male role model. *Does this mean Acaraho will also be this offspring's mentor?* she asked herself, somewhat alarmed. *How did I allow this to happen? And how am I going to cope with seeing him so often?*

Acaraho went on his way, and Adia went back to helping Nadiwani sort and process their large harvest bounty. She tried to keep her mind on their work but could not help reflecting that conversations with Acaraho were becoming longer and more relaxed.

CHAPTER 5

Hakani's time had come. She had complained of not feeling well for a few days now. She had gathered the materials she needed from the community kitchen area at a time when no one else was around to see what she was selecting. She only needed enough to convince Khon'Tor that she had indeed lost the offspring. She knew he would be relieved and so would not question it; why should he? He was aware that she needed this offspring to secure her continued position as his mate. He would have no reason to suspect she would fake a miscarriage.

Khon'Tor came back to the quarters as late as possible, but his timing was still fairly consistent. Hakani had left the evidence in the personal care area, not so apparent as to be blatant, but not hidden enough that he could not notice it at some point. She knew he would not inspect it and planned on disposing of it in the morning so no one else would be able to either. She was confident it was enough to back-up her story.

Hakani knew if her seeding had been real, and the miscarriage had happened, she would be beside herself with anger at having lost her hold over Khon'Tor. So she prepared her mindset along those lines.

She made sure she was sitting in direct line of sight so he could not miss her when he came in. She arranged her position to indicate discomfort.

As soon as he entered, she spoke to gain his attention.

"Well, this is your *lucky day*, Khon'Tor," she said, looking up at him as he walked across the room.

"Obviously, I do not know what you are talking about," he replied blankly.

"You are going to find out eventually so I may as well tell you now. I lost the offspring. I am no longer seeded," said Hakani, bringing as much disappointment into her voice as possible. She was watching him for the reaction she knew was coming.

Khon'Tor stopped walking and turned to look at her. "If this is another of your twisted games, Hakani, I am not interested in playing," and he turned away.

"It is not a game, Khon'Tor. You can see for yourself if you wish," she said, nodding toward the personal area where she had left the discarded evidence.

Khon'Tor continued to his sleeping mat, which he had located as far away from hers as possible.

Hakani had not counted on his not believing her. She needed Khon'Tor to spread the word throughout the community.

"Surely you do not think I would lie about something like this," she hissed.

🌀

Khon'Tor did not know what to believe any longer when it came to Hakani. He did *not* put it past her to lie about this as well, only to torment him again by telling him she was still with offspring.

When he entered, he had been surprised to find Hakani sitting up in her sleeping area. Usually, she was asleep—or feigning sleep—by that time. He did not want to speak to her, but he did notice the way she was sitting seemed to indicate she was uncomfortable.

And now she is saying she lost the offspring? He did not want to, but he arose and went to where she had indicated. Though he did not know what to expect, Khon'Tor started to accept that this might be true and that he might be freed of her someday after all.

"I am not going to say I am sorry," he said to her coldly as he came back out. "And I doubt you care that much either, other than that your hold over me has now been broken, and your spot in the limelight will now be dimmed," he added.

"I am sure you will not waste any time letting everyone know either," Hakani said.

"You are correct. However, instead of worrying about that, you should be considering your next move." Khon'Tor looked at his mate with cold eyes.

"Since you are obviously capable of being seeded, I suggest you reconsider your position about providing me with offspring. I meant what I said before. You are of only one use to me now. I have no qualms about setting you aside and choosing another mate. I would prefer it."

He stared blandly at Hakani.

She sat up straighter, her eyes blazing. "Just try to bring another female into these quarters, Khon'Tor. You think your life is miserable now? I would make you regret you ever met me!" Hakani spat out.

Khon'Tor laughed, "I already regret that, Hakani. And I have for some time. And do not worry—I would never try to live with two females under one roof. If I take a second mate, only one of you will be living here," he said.

She was staring at him, and he enjoyed her discomfort as she realized the implications of what he was saying.

Knowing he had her full attention and that his nonchalance enraged her, he continued,

"Of course, I will provide for you. You will have your own quarters, and your needs will be taken care of, but as for your position as my mate, that will be only a memory. And your position as Third Rank, of which I stripped you for the stunt you pulled with the Waschini, will naturally be transferred to the mother of my offspring."

He looked at her casually, as if they were discussing the most mundane of matters, almost beneath his attention.

Hakani flew up and lunged at him, her nails clawing at his face. As before, he easily caught her wrists, only this time brutally shoving her down onto her knees. He trapped and held her there, as she looked up at him with narrowed eyes.

She struggled, but Khon'Tor just tightened his grip, hurting her and causing her to stop squirming. He then leaned over, bringing his face just inches from hers.

His eyes burned into those of his mate. He bared his teeth and whispered to Hakani in the lowest of growls, "As I said, I suggest you rethink your position. If it were not for your current condition, I would suggest we start tonight. However, all things considered, I will give you two days to recover. I will then expect you to submit to me. Let me say, *I strongly suggest you do.*"

"I hate you," she spat at him, still trapped in his grip.

"As you will. I really do not care how you feel about me, or what you want."

"I cannot possibly be seeded this soon, Khon'Tor. There is no point this early," she offered up— anything to delay what seemed to be inevitable.

Khon'Tor chuckled. Then he leaned closer, and Hakani could feel his warm breath on her neck.

"Oh, Hakani. There is lots of time for you to be seeded. You are missing the point. I intend to enjoy my victory over you at *every* opportunity," he sneered.

She was furious. She struggled again to get free. This time Khon'Tor swept her knees out from under her with one of his legs and knocked her to the floor, where she lay on her back. He dropped to lean down over her, trapping her under the inescapable weight of his body, her wrists pinned over her head, leaving her powerless against him.

"Do not push me, Hakani. I said we could wait, but that was out of consideration for you. There is no benefit to me in not proceeding this very moment," and with that, he pressed himself against her with the clear intent of mating her right then.

Hakani broke. And as angry as he was with her right now, he was still nowhere near the level she had pushed him the night she had tried to provoke him to attack her. Even in that state, he had managed to back off when she revoked her consent. And yet he was sending her a message that he no longer cared whether he had her consent or not. *I have finally pushed him too far.*

And she said the words she never thought she

would say, "Khon'Tor. Stop, please. You win. Please, do not. Not now, not tonight," she asked, turning her head to avoid his piercing gaze.

She was practically begging him. He raised himself enough to bring her wrists down from over her head. But she could tell he was not done yet.

"Oh, and if you have any thoughts about repeating your little trick with whoever betrayed me, you can put that out of your mind. From now on, you will have a personal guard with you at every moment. You will never be alone with any other male again; you can be sure of that. The only one who will *ever* mate you will be me," he continued.

Khon'Tor released her wrists and got up, freeing her. The moment he let go, she rolled over on her side, instinctively curling into a fetal position.

Khon'Tor had been bluffing. He did not want to bring another female into his life. As much as he hated Hakani, his status as Leader came first on his list of priorities. Having a female around who would require attention and dialogue would be a drain. While he had wanted exactly that when he imagined being with Adia, he now saw a real relationship as a drawback and a hindrance.

The most straightforward path would be for her to produce an heir and focus her life on raising the offspring, letting them continue in their cold stale-mate of a union.

He looked down at Hakani, curled into a ball, and felt nothing but pleasure. *I finally crushed her. I finally won with her, too. And I enjoyed that. It seems I am developing a knack and an appetite for defeating these unruly females.*

He retired to his sleeping mat and envisioned the even more satisfying victory to come in three night's time.

The next morning, Khon'Tor spread the word that Hakani had miscarried. He started with the morning breakfast assembly. He knew it would pass through the community like wildfire.

It did not take long for the news to reach Acaraho. Honovi was in the Healer's Quarters when he came to tell them.

When Acaraho told Adia and Nadiwani, they could not but express concern for Hakani. It was a sad time for any female. No matter the tension or problems between them, Adia was the Healer. She prepared a mixture of sweet marjoram and sweet fennel for the ease of cramping and discomfort and asked to have it delivered to Hakani with instructions for how to take it. She expected Hakani would toss it away instead of using it, just because it came from her. But Adia wanted at least to try to help relieve Hakani's discomfort.

Adia also felt sorry for Honovi, who had no idea what she had stepped into. Though the Healer would shield her from as much of it as she could, Honovi would still no doubt feel the tension and stirring in the air. Adia hoped it would not run the young woman off. No matter what happened, it was still imperative that Oh'Dar learn Whitespeak and they had intentionally started very early with his training.

Three nights hence, Khon'Tor kept his appointment with Hakani. He came back to the quarters a little earlier than usual. Hakani was there, though he had half thought perhaps she might not be. When he saw her, it confirmed in his mind once again that he had beaten her spirit.

"Good evening, Hakani," he said, sliding the stone door after him and standing there in front of it for a moment as if symbolically saying there was no way out for her now. He wanted her to have no doubts he was in full command from now on.

"Did you forget our appointment?" he asked with a smug smile on his face. He walked slowly toward her, intending his approach to be menacing. Khon'-Tor's source of satisfaction had moved past the mere physical act itself to the pleasure of doing as he wanted to her.

"I did not, Khon'Tor," Hakani said quietly.

He continued his slow approach, savoring her reaction. *I have never seen her like this!*

"I will let you choose, Hakani. Your sleeping mat or mine?" he asked.

"Are you really going to do this? Are you really going to go through with this?" she asked.

Her eyes are wide, he thought. He found the fact that she was frightened fueled his enjoyment.

In answer to her, Khon'Tor came to where she was sitting on the edge of her mat. He stood towering over her and looked down. He was starting to breathe harder in anticipation of his next move, and he noticed her eyes were full of alarm.

"I will not hurt you. Well—not unless you *force* me to," he said.

With that, he pushed her backward on the mat and knelt next to her. He grabbed her hips and pulled her to him. Hakani said, "Khon'Tor, I do not give my consent!" to which Khon'Tor scoffed and replied, "You no longer have to, Hakani."

And with that, he took her easily, swiftly, and deliberately—completing his defeat of her with no regard for her pleasure, only his own.

When he was done, he unceremoniously rolled off her, got up, and went to his sleeping mat.

"Tomorrow night, we will discharge your obligation to me over here," he said nonchalantly, gesturing to where he was sitting.

Khon'Tor realized he found this arrangement immanently satisfying. Whereas he used to hate returning to their quarters, he would now look forward to it with burning anticipation. The more she defied him, the more miserable she was, the more she hated him, the more he enjoyed forcing himself on her. Khon'Tor had discovered his appetite for mating and how to satisfy it.

Acaraho was still busy with preparations for the High Council. Adia was spending as much time as possible deciding how she was going to proceed with her announcement when the time came. She made a mental note *not* to look at Khon'Tor when she told them she was with offspring. She knew it would be an easy mistake to make, unconsciously betraying him to the others.

Within days of his messenger's return, Acaraho called for an audience with Khon'Tor. They met in the meeting room Khon'Tor had appropriated for his personal use. Acaraho did not wish to drag this out because he was not at liberty to explain why the High Council was coming. He knew Khon'Tor knew this, but he expected the Leader to press him for details, nonetheless.

"Good Morning, Acaraho. You asked to meet with me. I assume this is a matter of some importance if it cannot wait for our regular time."

"Khon'Tor," started Acaraho, "I was asked to send a message to the High Council asking for their intervention in a matter affecting this community. The High Council members will be here within a day or so. I have been busy with logistics, and now that they have given me a commitment regarding the time of their arrival, I must notify you of their intercession."

It was all Acaraho could do to look at Khon'Tor without imagining his hands around the Leader's throat.

Khon'Tor's mind went immediately to Adia. *She is going to bring charges against me after all*, he thought. Despite the Rah-hora, despite the risk to herself and Oh'Dar, despite it all, she was turning him in. His heart started pounding in his chest.

He looked around the room as he collected his thoughts. Knowing he was not allowed to ask, he did anyway, "What is this about? Who requested you contact them?"

"You know I cannot disclose that. I understand your asking, however," he replied.

"Who is coming? Who on the High Council is coming?" he pressed.

This, Acaraho could disclose, and he recited the names. "You have the right as Leader of the People to have your Second Rank, and Hakani—though she is no longer officially Third Rank—in attendance if you so wish," he reminded Khon'Tor.

The Leader turned away from Acaraho, not wanting him to see any reaction. *He seldom misses anything. If ever.*

Khon'Tor took a deep breath. *I will know soon enough. A few days' notice will do nothing to prepare me for what is to come. If it was Adia who contacted them, I will find a way to deal with her later. If she is bringing charges against me, she is violating her part of the Rahhora. Regardless of what happens, she will still forfeit her life to me. And to whatever extent possible, I will find a way to enforce that agreement. Or find another way to make her pay.*

Unless, of course, they banish me from the community.

Banishment was the most severe penalty ever imposed by the People; a single Sasquatch living in isolation was condemned to a life of struggle and hardship, and usually an early death. The People depended on each other. They were communal by nature, so they thrived in a setting such as Kthama.

Once they knew what Khon'Tor had done to Adia, it would not take them long to figure that he had left her there to die. He would be ruined. But, as hard as it would be to remain in the community, humiliated and denigrated, it would be better than banishment.

Khon'Tor had become Leader of the High Rocks

at an early age and was used to being in a position of power; he did not know any other way to live. His greatest satisfaction was feeling he was looked up to, admired, perhaps even revered. To be stripped of his position of leadership, and to have his reputation and memory disparaged, would be anathema to him. He would go down in history, not as the great Leader he imagined he was, but remembered as the second ever to break the First Law: Never Without Consent.

He knew it had to be Adia. The Waschini offspring had been accepted into the community. The People were enjoying the cold weather activities; it was a time for socializing and reinforcing the bonds among them. The threat of the Waschini waxed and waned. He could think of no one else who would have a reason to call for the High Council's oversight.

He did briefly consider Hakani, but the request for the High Council must have been put in before she lost the offspring. There was no reason for her to have requested their presence when she still had the upper hand.

Khon'Tor looked at Acaraho. It was possible that Acaraho did not know what the allegation was. It was possible he that had only been asked to send the message. But Acaraho, at the very least, knew *who* had requested it.

Khon'Tor's mind was reeling.

Acaraho had said he could request Adia's presence as Second Rank. Did that mean it was not she who had lodged the complaint?

Perhaps the High Council had learned about the Waschini offspring. Both Ogima Adoeete and Is'Taqa of the Brothers knew about Oh'Dar because they were visiting when Hakani revealed his presence. *It would not be like the Brothers to interfere in our internal operations, though. They may sit on the High Council in consideration of a matter of the People, but they would not instigate an investigation.*

It is possible Hakani let the High Council know about Oh'Dar, but again, things were going well for Hakani at the time the request was made. There was no motivation for her to cause trouble.

An investigation; that's what it comes down to? thought Khon'Tor. *Having the High Council hear an issue against me as Leader is the worst thing I could imagine.*

Acaraho stood quietly while Khon'Tor was lost in silence. Finally, he walked around to face the Leader, forcing him to acknowledge that Acaraho was still there.

"You will need to let me know who you want in attendance, at least by the time they arrive," Acaraho said.

"I will," said the Leader.

Acaraho left, and Khon'Tor lowered himself to one of the seating boulders where he could try to clear his mind.

The process is underway, he thought. *There is nothing I can do to stop it.*

All he could do was wait for the High Council to arrive. And to figure out whether to have Hakani attend the High Council Meeting. In the end, he decided against it. Though her submissive attitude continued, he was not sure how long it would hold up.

He blamed both Hakani and Adia for his problems.

I am the Leader of the People of the High Rocks—the largest most expansive known community of the People. My ancestors have lived here for generations upon generations. It is my job to protect my community and our culture. Yes, I am a strong Leader, but I have to be. I only want what is best for them. I do not need to be challenged by these two females who do not understand the level of responsibility I carry. If they did not fight me, I would not be so tough on them. They have brought their problems on themselves.

That night, Khon'Tor was particularly hard on Hakani.

Acaraho was confident that Khon'Tor assumed Adia was, after all, going to hold him accountable for his crimes. Therefore, Acaraho was already on high alert for any signs of a pre-emptive strike against Adia, and he had placed additional guards throughout the corridors leading to her quarters. He did not have to give a reason; the males followed his orders without question. Khon'Tor would only discover them if he went to find Adia.

The day had come. The Watchers brought news of the High Council members' approach, and Acaraho was ready for them. In the meantime, he needed to know who of his command Khon'Tor had decided to have in attendance at the next day's meeting.

Khon'Tor had thought through it both ways, but if it turned out he was entirely wrong and the issue had nothing to do with Adia, it would be peculiar if he had not requested her presence at so critical a meeting. On that basis, he told Acaraho that Adia should be in attendance, but not Hakani. He used the excuse of his mate's miscarriage to leave her out.

Acaraho nodded and said he would let Khon'Tor know when they were assembling.

He next went to Adia to let her know they would be convening in the morning.

This was a volatile situation, and the outcome depended on how the High Council perceived her condition—as an act of disregard for her role as Healer, or the understandable failing of a robust young female who had been relegated to a loveless and barren way of life. One that ran counter-current to everything about a female's nature.

When Acaraho left, Adia sat alone with her thoughts.

Whether to deliver justice or mercy. My father taught me this is always the question for those with the power to judge others. Whether to deliver justice—the proper and fair administration of the law and the consequences of violating it—or mercy, which through compassion, tempers the punishment that justice demands.

Whatever happens, I will not receive justice—because I will not be judged on the truth. Because I have decided not to offer the whole truth, I will be judged as a willing, negligent participant in the creation of my own troubles. Mercy? I pray I might see what mercy would look like. I only know that in a few hours my life will be changed forever.

Acaraho received the High Council members and arranged guards to show them to their quarters. He knew they would wish to rest before tomorrow's hearing. It was customary for the Leader to greet them, and Khon'Tor met his obligation to be there. He knew word of their arrival would fly through the community even faster than had the word of Hakani's miscarriage. He hated that there would be rampant speculation about the purpose of the visit. All the People knew that the High Council only inserted itself into matters of the gravest concern.

As Khon'Tor greeted the members, he kept his behavior as normal as possible. There was still an outside chance this had nothing to do with him, and he was hanging onto that for all he was worth. Only a guilty male would avoid meeting them.

He had not told Hakani of their coming because he did not want her involved. There was no scenario he could imagine in which her presence would benefit him. She was a different person now, subdued and quiet, but he doubted he had doused her flame permanently. When and if it reignited, he did not want it to be in front of the High Council. Though, if they were here because Adia was bringing charges against him, he doubted there was anything Hakani could do to make the situation worse for him.

The next morning, some of Acaraho's guards brought the High Council members into the room he had prepared for the meeting.

It was not being conducted in the Great Chamber because that area was far too large, with no privacy, and would have lent an even more intimidating air to the meeting than was already present. Acaraho did not care about any of this for Khon'Tor's sake; he wished as much discomfort as possible on the Leader. But for Adia's sake, he wanted a more personable setting. And one as far away from curious eyes and listening ears as possible. He had found a venue suited to the purpose and staked several guards at various routes to the location.

He arranged the room with a table and seating at

what could be considered the back, with more seating facing the table for Adia and anyone else who might be in attendance with her. Acaraho intended to stand to the side where he had the best view of everyone involved. He wanted to make sure Adia could see him and hoped his being there would be a comfort to her.

As the one in charge of this operation, he should receive no resistance from anyone regarding his presence, but leaving nothing to chance, Acaraho met privately with the High Council members before the meeting began. He was concerned they might ask him to leave and had his vehement objection prepared. There was no way he was not going to be there for Adia. However, they confirmed to him that his presence would be necessary throughout the proceedings, as he was the intermediary as well as the head of security.

When they were ready, Acaraho sent first for Khon'Tor.

The Leader arrived and greeted the High Council members. They indicated that he was to take a seat at the front table with them. After seating Khon'Tor, Kurak'Kahn, High Council Overseer, spoke directly to him.

"Khon'Tor, Leader of the People of the High Rocks, we have been summoned to hear a matter of urgent importance to the welfare of your people. As Leader, you are permitted to be in attendance. You will be able to hear all the conversation and what the petitioning party has to say. However, since this involves your community directly, you will not be able to participate in our determination of whatever action might be necessary. We will, however, allow you to make whatever remarks you wish after we have heard the matter, and before we adjourn. Do you understand and accept these protocols?"

It was more a formality as every Leader everywhere knew the rules of engagement should an issue of this magnitude arise within his own walls. Khon'Tor nodded that he did.

Then Kurak'Kahn looked at Acaraho and announced, "Please have the People's Healer, Adia, Second Rank, and the Leader's Mate, Hakani, Third Rank, brought to this meeting."

Khon'Tor could not help but look across at the Overseer. He did not want Hakani there. But it was too late. They did not know he had stripped her of her rank, and the Overseer himself had ordered her attendance. Perhaps it was she after all who had lodged a complaint.

Time crept uncomfortably by. While they were waiting, Khon'Tor considered each of the High Council members and what their opinion of him might be.

First was Ogima Adoeete, High Chief of the Brothers. Though this was a matter for the People, the High Council requested Leaders of other tribes, who might have first-hand knowledge of the affected community, to participate in the hearings. Khon'Tor had no problems with Ogima Adoeete. The partnership between his people and theirs had been in place for generations. Khon'Tor almost thought of Ogima Adoeete as a friend, and in many ways looked at him as a mentor.

Because leadership of the High Rocks had been passed to Khon'Tor at an earlier age than most, after the loss of his father he had often turned to Ogima Adoeete for counsel. However, the Brothers were ruled by honor as much as were the People. Khon'Tor had broken the People's First Laws regarding unprovoked violence against another of the People, and specifically the First Law: Never Without Consent. Despite their previous good relations, Khon'Tor knew he would find no support from Chief Ogima.

Next was Is'Taqa, Second Chief to the Brothers and Ogima Adoeete's right hand. Is'Taqa was the one who had found Adia where Khon'Tor had left her for dead, and he had hurried to Kthama for help. The fact that Is'Taqa had first-hand knowledge of the condition in which Khon'Tor had left Adia would go harshly against him.

Then was Lesharo'Mok, from the People of the Deep Valley, who, in the absence of a male heir was the rightful successor to Apenimon Adoeete, Adia's father. Khon'Tor did not even linger in his consideration of what their position would be. Adia's father was a legendary Leader, and there would be no mercy here for an attack against his beloved daughter. Though not a direct offspring, Lesharo'Mok was blood-related to Apenimon Adoeete and therefore to Adia.

After him was Harak'Sar, Leader of the People of the Far High Hills. Harak'Sar was known to be a strong-willed Leader like himself. If anyone would understand the reasons for what had happened, Harak'Sar was his best bet.

Lastly was Kurak'Kahn, the High Council Overseer himself. Kurak'Kahn had been the Overseer for as long as Khon'Tor could remember. No doubt he had heard every possible excuse for the breaking of one of the People's laws. He doubted he would find any mercy there, either.

Looking at himself through their eyes, all Khon'Tor could see was a criminal. *But I am not! I am dedicated to the welfare of my people. I would do anything to maintain the peace and well-being of my community.*

He would have somehow to make them understand this, make them see he had lost control, yes. But that anyone in his position, with the stress he was under, could have done the same. If need be, he decided he would even go so far as to tell them of Hakani's cruel treatment of him, the vacant barren years of their relationship, the two females' ongoing defiance of his authority—whatever it took to make them understand this was not his fault.

Nothing was going to undo what he had done, but making it known would only destroy the peace just returning to his people. And they would lose his leadership—the leadership they needed to bring them through the impending threat of the Waschini. He had made a mistake, he would admit to that.

But was not the ongoing order of the People, and their future protection, more important than one life —even a Healer's? Nothing could undo what happened; leaving her to die was the appropriate choice for a Leader to protect his community.

Hakani and Adia finally arrived at the meeting room. Hakani was totally in the dark. Her mind was swirling with her crimes, and she wondered if perhaps this had something to do with her. Her eyes darted around the room suspiciously. She knew of all the High Council members but had only ever interacted with a few.

Adia and Hakani stood before the panel as Kurak'Kahn addressed them. He spoke to Adia first, as Second Rank.

"Adia, Healer of the People of the High Rocks, we have been summoned to hear a matter of urgent importance to the welfare of your people. As Healer and Second Rank, we welcome your attendance. You will be allowed to hear all the testimony offered; however, you will not be able to participate in our determination of whatever action might be necessary. We will give you an opportunity to make any comments you wish before we adjourn to consider our decision in this matter. Do you understand and accept these protocols?"

Adia nodded and remained standing as she had not been dismissed.

Kurak'Kahn then addressed Hakani with the same instructions. Hakani nodded, realizing no one had told them that Khon'Tor had stripped her of her Third Rank. Her mind was still racing to figure out what this could be about.

When the Overseer finished, he told both the females they could sit down. Adia took a seat and waited for the next direction.

Kurak'Kahn then turned to Acaraho, who had invited them.

"Acaraho, it was through you the request came for our attendance to this matter. Please bring the offended party to us now so we may hear their plea."

Adia stood up and stepped forward to address the High Council.

"High Council members. It was I who requested your intervention. Thank you for coming to hear my matter." Adia stood tall and composed. Her gaze was steady and unwavering. She addressed them with formality and presence.

Khon'Tor froze. He gripped the flesh of his thighs painfully under the table with his fists.

Hakani's head snapped over in Adia's direction. She could think of nothing about Adia that would warrant the involvement of the High Council.

Though it was improper, the High Council members stirred just the slightest bit in their seats. This was Adia, daughter of Apenimon Adoeete and the most respected Healer among the People. Even the Brothers revered her. Whatever crime had been committed against Adia would be met with the most severe consequences permissible.

"Adia," Kurak'Kahn addressed her again. "What crime has been committed against you?" he asked, cutting to the point.

"No, Kurak'Kahn, Overseer of the High Council. It is I who have committed the crime which requires your intervention," she stated plainly without emotion.

Eyebrows rose as the members of the panel exchanged glances. Never had a Healer of the People transgressed one of the laws, and certainly not Adia of the People of the High Rocks.

Is'Taqa stole a look at Ogima Adoeete, his brows knitted together in confusion. Khon'Tor sat rigid and unmoving. It took a moment for the High Council members to regain their focus.

Kurak'Kahn raised his hand to bring their attention back under control. The Overseer was required by protocol to address Adia next.

"Adia of the People of the High Rocks, whatever you tell us now will be taken into serious consideration. The other members of your leadership, Khon'Tor as Leader, and Hakani as Third Rank, will be allowed to make statements for or against you after you have finished speaking. We will then retire and come to an agreement about how to proceed. Our ruling will be binding on you and everyone here. Do you understand?"

"I do," she replied, making sure she made her voice heard and did not resort merely to nodding.

"Proceed," said Kurak'Kahn, and he nodded at her, keeping his eyes locked on hers.

It was time.

Adia had vowed she was not going to let herself cry. She would not let herself appear to play on their goodwill toward her—or their reverence for the females of the People and her position as Healer. But she would remind them of who she was and what she stood for, regardless of what else they were about to hear.

She had prayed for their understanding, but had prepared herself to receive none.

"I know you all know who I am. Many of you knew my father, Apenimon Adoeete, Leader of the People of the Deep Valley. Lesharo'Mok is here as their current Leader. My father's blood runs in my veins. My father's love for the People lives in my heart. My father's honor lives in my soul. When I was chosen as Healer for the People of the High Rocks, I was honored to be offered this great responsibility and opportunity. To serve and minister to the People here has been my life's greatest reward. I recognize the sacredness of the position which was entrusted me to discharge. I have administered my duties with reverence and gratitude. I hope you will remember this when you consider your judgment of my crime," Adia told them.

Nearly everyone in the room caught their breath. All eyes locked on her.

"High Council. It is with deepest regret and shame that I must inform you I am with offspring."

The room fell deathly silent. Not one of them, except for Acaraho, was prepared for what Adia had just said. Ignoring their blank stares, she continued.

"I know my condition violates the Second Law. No Healer may bear the risks of carrying and delivering an offspring. I come to you for your deliberation on the best course of action regarding my continued place here among my people as their Healer."

To ask the next question was on the border of impropriety but Kurak'Kahn leveraged his position as Overseer to ask it. "Adia, who seeded the offspring you carry?"

"The identity of the father is of no consequence to my situation, Overseer," she stated.

The Overseer leaned forward.

"I will ask you again, Adia. Name the father of the

offspring you bear." This time it was a demand, not a question.

"With all due respect, Overseer. I will not reveal the father's identity. Who he is has no bearing on the fact of my condition and that a Second Law has been broken." She locked her eyes to his in a message of immovability, making sure she did not glance in Khon'Tor's direction.

Khon'Tor could not move.

Adia was with offspring.

I seeded her that night? She is carrying my offspring —the lawful heir to my leadership? Hakani, thankfully, just lost the PetaQ offspring she was carrying, one who would *have had a claim to my leadership and whom I would not have been able to deny. This, this offspring is my lawful heir. But if I claim it, I will lose my position as Leader.*

And here was Adia, with his offspring growing inside her. The female who was his First Choice, the female whom he had envisioned as Mother Of His Offspring, standing here now, with offspring from the seed he had forced within her. His mind was bending at this cruel turn of events; the female he wanted was bearing his offspring. A female who would not have him, and an offspring he could never claim.

From the side, Acaraho was enjoying Khon'Tor's discomfort. It was a small price to pay for the burden Adia was shouldering.

A male like Khon'Tor would never understand the honor Adia embodied, the honor that gave her the strength to stand before the High Council and take the blame for his crime to the benefit of everyone but herself.

Lesharo'Mok spoke up. "Adia. He bears equal responsibility for your condition."

The softness in his voice reminded her of her father, and tears stung her eyes.

"By protecting the father, you bring more hardship on yourself," he said.

Adia looked into his kind eyes, realizing he had compassion for her situation, perhaps because he was very much like her father in understanding how difficult life could be, and how lost anyone could become on their path.

"Does he know you bear his offspring?" asked Lesharo'Mok.

Well, he certainly does now. She suppressed a little chuckle and surprised herself that she could find any humor in this situation at all.

"Yes," she replied.

"And the fact that he is not standing with you here now is not due to an inability to do so? But of his own volition?"

"No, he is able to do so, but chooses not to," was all Adia could think to say in an answer.

She then continued, "I will not give you my justification for withholding his identity, Adoeete Lesharo'Mok. I only hope you will trust that my reasons are honorable and not meant to impede justice in this matter in any way."

Realizing she was not going to give way on this matter, Kurak'Kahn continued to conduct the review.

"When is the offspring due, Adia?" he asked.

"By the time of the turning of the leaves, High Council Overseer."

"Is there anything you wish to add to your admission, Adia? You will not be given an opportunity to speak again in your defense," he told her.

She did have something to add, "I realize my condition compromises my position as Healer and puts my life at risk. For this, I am deeply sorry."

Kurak'Kahn turned to Khon'Tor and Hakani for their remarks.

Khon'Tor held his breath willing Hakani to stay silent. Instead, she stood up to address the High Council. Khon'Tor swore under his breath.

Acaraho visibly bristled when he saw Hakani rise. He was well aware of her ill intentions toward Adia.

"High Council. There is a contributing issue of

which I am not sure you are all aware. The Healer's position is already compromised by raising a Waschini offspring—an offspring which she willingly brought into our midst when it was very young."

Kurak'Kahn said, more of a statement than a question, "There is a Waschini offspring being raised among the People of the High Rocks."

Hakani looked over and sneered at Adia. *She has been told she may not speak again! I wonder how she is feeling now?*

Hakani's statement woke Khon'Tor out of his stoic trance. *I need to mitigate the damage Hakani is trying to inflict, lest the High Council's judgment against Adia is harsh enough to break her vow of silence on my behalf!*

Khon'Tor stood up and walked around to the front of the table, directly facing the High Council, and making sure he crossed in front of Hakani as if to dismiss her and her statement entirely. He had kicked into his Leader role and was addressing them with authority and finesse. This was the best of Khon'Tor—one of the abilities that had elevated him within his position as Leader of the People. Khon'Tor could be eloquent, convincing, and entirely credible. Hearts and minds were changed when he spoke with authority. And he brought all this gift to bear now, in what appeared to be on Adia's behalf.

"High Council. Hakani's statement that there is a Waschini offspring being raised among my people is factually correct, but does not convey the extenuating circumstances by which this came to pass.

"Adia came across the offspring when it was helpless; the sole survivor left amid a barbaric scene of the bloody and ruthless slaughter of its parents. Her choices were to leave it, or to take it with her; plain and simple. She would not be the revered Healer you all know her to be if she had been able to leave the offspring to die a horrible death of exposure, or at the teeth of predators. I do not know of any of the People's females, let alone a Healer, who could have done differently in her situation.

I put it to you that all offspring are innocent —*even those of the Waschini*. Adia was selected to become a Healer because the love of the Great Spirit runs through her so strongly. To condemn her for decisions she made because of that very same quality would be the height of injustice." He paused for a moment.

"The offspring is being raised as one of us. It has been accepted by our people. The Healer has the support of the community females, as does any other mother. She has faithfully continued to fulfill her role as Healer, and I have extended my protection to the offspring as I would any of the People's offspring. This was not a crime Adia committed, it was an act of mercy, and for that, she could not be condemned, *by anyone*," and as he spoke, he turned and scowled directly at Hakani.

Khon'Tor then turned back to face the High Council.

"I do not have to remind you of Adia's reputation as a Healer, nor her dedication to the People. She has given of her time and energy without fail, often against unreasonable burdens. Any punishment leveled against her for her condition would be an injustice. I submit that no one in this room has not made a serious mistake. We can sit here in innocence because our failings were not made public. Adia does not have that luxury, and instead of hiding from the consequences of *her* mistake, she has directly contacted the High Council and proactively sought your intervention. She has turned to you for wisdom and guidance, not judgment and condemnation. I hope her faith in you has not been misplaced."

Khon'Tor concluded his statement and then paused a moment for effect. Then, instead of taking up his seat at the table with the other High Council members, he took a seat facing them, symbolically sitting with Adia.

Kurak'Kahn, the Overseer, turned to look at each of the High Council members. He was looking for agreement that they had heard all they needed. They each nodded at him in turn, and Kurak'Kahn turned back to address Adia.

"This hearing is now completed. You may return to your regular activities. We will notify you when we have determined how best to proceed, and are ready to reconvene," concluded the Overseer of the High Council.

Acaraho moved away from his place and pushed the stone doors open so they could leave. Adia went first, passing by him without making eye contact.

Hakani filtered out next, followed by Khon'Tor, who conspicuously did not walk with his mate. Once all three had left, Acaraho turned back to the High Council to see if they needed anything else.

"Acaraho, may we use this room for deliberation with an assurance of privacy?" asked Kurak'Kahn.

"I have guards stationed in all directions at a distance which precludes their overhearing anything, Overseer. I give you my assurance that nothing you say here will be overheard. You may use the room as long as you wish; I will instruct the guards that no one, including them, is to approach, and only when you vacate may they surrender their posts. They will also show you the way back to your quarters," said Acaraho.

"Thank you. We will let you know when we are ready to reconvene."

Acaraho nodded to them, making eye contact with each one, and left the room, closing the door behind him. As promised, he went to each guard and gave them their explicit instructions.

Then he stood outside the room for a moment before going to catch up with Adia. His mind was churning. He had noticed Is'Taqa look over at his Chief when Adia brought her accusation against herself. From that reaction, it appeared the Second Chief knew something.

And as for Khon'Tor's defense of Adia, had Acaraho not known that everything Khon'Tor did was always ultimately in the Leader's own best interests, his estimation of Khon'Tor would have been raised to a new high. But he knew Khon'Tor was not genuinely speaking on Adia's behalf. Yes, he was working to mitigate their judgment of her, to soften whatever consequences they might levy against her for breaking one of the Second Laws. However, he had attempted to move them to mercy for the sole purpose of ensuring she had less to lose by keeping her silence than she had to gain by breaking it.

Acaraho followed behind Adia to ensure she made it safely to her quarters, but he kept his distance so as not to disturb her. More than anything else, he wanted to speak to her. He wanted to tell her how proud he was of her, how impressed with her resolve, and the honor and dignity with which she had delivered her message. He wanted to tell her that no matter what happened, her father would have been so very proud of her in every regard. And how deeply sorry he was that this terrible injustice had been committed against her. And what a coward Khon'Tor was, and a thousand other things.

But Acaraho knew it was not over, and if she wanted to see him, she would send for him. She was under tremendous strain, and he could not risk disturbing her tenuous control over herself. So he went back to his private quarters and weighed the possible penalties the High Council might impose upon her.

Khon'Tor was following behind Hakani, as was the guard he had assigned to accompany her every move. He wanted to make sure she went nowhere else but back to their quarters as he had business to conduct with her there. He closed the distance between them; his anger was undeniable, and he would have been surprised if she could not feel it emanating off him from several paces behind her. He knew Hakani had seen an opportunity to create more hardship for Adia, and it was only her sheer hatred of the Healer that had given her the strength to stand up and address the High Council. *She is going to pay for her act of rebellion.*

He caught up with her just as she was about to enter their quarters. The moment they were inside the room, Khon'Tor grabbed her arm roughly just above her elbow and jerked her over and up against him hard. As they cleared the door, he shoved it shut with only one hand.

"If you think I was hard on you last night, Hakani," he threatened her, "you had better brace yourself tonight."

"Khon'Tor—" She started to defend herself, but it only made him angrier.

"*Kah-tah!* *Shut up!* It is obvious from your performance in there that you still do not understand your place. *It's time for another lesson.*"

And with that, he dragged her over and shoved her down hard on his sleeping mat, and for the third night in a row, he unleashed his raw power on her repeatedly, violently, taking her Without Her Consent.

CHAPTER 6

Adia returned to an impatiently waiting Nadiwani. The two females sat together, and Adia recounted what had happened. Nadiwani's eyes narrowed as Adia recounted how Hakani had stood up and told the High Council about Oh'Dar. And when Adia repeated what she could of Khon'Tor's speech on her behalf, Nadiwani was as surprised as Adia herself had been.

"He spoke eloquently, Nadiwani. It was Khon'Tor at his best. He is an even greater Leader when he puts the People's best interests above his own," she added.

Nadiwani nodded in agreement. The People needed a Leader of great resolve, strong-willed, one who had the vision to get them through the trying times ahead, especially with Wrak-Ayya threatening their way of life. Khon'Tor was a powerful speaker who could not only persuade people, but also move them to action.

"Acaraho could equally be our Leader," Nadiwani said. "He is just as strong as Khon'Tor. Everyone looks up to him. There is no one who does not respect or trust him. And there is no male of more exceptional character. You have done well to secure him as mentor to Oh'Dar," she added.

What Nadiwani had not yet found a way to say to her friend, was that she had seen the looks passing between Adia and Acaraho. And though she did agree that Acaraho was the perfect choice of role model for Oh'Dar, his increased involvement in Adia's life could only create more and more conflict for Adia down the road.

Their conversation wound down, and they both retired to bed. Adia was asleep almost before her head hit the mat. Nadiwani stayed awake for a while, worrying what the High Council was going to decide in the matter of her friend's situation.

The next morning passed without a decision from the High Council. Acaraho made sure its members were well taken care of, arranging for food to be brought to their quarters and providing them with other matters of convenience. He let the Overseer know that if they wished to use the room again for further discussion, he would make sure the guards were placed as before to ensure their privacy.

The Overseer did not indicate that they needed the room but did ask Acaraho to check in after a few hours.

Before Acaraho could do so, however, one of the guards came to tell him that the High Council was ready to reconvene. They had asked that he assemble those who were in attendance yesterday and bring them to the meeting room.

Acaraho sent the guard to retrieve Khon'Tor and Hakani. He would go and find Adia himself. He wanted to time it so Khon'Tor and Hakani would already be in the room, and the session ready to convene, before he brought Adia in. It was going to be hard enough on her as it was, without having to sit in the room waiting for the others to arrive.

"It is time, Adia," he said.

Adia reached out her hand to Nadiwani who clasped it and squeezed her friend's fingers. Then Adia turned and left with Acaraho.

The two walked silently through the tunnels that stretched between her quarters and the meeting room. Acaraho could sense Adia was attempting to maintain the same detached composure she had shown yesterday. For that reason, he did not speak but waited for her to initiate conversation if she wished to.

When they arrived at the door, Acaraho stopped and waited for her to enter first. His timing was perfect; everyone was already in the room and appropriately seated as he ushered her in.

Kurak'Kahn, the Overseer, motioned for her to sit. Adia raised her hand and shook her head, indicating she would prefer to stand. Acaraho moved to the wall, to the same place as yesterday, where he would have an unobstructed view of everyone there.

Khon'Tor sat stiffly, as far away from Hakani as possible.

Kurak'Kahn began.

"We have come to a decision regarding the disposition of your situation, Adia," he said.

Disposition of my situation. She rolled the words over in her mind. She tried not to read too much into them, but they sounded clinical and cold, as if her being with offspring was a medical inconvenience and not the miracle of new life; the gift of the Great Mother.

"First of all, Khon'Tor spoke correctly yesterday. Adia, you should be commended for reaching out for our oversight. No doubt had you not, the situation would have come to our attention one way or the other. But, much like your father, you have not shied away from difficulty and instead stepped up to meet it head-on."

A soft start, but Adia braced herself for the rest.

"The First and Second Laws of the People have been passed down from generation to generation. The laws reflect our values and our motivations. The First Law states that the needs of the community supersede the needs of the individual. The second of the First Laws reflects the position of honor and respect our females hold. It is through the females that new life is brought into our world; into Etera. Females embody the essence of the feminine aspect of the Great Spirit —which Healers call the Great Mother—and remind us there is nothing more important or more powerful than love. The third of the First Laws requires us to show forbearance for each other's failings," he said, pausing before continuing.

"The Second Laws guide the execution of the overseeing roles within the community. It is these laws which state that a Leader may choose his mate and that the Healer may not be paired nor bear offspring. Though we do not recognize a hierarchy of the laws, when there has been a violation, we do consider them all," he continued, setting the stage for what was to come next.

"Adia Adoeete," he addressed her, for the second time in a row honoring her with the formal title of Great Leader. "You are revered among not only your people, the People of the High Rocks, but throughout all the adjoining communities. Your actions affect not only your people, but those of us all. For that reason, your failure in this regard has more far-reaching consequences than among the People of the High Rocks,"

Adia's emotions rose and fell with his statements, which on the one hand seemed to be praising her, and then on the next admonishing her.

"You, as a Healer, are obliged to uphold the First and Second Laws and to conduct yourself with the highest level of honor possible. You have failed in this regard, bringing risk to yourself, as well as the potential and devastating loss of a great Healer," he continued.

Acaraho clenched his jaws and tightened one fist behind his back.

"However," continued the Overseer.

Adia's heart leapt; there was a *however*?

"However," he repeated, "As members of the High Council we have an even greater responsibility to uphold the laws of the People. Just as your actions have far-reaching consequences, so do ours, only more so.

"As Khon'Tor said yesterday, there is not one of us who has not suffered consequences from a lapse in good judgment. There is not one of us who does not deserve judgment under the laws. Your record of service has been exemplary. We recognize your regret over the situation, and that you admit you have failed to live up to the restrictions placed upon your position—restrictions put in place for your own welfare as well as that of the People. The loss of a

Healer is disastrous—and especially one of your caliber."

"I have said there is not one of us who does not deserve judgment for breaking the laws. And there are few of us who do not deserve mercy. The First Laws remind us to show forbearance for each other's failings. It is our role as members of the High Council to determine when to apply which—justice or mercy."

"Adia of the People of the High Rocks, you have broken one of the most important of the laws of the People. You stand before us repentant yet defiant, in that you refuse to disclose the name of the father of your offspring. We cannot force you to, but we must state that his cowardice in not standing with you does not speak well of your choice in mating. It is our hope that in time, he will come forward and bear with you the burden in which he shares equal responsibility."

Adia kept her eyes fixed on the Overseer just as she had yesterday, lest she betray Khon'Tor with even the quickest of glances in his direction.

She noticed the Overseer's voice softened just the slightest bit as he continued, "Adia, your services as Healer are critical to the welfare of the People. We would be negligent not to recognize the risk presented by your being with offspring.

When we leave here, we will make arrangements to locate an experienced Healer who can come to tend to you from now on and be present for your offspring's delivery. It will have to be someone close enough to return to her people if the need should suddenly arise. And that Healer's Helper must be highly skilled and able to fill in for her absence in all but the direst of circumstances. When we have made our selection, we will send word to the High Protector Acaraho, that he may make preparations for her arrival."

As he mentioned Acaraho's name, Kurak'Kahn looked over at him, and Acaraho nodded his acceptance of the responsibility.

"As to the matter of justice versus mercy, the members of the High Council have determined that as you stand before us alone, we do not accept the right to impose any penalty on you. We refuse to acknowledge any fault on your behalf in this matter since the father of your offspring—who should share equally in your burden—does not have the courage to come forward," said Kurak'Kahn.

If Adia had heard correctly, they were not going to impose a penalty on her. The fact that she had to stand here and bear the burden of her situation on her own had softened their hearts in the matter.

"I speak now as a male and not as the Overseer of the High Council," said Kurak'Kahn with iron in his voice.

"Whoever is the father of your offspring, I wish he were in this room so that I could admonish him man-to-man for his gutlessness. Whatever the cost to him in admitting his part, he has burdened you with bearing in his stead. And not only that, he has self-ishly put your life at risk. It is well known that *your mother died while birthing you*."

It was not lost on Adia that Kurak'Kahn had stepped outside of his role as Overseer. It was unprecedented, and she interpreted that it under-scored the distaste he felt for the situation into which a male had put Adia.

Kurak'Kahn continued again, with some softness returning to his voice.

"Unfortunately for you, Adia, a male who will take the pleasure of seeding an offspring but avoid his responsibility for it, will neither show up to father it—nor share the burden of providing for it. This leaves us in an untenable situation. Though we will not pass judgment on you, we must deal with the realities of the situation."

"Hakani, Second Rank to the People of the High Rocks, and mate to Khon'Tor, stood up yesterday and informed us you were already raising one offspring—the Waschini you rescued. The laws remove a Healer's right to pair or produce offspring for the physical risk it presents to her, but also in recognition of the responsibilities that come with raising offspring. The Healer is meant to be dedi-cated solely to the wellbeing and needs of her people. The Waschini offspring is already estab-lished in your life, and we do not have the heart to force you to give it up. However, we cannot allow your energies and focus to be further divided by adding the responsibilities of yet another offspring."

"Therefore, it is the determination of the High Council in this matter, that you, Adia, must surrender the care of one of these offspring to another female. We will not make the choice for you, but you must choose. You must give up either the Waschini offspring or the offspring you carry now," he stated.

Had this been a general assembly of the People, chaos would have broken out. The room would have been filled with chatter and gasps and heightened disbelief at what they had just heard. Instead, everyone in the room froze, including Adia.

Adia's blood ran cold. Had Kurak'Kahn just said what she thought he had? Must she give up one of the offspring? Either Oh'Dar or this one she carried now? Give up to whom? And when was she expected to make this impossible decision?

"Kurak'Kahn, please. I do not understand," she stammered, her composure starting to crumble under the felling blow the Overseer had just delivered.

"Adia, it is to your credit that you have been able to discharge your duties as Healer while saddled with the care of one offspring. No doubt, the support of the other females has gone a long way toward enabling you to that end. However, despite their help, the responsibilities of raising two offspring would be too much. Therefore, it is the decision of the High Council that *you must surrender one of your offspring to another female of the People.*

In recognition of the difficulty of this situation, we will let the offspring remain among the People of the High Rocks where at least you will have knowledge of its care and its wellbeing. Be aware this is a compromise on our part; we could have decided the offspring should be removed to another community entirely," he added.

She heard him. Essentially, she *must* take the deal because they could make it even harder on her.

Acaraho's eyes were glued on Adia as she swayed the slightest bit on her feet.

"When am I expected to decide? When do you expect me to decide *which of my offspring I will give up*?" she said, pressing a hand to her forehead.

"We recognize this is hard on you, Adia. And we find difficult decisions are not any easier made later as opposed to sooner. We ask you to decide before us now. We will give you a moment to collect your thoughts before you choose," said Kurak'Kahn.

It was all Adia could do not to cry. She felt herself weaving and was afraid she would pass out in front of them. *They said they would not administer punishment, but what is this? I must give up one of my offspring —either Oh'Dar, the frail and disadvantaged Waschini offspring, or the one I carry within me? Blood of my blood? Regardless of who the father is, this is my offspring, my direct offspring; a blessing denied to all Healers.*

While all this was taking place, Hakani's mental wheels had been turning. She had not recovered from Khon'Tor's ongoing denigration of her. Trapped within their quarters, she did not have the fortitude to oppose or defy him, but this situation was different. Just as she had found the strength to stand up yesterday and tell them about the Waschini offspring, she could not resist the opportunity presented before her now to make Adia suffer even more.

Before she could lose her nerve, Hakani stood up, stepped forward, and turned to address the High Council again. She could see Khon'Tor looking at her, aghast.

Oh, I know I will pay for this later, perhaps dearly, but I am not going to pass up the chance to deal her another blow. Brace yourself, Healer. I am not done with you yet.

"Kurak'Kahn," she said boldly and loudly so there would be no mistake, "I, Hakani, Third Rank and mate to Khon'Tor, Leader of the People of the High Rocks, I claim the right to whichever offspring she relinquishes."

Hakani did not dare look over at Khon'Tor, knowing he would be incensed. And she knew he would take this out on her later, most likely as painfully and as slowly as possible. But no one could make her withdraw her claim, and no matter how angry he was, Khon'Tor would not do her any serious bodily harm considering there were so many eyes on the situation. No matter what she had to endure later, the offspring—whichever offspring—would be a priceless tool through which to torture both her mate and the Healer.

Decorum shattered and the High Council members turned and looked at each other, then at Khon'Tor, then at Adia, and then back to Hakani.

Adia's hand flew to her mouth in disbelief.

"No!" said Adia, marching toward the council table. "You said it would be *my choice!*"

Kurak'Kahn replied, "I said that which offspring you gave up would be your choice. We did not say that who took the offspring would be your choice. Hakani is within her rights to claim the offspring."

Adia knew what Kurak'Kahn said was true. In the rare situation where an offspring was orphaned, the other females of the community had a right to put claim to the offspring. Ordinarily, there were always a few who stepped up, though never the mate of the Leader—but it *was* within her right.

What? thought Khon'Tor, *Hakani has just laid claim to the offspring I seeded in Adia? I will need the protection of all Acaraho's guards should Hakani find out the offspring is mine!*

It had taken all he had not to fly to his feet when

she first spoke, but he had contained himself. However, now Khon'Tor stood. He walked over to his mate, took her arm, and turned her to face him.

"Hakani, *what are you doing*?" he spoke bluntly.

"I have lost our offspring, Khon'Tor," she said, patting her stomach and lying unabashedly in front of the High Council. "I deserve a chance to have another."

"Hakani," he continued, also lying, "This offspring is not heir to my leadership. It is my expectation that in time you will bear me offspring and have those to raise," he said.

"I have every intention of doing so, Khon'Tor. I understand that neither of whichever offspring she relinquishes will satisfy the requirement for an offspring of yours. But I do not remove my claim." And, shored up by the presence of others in the room and her hatred of Adia, she stood her ground.

It was within Hakani's rights, and no one had the authority to repudiate or force her to withdraw her claim. Since the matter was being considered before the High Council and not before the local community, there were no other females present to lay claim, and so Hakani's stood by default.

Adia was having trouble standing. Acaraho could see she was faltering. He stepped forward and addressed the High Council. "High Council members. Clearly, this is an extraordinary situation, and the stress on everyone here is very high. Could we take a brief recess to let emotions settle before we continue?"

"Alright, Commander. You make a fair point. Anyone who wishes to leave the room may do so; however, I ask the High Council members to remain. Please do not be gone more than the minimal time any of you might need," agreed Kurak'Kahn.

Acaraho stood, waiting for Adia. She remained in her position a moment and then finally went out into the hallway. Acaraho did not follow her, realizing it would be improper, and there would be no reason for it unless their relationship was closer than currently understood to be.

Adia walked down the hallway far enough almost to reach the guards posted there. She wished she could be utterly alone, but at least the guard had the presence of mind to turn his back to her—not out of disrespect but to give her some privacy.

I expected punishment, but then it looked like they were showing me mercy. But to have to give up one of my offspring, and to Hakani who hates me? How is this anything but punishment? Oh, Great Mother, please let this be a bad dream from which I will wake at any moment.

My father's words are coming back to me; I must balance the leadings of my heart with reason. I need to try to think this through logically because the future of two offspring depends on the wisdom of my decision.

It did not take her long.

The moment she thought of Oh'Dar in the care

of that heartless female, she knew she could not give him up to her. *He is such a happy offspring, very full of life. But he is frail and at risk of harm by the nature of his delicate build. And he is also immanently vulnerable to harm by other offspring in the community. There would never be a Waschini—or a Brother for that matter—who could match one of the People for height, build, strength, or speed. He could be harmed—or worse—while playing with one of Khon'Tor's other offspring, or those of the community.*

And Hakani had no love for Oh'Dar. She had risked his life even from the start, dangling him high in her outstretched arm for everyone in the assembly to see while she called out Adia's sin. She could never allow Oh'Dar to fall into Hakani's hands again.

That meant Adia had to relinquish Khon'Tor's offspring to Hakani. But not just Khon'Tor's offspring. Her offspring. The only offspring she would ever bear; she would have to stand by and watch it raised by a mother who most likely would never love it, and a father who would never claim it. Adia had no illusions about Hakani's motivation for claiming the offspring, though why the Leader's mate hated her so much, Adia still did not know.

She had made up her mind, making the only choice she could make in the situation. Oh'Dar needed her more. And the truth was, Adia had not chosen to be seeded with the offspring growing in her now. Oh'Dar was the offspring she had chosen. And she must now choose him again.

. . .

Adia was so grateful to Acaraho for the brief respite. She had regained her composure and was now ready to face the consequences the High Council had imposed on her.

She turned and walked back to the Council meeting room. Acaraho, who had been watching, opened the door as she approached and gently ushered her back into the room.

All eyes turned her way as she entered.

She walked up and stood in front of the High Council. She did not have to wait long for their undivided attention.

Looking directly at Kurak'Kahn, she calmly stated, "I will relinquish the offspring I carry."

Khon'Tor's stare was all but burning a hole into Hakani. She averted her eyes and ignored him as best she could, silently gloating over the coup she had just pulled off. It was all she could do to keep a smile off her face. *I knew without a doubt that Adia would never relinquish the Waschini offspring. I knew Adia's choice even before I staked my claim.*

Kurak'Kahn spoke. "The matter brought to the High Council by Adia, Healer of the People of the High Rocks, has been heard. As a result of the situation, at the age at which the offspring can safely be removed from his or her birth mother, Adia will surrender the offspring she carries into the care of Hakani, Third Rank and mate of

Khon'Tor, Leader of the People of the High Rocks."

But then he turned to address Hakani, "Hakani, at this moment, the High Council has no jurisdiction or grounds on which to deny your claim to the Healer's offspring. However, should evidence be brought to our attention that you are not caring for this offspring as if it were your own, we *will* have jurisdiction at that point, and we *will* vacate your claim. Should it come to this, I assure you, you can count on justice alone and no mercy from this Council."

The sting and weight of Kurak'Kahn's words were not lost on Hakani. It was clear he questioned her motives and was letting her—and everyone else in the room—know it.

Then he turned and spoke to Adia directly, "Adia Adoeete. I know this may feel like a punishment to you. Please trust that it is not intended as such. What I stated earlier stands; we do not sit in judgment of you. We recognize that this is an extremely difficult situation for you, and our decision is meant to allow you to continue in your calling as the Healer to your people. It is meant to lessen your burdens, not add to them," he continued.

"However, I will offer you an alternative solution. Should you decide before the birth of your offspring that the burden of our resolution is too high and you wish to relinquish your position as Healer of the People of the High Rocks to keep the offspring you carry, please send word through Commander

Acaraho at the earliest possible moment. We will then attend to the matter of selecting a new Healer for your people."

Then the Overseer added, dropping his voice, "That is the best I can do, Adia."

With that, Kurak'Kahn stood up, signaling the end of the official hearing.

"Someone will be in touch with you, Commander Acaraho, about the identity of the Healer who will come to tend to Adia Adoeete during her carrying of the offspring and the offspring's delivery. In addition, I am ordering you, Commander Acaraho, to select a helpmate to assist Hakani in caring for Adia's offspring—should Adia elect to surrender the offspring to Hakani and continue in her role as Healer to the People of the High Rocks. The meeting of the High Council on this matter is resolved."

Everyone in the room, including Hakani, knew that the Overseer had just assigned a spy to make sure the offspring was never in danger. He wanted a direct line of information coming to Acaraho regarding the care the offspring was receiving.

The rest of the High Council members then rose from behind the table.

The Overseer came up to Acaraho and thanked him again for his part and for all the arrangements he had put in place. Kurak'Kahn then placed his right hand on Acaraho's shoulder in the People's sign of brotherhood and respect, and Acaraho placed his left hand on Kurak'Kahn's shoulder in return. The Overseer had paid Acaraho a great tribute. The other Council members also came forward to thank him for the hospitality he had shown them.

Despite her raw emotions, Adia smiled at seeing Acaraho receive such an honor from Kurak'Kahn. Khon'Tor watched the same display with narrowed eyes and a jealous heart.

As they all left, one of the guards came up to Adia and explained that he was under Acaraho's orders to see her safely wherever she wished to go for the balance of the day. She turned back to catch Acaraho's eye, but he was busy talking with the Council members. So she thanked the guard and made her way back to her quarters. She very much wanted to go to her private hideaway, but she did not want anyone knowing she took solace there. It would have to wait.

Nadiwani was waiting for Adia. Honovi was also there, and when Adia came through the door, Oh'Dar pointed to her and gave the sign for *Mama*. He now reserved it for Adia only, using the *Auntie Mama* sign taught to him by Honovi for Nadiwani.

Adia went over and embraced the small, frail thing whom she now loved so much. Her tears fell as she hugged him gingerly, and she knew she had made the right decision.

No one will care for him as I will. He is all alone in the world, more alone than I am, for he has only me. He is an orphan and does not yet realize how different he is from everyone around him. In the end, he will always be an Outsider. Adia's tears fell now for the helpless offspring entrusted to her care, and she vowed again never to let anything harm him.

She suddenly remembered the locket. She had forgotten about it—the very reason she had been out there the night Khon'Tor attacked her. She was so relieved when Is'Taqa returned it. She knew Khon'Tor had destroyed the little pouch the locket had been in—tearing it apart with his teeth and tossing it unceremoniously over into the treetops along the path's edge. The locket, the little blanket, and the stuffed brown toy that looked like a bear were Oh'Dar's only ties back to his original family. She did not know how they could ever be important to him, but like his learning Whitespeak, somehow she knew they would be.

Adia realized her judgment was impaired that terrible night. As much as she valued the locket, she knew it had been safe where it was. There was no reason for her to venture out to fetch it. Her mind had been clear enough to devise the plan to lose Awan, but not clear enough to realize there was no need to retrieve the locket at that moment. It nearly broke her heart that such an unnecessary trip should have ended so tragically.

Adia signed to Oh'Dar that she loved him and set

him down. He toddled back to Honovi, giggling and flapping his pale little arms all the way. *He is such a free spirit. I hope I can protect his carefree heart as he grows into adulthood. Thank the Great Mother that Acaraho will be the one helping me raise him.*

She knew it created complications for both her and Acaraho, but they would somehow have to manage these along with everything else going on.

Honovi scooped Oh'Dar up and told the others she was taking him to visit Mapiya or Donoma. With Adia's permission, she had begun enlarging his world. Oh'Dar signed goodbye as they went out of the door.

The High Council meeting had drained Adia. She was grateful to Honovi for giving her some time to process what had taken place.

She asked Nadiwani to sit with her while she went over the events in the order they had occurred. When Adia got to the point where Kurak'Kahn declared she must give up one of the two offspring, the Helper's jaw dropped. Then Adia told Nadiwani that Hakani had claimed and won the right to raise whichever offspring she gave up.

"Hakani is only doing this to torment you, Adia. We both know that. She wants to see you suffer, though for what reason I have no idea. I have gone over this and over this, and I cannot remember a single incident that would have caused her to dislike you so much. But take heart. There is no love lost between Khon'Tor and Hakani. Despite the tension existing between you and him, I doubt he would let any harm come to an offspring because of her. It would not be a good reflection on him, shall we say."

Adia then told Nadiwani about Kurak'Kahn's statement that they were assigning a helper to Hakani, and if there were even an inkling that Hakani was not doing right by the offspring, they would vacate her claim in an instant.

"That was a very wise move, Adia. And aside from that, you know Acaraho is going to be monitoring the situation very carefully, as will we," she added. "Your offspring will be safe."

When Nadiwani said the word *offspring*, Adia finally broke down. The thought of handing a helpless offspring—any offspring but yes, *her* offspring—over to that person was unbearable. Nadiwani sat with her arms around her friend while Adia sobbed out all the stress, tension, and heartache of the last two days.

CHAPTER 7

Acaraho saw the High Council members out. He then met with all the guards and thanked them for their exemplary service. He dismissed them but signaled to Awan to stay.

"I need you to assume a post at the beginning of the tunnel leading to the Healer's Quarters. No one, and I mean no one, other than the Healer's Helper, Nadiwani, the Whitespeak teacher Honovi, and Mapiya and Haiwee is allowed in unless escorted by me," said Acaraho.

Awan nodded.

But Acaraho continued, "Do you understand by my use of the term *no one* I am including Khon'Tor?" he asked.

"I do now, Commander," answered Awan.

"You are under no obligation to do what I am directing you to do," said Acaraho, making sure that

Awan understood his charge and was willing to fulfill it.

"I need to ask, Commander. What is my response should someone, *anyone*, attempt to breach the corridor?"

"I am authorizing you to use whatever force is necessary to keep *whoever* that is from reaching the Healer's Quarters, Awan. Do I make myself clear?" stated Acaraho, never taking his eyes off Awan, watching for any wavering or resistance.

"I understand, Adik'Tar. I have no problem with this. I assure you I will carry out your orders with no hesitation," he replied.

Of all Acaraho's guards and watchers, his First Guard was always the one Acaraho chose for the most challenging assignments, and Awan had never wavered and had never failed. Acaraho did not blame his First Guard for being taken in by Adia when she escaped through the females' bathing area almost a season ago. He and Awan had a bond from years of shared experiences. They had been raised together and were like brothers to each other.

By issuing that order, I just committed treason. But Khon'Tor is trapped in an untenable situation, and trapped people often go to terrible extremes to free themselves. Now that I have involved Awan in this act, I will owe him for the rest of my life—as if I did not already.

Acaraho now knew the lines Khon'Tor had crossed with Adia; he did not want to test how much further Khon'Tor was willing to go to protect his position of power.

Khon'Tor was indeed feeling trapped. The day had ended too early to return to his quarters, though he had no intention of going there anyway. He did not trust himself with Hakani at this moment; he needed time to calm down.

The Leader headed for the Great Chamber and then onward outside. He had much to sort out, and he wanted no chance of anyone observing him in his agitated state.

Despite everything, Hakani had still found a way to thwart him; to bring strain and misery back into his life. Though what Khon'Tor said was true—her claim of this offspring did not meet his demand for an heir—he also knew it effectively tied his hands. He could not put her out of his quarters and select another mate; the court of public opinion would never forgive him for such a callous move.

And on top of all that, the High Council was questioning her motives. As a result, he would have to put up with not only an offspring under his roof but another adult—a helpmate of some type. No matter what they called it, he knew they meant it as an objective set of eyes to report on what was happening behind his closed doors. In other words, a spy.

And Khon'Tor did not like the relationship that was forming between the High Council members and Acaraho. He did not like the honor Kurak'Kahn had bestowed on the High Protector with his gesture of brotherhood as they were dispersing.

He did not like that Acaraho would be the one to select the helpmate for Hakani. All in all, Acaraho was becoming too powerful—and too popular—for Khon'Tor's taste.

Khon'Tor walked for what seemed like hours. The cold air helped clear the angry fog clouding his thoughts. Mindless physical activity always seemed to help him sort out his thinking and decide his next course of action. There might be months between now and when Adia would deliver her offspring—their offspring—but it did not mean he had months to decide what to do next.

The longer Khon'Tor walked, the clearer his thinking became.

This offspring serves no purpose to me, he realized. *I can never claim it. Even if it is a male, it can never assume a place as heir to my leadership. It is nothing but a complication. And it will re-establish Hakani's position as my mate. I will never be rid of her after that point, regardless of whether she produces me an offspring or not.*

When Hakani assumes care of that offspring, all my control over her is lost. She has made my life miserable already; but then all bets will be off, especially after what I have put her through the last few nights.

Khon'Tor's outrage at what Hakani had achieved

returned to him as he walked back. As much as he wanted to take his anger out on her, he also realized his punishment was becoming too predictable. And the more predictable it became, the more she could armor herself against its effects. And that he did not want.

Khon'Tor admitted he had never enjoyed mating a female as much as he did with this new approach. His appetites had taken a turn down a dark path. He found himself looking forward more and more to punishing Hakani. And the more she fought him and the more she hated him, the more pleasure it brought him.

And to reward her for what she had done now, he would take some time and plan out an exceptional experience for her. For them both.

While Khon'Tor was out walking and making plans to the detriment of Hakani, she was considering the consequences of her actions. If Khon'Tor had been angry with her before, he was livid now. She knew she was in for it that evening, and felt real fear brewing in the pit of her stomach.

Maybe I should leave. But where would I go? I cannot give up living here, not now, when I am only months away from establishing complete control over him. Hakani knew the offspring Adia was carrying was her ticket to freedom. She knew once the offspring was established in their lives, there was nothing Khon'Tor could do to her after that. There would be too much attention on them. And while she had at first railed against the idea of a helpmate, she realized that while this would fix another set of eyes on her, it would also put his actions under the same scrutiny.

Khon'Tor can have his way with me all he wants over the next few months. I know what to expect now. I can get through it. Eventually, his control over me will come to an end, and when it does, the tables will turn my way again, with a vengeance.

Honovi and Oh'Dar sat in the middle of Mapiya's living area. Oh'Dar was happily playing with a set of cooking utensils Mapiya had given him—stacking them, knocking them over, and then doing it all again. Each time he toppled them, and they scattered about, he laughed with delight, looking up at the females, his blue eyes sparkling.

As Oh'Dar continued to demonstrate how clever he was, the females shared their thoughts on the rearing of offspring and other female matters. Mapiya had opened her quarters and her heart to the young Whitespeak teacher. And Mapiya's kindness had helped Honovi tremendously in her adjustment to life among the People. Honovi had ceased to see them as disquieting giants. She no longer thought of them as Sasquatch and herself as one of the Brothers. She saw them as people, and she related to Mapiya, Nadiwani, Adia, and all the others she was getting to know as the individuals they were.

It was some time since Honovi had come to live with them, and today she was very quiet. Mapiya wondered if perhaps she was becoming homesick?

"How are you coping here? It has been some time since you came; are you homesick?"

"Oh, I am, yes, Mapiya. I have been thinking about going home for a little while, assuming Adia would be comfortable with it."

Mapiya knew Honovi no longer had a mother and surmised that Honovi was starting to turn to her for motherly advice because of the age difference between them.

"Mapiya, may I ask you a question, female to female?"

The older female was flattered that Honovi would ask her a question on anything. "Of course. Whatever you want to ask," she replied.

"You know I am not bonded to a man," Honovi continued.

Mapiya nodded.

"There is a man—" she started.

Mapiya could not help but smile. *How many of the females' problems start with, "There is a man,"* she thought.

"And he does not seem to know you exist?"

Mapiya interrupted, at the same time giving Honovi a sweet smile.

"Yes! How did you know?" laughed the young woman in response.

"You know, a lot has happened here since Oh'Dar came to join us. There have been many changes and many challenges. And now you are here. And the more I learn about us all—the Brothers, the People, even the Waschini—the more I realize that, as females, our similarities are far greater than our differences." Mapiya paused.

"So tell me about this man," she encouraged, a sparkle in her eye. "Was it by chance one of the two Brothers who came to visit you while they were here for the High Council meeting?"

Honovi blushed and nodded. "He is a great man. He is a man of honor and courage. He is smart and kind and a great hunter. He shows kindness to the sick and the helpless. He plays with the offspring when he has time. He can build a fire quicker than any other man in the village," she explained.

"And you have feelings for him."

"Yes. I have had for some time. Unfortunately, he does not seem to take much notice of me. The only time he did was when I was asked to come here to teach Whitespeak to Oh'Dar," continued Honovi.

"Has he noticed any other woman in your tribe? Is there someone else already in his heart?" asked Mapiya.

Honovi thought for a moment and then answered, "No, I would have to say there is not."

"Men are many great things. They are truly a gift from the Mother. They are our protectors, our providers, our friends, our lovers, and our companions. The Mother gave them many wonderful skills and abilities, but the one thing she seems to have left out is an ability to recognize when a female is interested in them." said Mapiya. "Unless, of course, she practically hits him over the head," she added, and they both laughed.

"Unfortunately, if you want this man you are going to have to let him know how you feel about him. Short of that, you run the risk that he will take an interest in someone else—or at the very least, you may never discover if he returns your feelings."

Honovi scrunched her face up at Mapiya's answer.

"If I wanted to know, how would I go about finding out?"

"Tell me, when you go back, what will be the first opportunity for you to be alone with this man?"

As their conversation continued, Mapiya gave Honovi a couple of ideas on how to look for signs if this man cared for her or not. Now sharing a secret, the two were becoming even closer.

Meanwhile, Is'Taqa and Ogima Adoeete had returned to their people.

Ogima Adoeete shared Kurak'Kahn's reservations about Hakani's motives in claiming Adia's unborn child. He had been there when she recklessly revealed the presence of the Waschini infant to cause trouble for both Khon'Tor and Adia. He knew Acaraho's selection of the helpmate for Hakani would be critical in monitoring the baby's wellbeing.

The Chief was a great and wise Leader. He had seen many troublesome situations, but the fact of the Healer's pregnancy shocked him. Adia was revered among the People as well as the Brothers. Ogima Adoeete knew every Healer alive understood the reproductive cycle. So, either Adia had chosen this mating and pregnancy of her own accord—or it had been forced upon her. Under no circumstances was it an accident. The problem was that Ogima Adoeete had difficulty thinking of either option being the case. He continued to roll the events over in his mind as he walked, and came to the only conclusion possible.

Now nearly home, Ogima Adoeete and Is'Taqa stopped for a moment to share their final thoughts on the matter before returning to their responsibilities.

The Chief leaned on his staff. "The father should have stepped forward before the Council then and there, Is'Taqa. It will prove to be his greatest shame that he did not."

Is'Taqa looked at Ogima Adoeete and blinked.

The Chief looked back at Is'Taqa and continued. "This. *This* will be Khon'Tor's undoing."

Is'Taqa was speechless. He knew Khon'Tor was the father because he had watched the attack on Adia. He had waited throughout the hearing hoping Khon'Tor would step forward and confess what he had done. But he did not. Khon'Tor had abandoned Adia to bear the brunt of the High Council's condemnation just as he had abandoned her to die out in the elements that night. The Second Chief was stunned by Ogima Adoeete's statement that he knew the father to be in the room during the hearing.

At that moment, Is'Taqa almost did admit to Ogima Adoeete that he had seen Khon'Tor's attack on Adia. But he kept his silence. The burden was still his to bear—and what to do about it was something he had to decide for himself. No other man could lift the responsibility from his shoulders, nor could he shift the burden to someone else's to lighten his own load. To tell Chief Ogima would be to do just that.

Upon her return to the Healer's Quarters, Honovi asked to speak with Adia and Nadiwani before Oh'Dar was put to bed and she returned to her quarters.

The three sat together, and Adia and Nadiwani waited for her to begin.

"I want you to know how much I appreciate your bringing me here. I am very happy that I can help you, and Oh'Dar is a delightful child. I have been here for some time now, however, and I would like your permission to go home for just a little while. I have every intention of returning; I do not want you to think I will not come back. But I would like to go home for a brief visit. I hope you can understand," she said.

"Are you homesick, Honovi?" asked Adia kindly.

Honovi laughed a little bit and nodded, "Yes, I suppose I am. I know you will need me back here, especially with another baby coming. I know you only wanted me here to teach Whitespeak to Oh'Dar, but I feel like I have become part of your family, and I do not mind helping out with Oh'Dar's care as well. I want you to know that," she said.

Adia and Nadiwani had both become very fond of Honovi. They had nothing but respect for the young woman. They appreciated the patience she showed toward Oh'Dar, and it was evident she genuinely liked him and enjoyed spending time with him. She also often willingly stayed longer than her assigned hours to share food preparation and evening meals with them.

Adia had told Honovi that she was expecting an offspring. There had been too many emotional conversations between the Healer and her Helper for Honovi not to have guessed something was amiss. Honovi did not pry or ask directly, but she knew enough to realize it was unacceptable for the Healer to be with offspring.

"We certainly understand. When would you like to return home? How soon?" Adia asked.

"If you do not mind, I would like to leave in the next day or so. I would plan to stay no more than a few days."

"I will let Acaraho know so he can get word to Is'Taqa regarding your return," said Adia.

"Thank you. Thank you for understanding."

"Before you go, we will prepare you a basket of the harvest medicines to take back, as well as one for Ithua," said Adia.

"Oh, that is very generous. Thank you, I greatly appreciate it, and I know Ithua will too!"

They rose, and Honovi left for her quarters.

Is'Taqa received word that Honovi would be returning home for a while. He, his sister Ithua, and High Chief Ogima Adoeete all looked forward to her return. Ithua was particularly interested in hearing how Adia was doing and what Honovi had been studying with her.

Is'Taqa realized there was a good chance Honovi knew Adia was pregnant. He also realized that the pregnancy would become apparent in very short order. However, he needed to know exactly how much information Honovi had before he was comfortable for her to share anything with Ithua. Adia had not revealed much in the High Council meeting, but he could not take a chance that Honovi might innocently share information and create the appearance that either he or the High Chief had betrayed the sanctity of the hearing.

Honovi's return would also allow him to learn more about how the Waschini offspring was doing. He wondered if she would invite him to meals as she had done in the past. It would be an excellent time to sit and chat casually about her experiences there. He did enjoy her company, and he would be glad for the excuse to share in it again.

The day for Honovi's departure came too soon. She said her goodbyes to Adia, Nadiwani, Mapiya, and the other females and made her way to where she was to meet Acaraho. Honovi no longer had trouble navigating the tunnels as long as she stayed on the brighter upper level. Acaraho had taught her the meaning of the symbols on the walls. She told him he was an excellent teacher and in return, he said she was a bright student.

Acaraho took the two satchels of herbs and powders she was carrying, and they left together. Honovi thought back to the first time she saw Acaraho and how taken aback she had been by his enormous size and strident approach. What had worried her before was now a comfort. She knew nothing could harm her while he was around.

Honovi did not have the speed or stamina of Acaraho, so they had to stop for her to rest several times along the way.

"I hope you have an enjoyable stay, Honovi," said Acaraho.

"I will not stay away too long, Commander. I know Adia needs me and even more so with the offspring coming. I will be back soon enough."

Honovi has just casually mentioned that Adia is with offspring, thought Acaraho. *How would she know that I already have the information? This is how easily Adia's situation can be made known. When I return, I must make sure that Khon'Tor announces her condition with urgency.*

Finally, they approached the last valley, and Is'Taqa was waiting for them to arrive.

"Welcome back, Honovi," he said, taking her bag from Acaraho. "Thank you for bringing her safely. I will send word when she is ready to return to Kthama."

Honovi was very tired by the time they arrived back at the village.

Ithua came over to greet them as she saw them enter. "Honovi, we are so glad to have you back home. You must be exhausted. Please, share our evening meal with us before turning in. We have prepared your shelter, so it is all ready for your homecoming."

Ithua had many questions but knew Honovi was tired and probably needed some quiet time to herself.

Honovi was grateful, and also pleased that Is'Taqa was joining them. Though there was little conversation, Honovi enjoyed their evening together. There was something about the three of them before a warm fire, sharing the meal Ithua had prepared, that provided a level of intimacy. It made her feel as if she were part of their family. And with the closeness that had developed between her, Mapiya, Nadiwani, and Adia, she now had two. Tears welled up in Honovi's eyes, and Is'Taqa and Ithua quietly exchanged glances with each other.

When they were finished eating, Honovi showed Ithua the bag of herbs, roots, powders, and tinctures Adia had sent back for her.

"This is very generous and thoughtful. I must send something back with you for Adia in return," said Ithua.

"You look exhausted Honovi. Please, let me walk you to your shelter," Is'Taqa offered.

She gladly accepted, not trusting herself in the dark as tired as she was. When they got to her dwelling, she was delighted to see someone had filled it with fresh bedding, and there was an enormous, beautiful silver wolf skin waiting for her.

"Oh! How lovely! Who left this for me?"

"I thought you would need it; no doubt even the

cooler caves at Kthama are not as cold as the temperatures outside at night."

"Thank you, Is'Taqa. That was very kind of you," she said.

Is'Taqa just smiled and said, "I hope you sleep well. Welcome back." Then he left.

Maybe he does like me, she thought to herself. *It was a very generous gift and very thoughtful. But it was also just as likely that Ithua had thought of it and Is'Taqa had followed through with her idea.*

The next morning, Honovi was not sure what to do with herself. She was used to being on a schedule. After she had left, her community chores were assumed by others. Ithua had told her the previous night that there was no need to bother herself with them for the short period she would be home. This left her with a great deal of time on her hands.

Honovi decided to go and visit Ithua to see if she had any questions about Adia's gift and if there was anything with which she could help the Medicine Woman.

Ithua was outside warming herself by the morning fire. She smiled when she saw Honovi approaching and motioned for her to sit down. Honovi put her hands out to capture the warmth of the flames.

"So how did your stay go, Honovi?" asked Ithua.

"Did you make progress with the Waschini child? — What is his name?"

"His name is Oh'Dar, and yes, I believe I did, but I will not really know until he starts forming words instead of babbling. He knows quite a few Hand-speak words already and is learning more every day. It makes it so much easier, as I can use the signs he already knows to associate with the Whitespeak words. Nadiwani and I work together. First, she speaks the words to him in our language, and I then speak them to him in Whitespeak. That way, he is learning both languages at once.

"He is very bright, Ithua. It frightens me how inventive he is. Our people and the Waschini do not seem so different on the surface—we are certainly closer in nature to the Waschini than the Sasquatch are, that's for sure. But I worry a bit that perhaps the Waschini are even more different, in ways we do not realize," she said. "If the Waschini ever do come in large numbers, I worry they will unseat our place in the order of things as they are now and always have been."

"That seems to be a fairly large assumption based on one little boy," said Ithua.

"I know. But still—" Honovi's voice trailed off, underscoring her concern.

"How are Adia and Nadiwani?" asked Ithua.

"They are doing well. Oh'Dar takes up a lot of their time, you can imagine. It is difficult for them to get it all done, so I have been doing more than working with Oh'Dar on Whitespeak; I have been helping them with his general care also," she explained.

And then, there it was.

"I hope I will be a big help to Adia when her baby is born."

Ithua blinked a couple of times and tilted her head. "Baby? What baby, Honovi?" she asked.

At that point, Honovi realized she had just revealed something she probably should not have. She had gotten so comfortable with Adia and Nadiwani talking about it among themselves that she had forgotten she was no longer there with them.

"Ithua, I am so sorry. I do not know what the matter with me is. I should not have said that. Oh no, I cannot believe I did that. I meant no harm to Adia; I am so sorry—" she stammered.

Is'Taqa had come up behind them while they were speaking and heard everything. He startled them when he spoke, and they both turned around at once.

"It is alright, Honovi. At the moment, only a tiny circle of people know of her being pregnant. But the word will be out soon enough. In fact, Adia will need to let her people know very soon. But I think you and I need to talk before you say anything else about the matter, even to Ithua," he added and nodded his apology to his sister.

"Is'Taqa is right," said the Medicine Woman. "They have taken you into their confidence; you have heard and witnessed things in their private quarters. It is possible you know things about this situation that you should not share with others. You and Is'Taqa do need to speak. You can trust him; he would never use anything you might tell him to harm either Adia or the People. But he does need to know what you know."

So, this is the result of Khon'Tor's rape of Adia? thought Ithua. *As if that was not bad enough? It is against their laws for a Healer to risk carrying and delivering an offspring. And Adia's mother herself died giving birth. But if Adia had come forward about Khon'Tor's attack on her, I am sure Honovi would not be talking calmly about her pregnancy.*

She and Is'Taqa exchanged a quick, knowing glance.

"Sit by the fire here, you two," she said. "I have chores to attend to, and I am anxious to go through and sort what Adia sent over," and she rose and walked a distance away.

"Alright, Honovi. Just start telling me what you know. I doubt there is anything I do not already know about Adia's situation, but if there is, I will keep it in confidence," said Is'Taqa.

Honovi trusted Is'Taqa. And Mapiya had suggested she spend as much time with him as possible, so this was as good a way as any.

It was hard for her to know what the Second Chief did and did not know, so Honovi did as he said and started talking. She told him how they had first thought Adia might be with offspring when the morning sickness started. She told him how distraught Adia was, and how often Nadiwani sat with her, trying to bring some comfort.

Honovi told him how much Adia loved Oh'Dar and how gentle and kind she was with the Waschini child.

"And I have taught Oh'Dar two different signs, one for Adia and one for Nadiwani, as he was calling them both Mama," she added, not knowing what was important and what was not.

"Sometimes, Adia disappears for long periods. We do not know where she goes or when she will be back. Usually, it is when she is upset, and when she does finally come back, she seems to be better. She is very strong, Is'Taqa. But she also looks as if she is carrying a tremendous burden.

"I know the Healer is not supposed to bond, is not supposed to have children, and that this is a very controversial situation. Of course, I know the High Council met about an important matter; I am assuming it was about her condition."

"Honovi, forgive my questions, but it might help if I can ask you about some things directly. Who else is close to her? Who does she spend time with?" he asked.

172 | LEIGH ROBERTS

Honovi shifted a bit before deciding it was acceptable to answer.

"Well, there are two women who also help care for Oh'Dar. One is older, and the other is younger. The older one has become a friend to me. I sometimes take Oh'Dar over to her quarters to play when I feel Adia needs some privacy in her own living space. The only other one who is around is Acaraho. That is pretty much it," she explained.

Is'Taqa listened carefully. He was becoming concerned about Acaraho's frequent interactions with Adia.

"What is Acaraho's role, from what you can see?"

"At first, I thought he was only setting things up, arranging for my coming, and having my quarters prepared ahead of time. Then at one point, I thought perhaps he was serving as a guard for her. Now lately, I am not sure. They spend a lot of time *not* looking at each other—if that makes any sense," she added.

It made perfect sense. Is'Taqa knew he had to ask the next question. He unconsciously took a deep breath and let it back out.

"Do you know who the father of Adia's child is?" he asked directly.

Honovi let out a deep, long sigh.

"No, Is'Taqa, I do not. I do not think even Nadiwani knows that. Adia is very careful never to talk about any of it. Even her accident a while back—she never talks about that either. But of course, she does not remember much, from hitting her head."

"Do you think it is Acaraho?" Is'Taqa hated to put the idea into her mind in case it had not already occurred to her. He knew Acaraho was not the father —but he wanted to see if there might be an appearance that he was.

"I do not know Is'Taqa. Sometimes I do, and sometimes I do not. If you could see the looks they exchange; there is something there. I think for people who do not know them well enough, it would be an easy assumption. As I said, they spend a lot of time making a point not to look at each other. And when he walks by, I can feel the energy pass between them. Does that make sense?" she asked.

"It does, Honovi. Thank you," he replied. Is'Taqa put his hand to his mouth and closed his eyes, thinking. If Honovi had noticed tension between Acaraho and Adia, then there was a good chance that others also had. He knew Adia would have to announce her pregnancy soon.

It would be very convenient and in Khon'Tor's best interests to let people think Acaraho was the father. *And it would not be above Khon'Tor either to encourage such an assumption*, thought Is'Taqa.

Is'Taqa had seen Khon'Tor's reaction when Kurak'Kahn of the High Council spoke to Acaraho at the end of the session. He sensed Khon'Tor was feeling some jealousy over the positive attention Acaraho was receiving—especially at a time when the Leader was being so challenged and was probably worrying every day about his secret being revealed.

For the first time, Is'Taqa was starting to worry about the stability of the People and their future. Both the People and the Brothers would likely face increasing intrusion of the Waschini into their land. A Waschini presence would have an enormous impact on the People's ways. It was different for the Brothers; the Waschini knew they existed. But no one other than the Brothers knew of the Sasquatch.

How the People came to be was a secret known only within a select circle. For many generations, the Sasquatch and the Brothers had lived peacefully side-by-side, but that had not always been the case.

According to the stories passed down from the Ancients, eons ago the Sasquatch were not the People as the Brothers knew them to be now. They were the Nu'numic Sasquatch of other regions. Far larger than the People, they were huge, hulking creatures with thick, heavy coats and broad features. The Brothers called them the Nu'numics, but the People also knew them as the Sarnonn.

At that time, the Brothers and the Sarnonn Sasquatch did not live in direct relationship. The different groups kept to themselves, respecting each other but having little interaction. They shared no language and almost exclusively remained in their respective territories. A glimpse of a Sarnonn by the Brothers was a rare occurrence.

During that period, a disease spread through the Sasquatch communities, up and down between those next to the Mother Stream and even to the communities slightly beyond. It left most of the males sterile. No longer able to reliably impregnate their females, the population was reduced to alarming levels. Out of desperation the Sasquatch females cross-bred with the Brothers. Because physical mating was impossible, the Sasquatch used a long-forgotten method to extract the Brothers' seed, through a means which bought the males' silence. It was another of the mysteries of the Age of Darkness, the answer to which would most likely never be known.

When they discovered that the two tribes could interbreed, word traveled to the others in the area. Slowly, over time, the population was re-established, except that the offspring were mixed—part Brother and part Sasquatch. Once their numbers were strong enough, and the following generations were producing consistently healthy offspring, the People abandoned this practice against the Brothers.

Smaller than the original Sasquatch, and built more like the Brothers, they inherited the best attributes of each. They still had incredible strength but in a smaller, less bulky package than the Sarnonn. According to the ancient stories they were also smarter than the Sarnonn, and though still somewhat resistant to change, they were more inclined to innovate. The thick, heavy coat was gone, replaced with a much lighter almost down-like undercoat, combined with a thicker covering in specific areas, but which still provided protection from the elements. Manual dexterity was greatly improved. As a result of the physical changes, cultural changes followed.

They became known to themselves and the Brothers as the People.

It was a dark age for the Sasquatch. There was great turmoil within their communities, and it took many generations for both the Sasquatch and the Brothers to make peace with what the Sasquatch had done.

As their culture changed, the People formed the High Council and the Second Laws. And from then on, pairings were controlled by the High Council to ensure that new bloodlines were dispersed through their communities. Only the Leaders were allowed to select their own mates.

It was the single time in history that the Sasquatch had betrayed the Brothers' trust. The details of the story were lost—or discarded—over time; perhaps out of embarrassment or possibly to keep the peace between the two tribes. In the Brothers' villages, the story was passed down to the Chiefs and Medicine Women only.

Among the People, what survived of the story was also known only to a very small circle. It was a period of deep disgrace for them and was rarely spoken of: the Wrak-Wavara, the Age of Darkness.

Eventually, the Brothers and the People developed a beneficial relationship. They developed a common language; they exchanged innovations and knowledge. For the wounds inflicted by the Sasquatch to heal had taken a great deal of effort, goodwill, forgiveness, and the intention to understand and embrace their differences.

The Waschini did not seem to have any interest in embracing differences. From what the Brothers and the People knew of them, they were marauders at heart, taking what they wanted and destroying whatever got in their way. They were more adaptable, and they were wilier than both the Brothers and the People. And they did not seek to understand what they were afraid of; they attacked it, subdued it, and kept on going.

Is'Taqa feared that of the three tribes, the future belonged to the Waschini for their ruthlessness.

He turned his thoughts back to the issues at hand.

The problems between the Leaders of the People were becoming critical. The tension between Khon'Tor and Hakani seemed only to be worsening. The Leader's mate appeared to want to cause as much trouble and anguish for Adia as possible. Hakani had still not produced an heir and had just lost the one she was carrying. Now, on top of all that, she was going to raise Adia's offspring—not knowing that her mate was the father and that the offspring, if a male, was the rightful heir to Khon'Tor's position.

Everywhere Is'Taqa looked, there was explosive tension building between the three.

Up until now, Acaraho had been the stabilizing force—well thought of, revered even. He had been uncontaminated by whatever was going on with the leadership trinity. But now, with Adia's pregnancy and Khon'Tor's growing jealousy of Acaraho, Is'Taqa was confident that Acaraho's character was soon to be brought into question.

And, having witnessed Khon'Tor's attack on Adia, Is'Taqa knew the truth that could blow it all wide open.

What would happen to the People of the High Rocks? Ogima Adoeete is right; somehow, this will end up being Khon'Tor's undoing. *People will follow a corrupt Leader, but only if they do not know he is corrupt. And eventually, the truth has a way of coming out.*

Is'Taqa could not decide whether it was best for the People to let it unfold in its own time, or if he should come forward and bring it all to a head. And did he have a right to intervene? Was it not for Adia to choose how to handle what Khon'Tor had done to her? Realizing how dangerous the dynamic truly was between Khon'Tor, Hakani, Adia, and now Acaraho, the burden of what he knew was becoming unbearable.

Over the next few days, Honovi spent as much time as possible with Ithua. It did not take her as long as she thought it would, though, before she felt she should return to Kthama. She knew Adia would be missing her help more and more with each passing day. Reluctantly, she let Is'Taqa know she would be ready to go back in a few days. She and Ithua prepared a special meal for her last night there. After they had enjoyed it, the three once again sat around the warm fire that chased away the slight chill in the night air.

Is'Taqa looked over at Honovi and noticed again how beautiful she was, softly highlighted by the fire's glow. *I am sorry she is returning to the People. I will be glad when she visits again. I have missed her.*

The next day, Is'Taqa made the trip back to the meeting place with Honovi. She had a bag packed by Ithua for Adia and Nadiwani. Is'Taqa handed Acaraho the bag and watched the two of them leave, feeling sad that he would possibly not see Honovi for some time.

CHAPTER 8

Adia and Nadiwani were glad to see Honovi
return. When Oh'Dar saw her, he trun-
dled directly over and flung himself into
her arms. Honovi grabbed him up and hugged him
tightly. She was back in her second home.

In the small space of her absence, Honovi could
see a difference in Adia's figure; changes that were
becoming undeniable. If the Healer had been a
regular paired female of the population, there was
no doubt the others would have figured out by now
that she was with offspring.

Adia saw Honovi looking at her. *Time is up.* Adia
had to let the community know of her condition.
Facing the High Council had been very hard, and
this was not going to be any easier. She waited until
Honovi was away to figure out with Nadiwani how
best to make such an announcement.

"This should be a time of joy," sighed Adia.

"I am sorry. But perhaps the People will surprise you. They know how dedicated you have been to them. None of us is above making a mistake," said Nadiwani, reaching out to cover Adia's hand in her own.

"In their eyes, I have let them all down. I have violated the basic tenets of my position. This is a time of shame for me, not one of celebration."

Nadiwani waited.

"My failing is going to be a shadow hanging over me and this poor offspring for the remainder of both our lives. Yes, every offspring is innocent, but this one will enter Etera already shackled by a heritage of shame." Adia sighed again.

"I wish I had asked the High Council to stay and make the announcement. After all, it is a result of my committing a crime. Any attempt to make it otherwise is going to be a disaster."

There would be no showering of congratulations and smiles for her, as there had been for Hakani when Khon'Tor announced that she was with offspring. And there was the matter that her offspring was to be handed over to Hakani. Adia remembered the last few words between Kurak'Kahn of the High Council and Acaraho.

"I am going to talk to Acaraho and see if he thinks rather that a general assembly should convene and someone from the High Council announce my condition. They could also explain why another Healer is coming and that eventually, Hakani will be raising the offspring." Tears rolled down her cheeks.

"I think you are right," replied Nadiwani. "The gossip and undercurrent of speculation and conjecture will run rampant without some formal declaration. I can already feel a shift since the High Council's visit. Everyone knows something serious is afoot; there is no reason otherwise for the High Council to have traveled to meet with our Leaders. There is already uneasiness and concern circulating over this."

Adia was still keeping Khon'Tor's secret for fear of destroying her people through the loss of the powerful Leader they so desperately needed; a Leader who could get them through the trying times ahead. She still believed it would be worse if they knew the truth, but this was not going to be an easy path either.

The next morning, she sent word that she wanted to meet with Acaraho.

Adia considered meeting at one of the many tables in the community eating area. She debated whether it was better to meet him openly or to have him keep coming to her quarters. Since he would be mentoring Oh'Dar, she felt everyone might as well get used to seeing them interact, which meant they should meet publicly. They were both in positions of authority, so no one would sit close by or interrupt their conversation. Still, they would have to keep their voices reasonably low. She was starting to second guess every move she made, as speaking quietly could also be misconstrued. In the end, she decided to have him come to her quarters as he had been doing up to now.

Acaraho listened carefully to everything Adia said, and when she was finished, he sat back for a moment before commenting.

"I understand all your concerns, and I think they are very valid. There is already too much conjecture among the People regarding the High Council's visit. They know something important has happened or is about to happen. It does no good to prolong the announcement and let them continue to worry and frighten each other.

"I also agree that there must be a formal announcement. Though I understand that this is not a matter you want to draw attention to, it is going to be at the forefront of everyone's minds, regardless of how they learn about it. Better to have it framed appropriately, as you have said—so they have something definitive to think about instead of reacting emotionally to the situation," continued Acaraho in rational assessment of Adia's reasoning.

He went on, "Having the High Council here would certainly create the formal atmosphere and gain everyone's attention. It would probably also reassure them that despite the recent turmoil, there is still order and structure; we are not isolated, because we are still part of a larger culture. And in a general assembly, they would all hear the same message at the same time.

"It is well thought out, Adia. I am impressed."

She let a little smile escape and lowered her eyes for a second.

"Let us talk about it a bit more, though," he continued. "This is a volatile time for everyone. I think you will agree that things were settling down before the High Council visit. Even the news of Hakani's miscarriage had a unifying effect. But since the High Council came, everyone is stirred up again, and the reason for that, ultimately, is the tension between the Leaders. You, Khon'Tor, and Hakani. I include myself in the leadership circle, but I have so far not been directly involved in the discord.

"Yes, I know Khon'Tor stripped Hakani of her rank, but the dynamics continue between the three of you regardless of whether she holds that title or not," he added.

"I am sure Khon'Tor's decision only made matters worse in some ways," she remarked.

"Yes. It is clear Hakani has been harboring animosity toward both you and Khon'Tor for some time. I pride myself on knowing what is going on around here, but even I have no idea what the reason is. It seems to have been present almost from the very beginning of their pairing and has only grown worse with time. At this point, I am not sure where she would draw the line in trying to create trouble. You know better than anyone how she handled the news of Oh'Dar—clearly designed to inflame everyone's opinion against you, and probably also against Khon'Tor. Her performance was inexcusably disrespectful of Khon'Tor as Leader, let alone as her mate. I will share with you that I was astonished that she was carrying his offspring, considering the tension between them," he said gingerly.

At so intimate a remark, Adia had to look away again for a moment.

They had never had such a drawn-out conversation. Despite the highly charged topic, they were both enjoying the time together. They had taken the next step toward a more casual level of interaction. For the first time they were Acaraho and Adia having a discussion—no longer High Protector Acaraho and Adia, Healer of the People and Second Rank.

Adia surmised that Acaraho also felt the shift because his inflection changed.

"Adia," he said, turning so he was more directly facing her. "Our people truly do need to hear about this together, all at once, and from someone in authority. But considering that Khon'Tor very likely feels disempowered by your asking the High Council to step in, asking them back again will, in his own eyes, only discredit him more." He stretched his arm out across the back of the seat, so it reached behind her, almost touching her but not quite.

It was a distraction difficult to ignore. Adia's imagination started to slip to possibilities unwise for a Healer to entertain.

She nodded in agreement. The most important thing to Khon'Tor *was* his image in the eyes of the People.

Following Acaraho's train of thought, she answered, "You think the announcement should come from Khon'Tor."

"Yes. As Leader, it should come from him. Whether he can do it, I am not sure. And by that, I mean do it justice, so it calms reactions instead of inflaming them. If he can see the value of that outcome to himself, I believe he will. He is an excellent orator."

"You are right. You are right. It should come from him, as Leader," she agreed.

In support of his next point, Acaraho glanced down at Adia's growing figure and then back up to Adia.

"I know there is not much time. Let me approach Khon'Tor with this. If he refuses or reacts so badly that I do not think he can carry it off properly, I will take your request to the High Council myself," he said, offering to travel in person to the Overseer.

They rose, and Adia thanked Acaraho, who left to find Khon'Tor.

Acaraho had not mentioned it, but there was also the possibility that Hakani would leak out the news that Adia was with offspring. He did not know her limits but had to assume that, like Khon'Tor, she had no limits at all.

As he listened to Adia explain her thoughts and her concerns, Acaraho had reflected on how she never took the easy way out; even in this, she was putting the needs of the community above whatever additional embarrassment or hardship this would cause her.

Acaraho found Khon'Tor in the general eating area. It was early enough that he had just finished the morning meal. He was sitting alone and aimlessly pushing the foodstuff around on the catalpa leaf in front of him.

Acaraho was careful to make sure Khon'Tor would see him coming. The Leader looked up and signaled for him to sit down. Khon'Tor was still feeling threatened by the camaraderie demonstrated between Acaraho and Kurak'Kahn of the High Council. But Khon'Tor did not much like anyone right now, and he still needed the cooperation of the High Protector.

So he spoke first. "How are you? I have not thanked you yet for making all the arrangements for the High Council, but I am grateful," he tried, saying the opposite of what he was thinking.

"I am well, Khon'Tor," replied Acaraho, following social convention. "And you are welcome. So much has happened in the past few seasons. It seems we have barely had a chance for things to settle down when something else happens. If they have not already, I fear it will not be very long before someone figures it out or someone lets on that Adia is with offspring," he said.

Khon'Tor knew Acaraho was alluding to Hakani, and he also knew the High Protector was right. It was not beneath her to let the news slip out—anything to create more trouble. *What is wrong with that female?* He still did not have the answer to that.

"Knowing you as I do, Commander, I am sure you have a suggestion. Please go on," said Khon'Tor.

"It is going to come out sooner or later—and most likely sooner—and is too volatile to leave to unchecked speculation. As you well know, it is unusual for the High Council to intervene in the affairs of any of the People's communities. Someone needs to explain why the High Council was here, why it was appropriate that they came, what the situation is, and what will happen after the offspring is born. And it needs to be presented in a way that calms them instead of igniting more worry and concern," said Acaraho plainly.

Khon'Tor might be many things—arrogant, strong-willed, driven, self-centered—but he was not stupid. *Acaraho is right. They need to hear an official statement from someone in authority. And they need to hear it from me. Nothing good is going to come of the continued disruption of their peace of mind with external worries.*

He let out a heavy sigh. *This war with Adia must end. If she were going to turn me in to the High Council, she would already have done so. Instead, she stood there and took the brunt of everything; all the shame, the repercussions. Even when Kurak'Kahn pressed her about who the father is, she stood her ground.*

He knew Adia still had negative feelings about him, but she had a long road ahead, and nothing good would come of his continuing to work against her.

I wanted to discredit her by allowing the Waschini offspring to learn Whitespeak, but she seems to have accepted what happened and is trying to move on. It is in my best interest to do the same.

The Leader turned his attention back to Acaraho and said, "I agree with you. I will put thought to it and call a general meeting. If there is anything else you think of, please let me know."

"Khon'Tor, there is not a lot of time," said Acaraho, and the Leader knew he was referring to Adia's changing figure, which he had noticed himself.

After Acaraho left, Khon'Tor started formulating the major points he needed to make. Adia was with offspring, the identity of the father was of no importance, and everyone should respect her privacy. He had to make sure they knew the High Council's decision was not meant as punishment. Somehow, he had to do this while presenting her in the most favorable light possible. Khon'Tor knew she was immensely popular with the People. If he did not speak in line with their reverence for her, they might turn against him.

Confident he had a general idea of what to convey, he sent out word that there would be a general assembly before the end of the next day, at which everyone was required to be in attendance.

Adia received the news with mixed feelings. She believed Acaraho when he told her he felt Khon'Tor would give a unifying and rallying speech. That part was reassuring to her. The unsettling part was that now it would begin. The sideways glances, conversations that stopped mid-sentence when she entered a room, the constant speculation about who the father was.

I believe I will have the support of the other females because they have experienced the longing to have offspring. But there will still be the question about how I could have let something like this happen. However, as far as her role as Healer went, she believed it could take the hit.

Adia was glad Honovi had returned in time for the general meeting, and said to her, "You are part of our community now, so you should be there with everyone else."

Khon'Tor did not move back to his quarters after the High Council meeting. In fact, he had still not moved back. He continued to live in the meeting room he had requisitioned.

Hakani waited every night for his return, bracing herself for the aftermath to her claim of Adia's unborn offspring. Days passed, and she neither saw him nor heard word from him or from anyone about his whereabouts. She would have liked to see him accidentally, to gauge his mood, but that did not happen either.

Finally, the day he announced the general assembly, Khon'Tor came to their quarters. He stood just inside the door, making it obvious he was not staying long. Hakani rose as soon as she saw him. She told herself to relax because it was doubtful he would do anything drastic the day before the meeting; though this was the first time they had seen each other since the High Council.

Khon'Tor's posture was rigid. "I am sure you have heard that I called a meeting for tomorrow. I am going to cover some high-level items affecting everyone. I am going to tell them the purpose of the recent visit from the High Council. I am also going to tell them that Adia is with offspring and the reason why that offspring will be turned over to you after it is born," he said matter-of-factly.

Then he took a couple of steps toward her. Hakani, despite her self-assurance of a moment earlier, stiffened and unconsciously took a step backward.

"Relax, Hakani. You are safe—*for the moment*. However, let me make this *very* clear. Do *not* act up tomorrow. I expect you to attend, listen attentively, and behave like the Leader's Mate. You are getting what you want. I suggest you behave accordingly," he said.

Hakani did not answer.

Khon'Tor stared her down a little while longer, intentionally trying to make her uncomfortable. Then, just to let her know he had not forgotten her acts of defiance, he narrowed his eyes and curled his left upper lip into a snarl—just noticeable enough— and left.

Despite her silence, Khon'Tor knew Hakani well enough to tell that her earlier bravado in front of the High Council was gone. He was disappointed, for it would have made what he was planning for her later so much more sporting.

The next afternoon came soon enough. Acaraho was there early. There was not much talk among the crowd once they got seated. They were subdued, which told him they were lost in their own thoughts, wondering about the reason for this meeting.

Adia, Honovi, and Nadiwani came in and took seats not too far from Acaraho. Mapiya sat next to Honovi.

Hakani was one of the last to get there, keeping to the back. Soon everyone was seated, and it was not long before Khon'Tor arrived and walked confidently up to the front. He had brought the Leader's Staff, indicating that this was a matter of great importance. A chill went through most members in attendance once they noticed he was carrying it. As was his practice, Khon'Tor raised his left hand to indicate he was about to speak.

Adia suddenly felt light-headed and was concerned she might faint. She prayed to the Mother that she would not and focused on controlling her breathing.

Khon'Tor spoke. "Thank you for coming. You all need to hear this at the same time, so there is no conjecture later over what I said. No doubt you are aware that recently the High Council came to Kthama, something which has only happened a handful of times in our memory. Only matters of the highest importance are attended to by the High Council. Matters which affect a community at a deep level and those which need the combined wisdom of many to decide. For several seasons our community has faced many challenges. Those challenges are not over, but that is the nature of life; the challenges will never be over."

There was a murmur in the crowd until he continued.

"Change is the nature of life. As much as we would like everything to stay the same, it never will. Our people do not easily accept change. It has always proven hard for us, regardless of what it has been. But no matter how hard, we have made it through each one—all of them. And we will make it through the changes to come," he said.

Then he took a few steps over to the side, something Khon'Tor never did. He usually stood in the same place once he started speaking and never left it.

"Our Ancestors created the laws of the People. The laws are here to guide us and direct us. They are meant for our benefit, not for our persecution. I will start by quoting one of the First Laws. In all things, show forbearance for each other's failings.

"The High Council came to hear a very difficult situation. One that will challenge our ability as a People to obey the law I just quoted. I have no doubt you will be affected by what I am about to tell you, perhaps deeply. But I ask you to hear me out before you pass judgment, and to keep in mind that none of us—no matter who it is—is infallible, and nor should we be expected to be."

Then he walked back to his original starting position.

"The High Council came here to sit in judgment

of a crime. A crime that was committed by one of our most revered and respected Leaders. As you know, a crime committed by one of the high ranks cannot be heard within the community concerned—it must be heard by the High Council," he continued.

"This was not a crime as you might think. But because what has happened goes against one of the Second Laws, it is still technically a crime. Although a law was broken, the High Council did not pass judgment. They did hand down a ruling on what should happen as a result of this situation, but it was not a judgment. They were very clear about that."

Everyone was shifting in their seats by now.

"Under any other circumstance, were it anyone else, what I am about to tell you would be an occasion for joy. I hope that by the time I have finished speaking, you will be able to embrace it as just that.

"Adia," and he held out his free hand as if he were expecting her to join him. Adia startled, then froze and looked at Acaraho.

Seeing her discomfort, Acaraho stepped over and extended his hand out to hers, to help her up. She took his hand and rose to walk to Khon'Tor. The High Protector walked a few steps with her, and then she took Khon'Tor's hand and stood beside him.

By having Adia join him, Khon'Tor sent a clear message that they were standing together in this matter. Those in the crowd were looking at each other now, trying to understand.

Khon'Tor paused a moment before continuing.

"Adia Adoeete, revered and respected Healer of the People of the High Rocks, is with offspring," he said, still holding her hand.

Nothing could contain the outbreak that followed. It was not riotous, and it was not contentious; it was just that they could not control their reactions.

Khon'Tor let it continue for a few moments. He knew this was part of their comprehending what he had just told them. He knew that if he interrupted this flow of energy at this moment, it would turn against him out of frustration. And frustration often turned to anger.

Finally, as the conversation slowed, he raised his staff, commanding everyone's attention.

They slowly stopped talking and turned to look back at him.

"I do not have to tell you about Adia's spotless record. I do not have to tell you how she has served every one of us diligently and with love. How many of us here have been healed by her care? How many of our Elders has she tended to in their Twilight, and even through their Return to the Great Spirit? She has been here for us in joy and tragedy. She has never turned her back on us, no matter what our need. I am asking you not to turn your backs on her now in *her* time of need."

Silence.

"I told you earlier that the High Council did not pass judgment on Adia. They recognize none of us is infallible. I hope each of you accepts that truth for yourselves at this moment.

"The High Council is sending a Healer to help Adia through the next few months of waiting. As you know, the Healer is one of the most important members of a community; even more so one of Adia's heart and talent. We all know that carrying and delivering an offspring can be trying and dangerous, so Adia must receive the best support and care through the next few months," he said.

Acaraho shook his head at Khon'Tor's instincts and abilities when it came to unifying and motivating people.

The Leader continued. "It would be an understatement for me to say there are circumstances regarding her situation about which you are no doubt curious, and questions for which you want answers. There will be times where you may even find yourselves feeling driven to seek out these answers. I am asking you now to find it within yourselves to let that pass and commit to not having all the answers you want. Respect Adia's privacy. Focus instead on the joy of a new life coming into our community.

"The offspring of a Healer is, in many ways, an event to be celebrated. It is in truth, a sacred event— not a shameful one. Adia is our Healer, and we are blessed to have her. But Adia is also a female, and she is about to experience one of the greatest blessings of being a female. Let us share her joy with her and let us practice the law of forbearance for each other."

Khon'Tor paused. Instinctively, he decided to leave out the part where the offspring would be turned over to Hakani.

And so, with that, Khon'Tor raised Adia's hand in his and slammed his staff into the floor.

Slowly, a single thought must have passed through the People because as if on cue, each raised a hand toward Adia, returning the gesture. It was a spontaneous act and one that had never occurred before. In the same moment, Adia felt warmth pass through her, and she was convinced it was the Spirit of the Great Mother moving through them all that had stirred the moment of unity.

Acaraho stepped forward, and Khon'Tor passed Adia's hand back to him. Acaraho helped her to her seat.

Just as she sat, Khon'Tor raised his hand again and said, "Thank you, People of the High Rocks. That is all," and he looked straight ahead as he walked through the crowd to the back of the room and left.

The mood had changed from one of anticipation and concern to shock and alarm when Khon'Tor had made his announcement, and now it changed again, to one of reverence. The People talked among themselves in hushed tones. As they got up to leave, nearly every one of them went past Adia and took her hand; even those at the back who had to come forward to do so.

Acaraho kept his position and took his eyes off her only to assimilate everyone's reactions.

People came up to her and gave her their congratulations, or simply looked at her with kindness and smiled at her. Adia was moved to tears and let them roll silently down her face. But these were not tears of sadness; they were tears of relief and gratitude at the outpouring of love and acceptance toward her.

Nadiwani, Honovi, and Mapiya stayed seated at Adia's side throughout. It seemed to take forever, but eventually, everyone had left except the five of them.

Acaraho came over and knelt in front of Adia, so he was at eye level with her. He placed one hand over hers as they lay folded in her lap. He did not say a word; he just looked into her eyes.

They stayed there for a few more moments until suddenly Adia sat up a little straighter and her hand went to her midsection. She looked around at them, her eyes a little wide, and said, "The offspring just moved."

And they all broke out in joyful smiles, even the usually stoic Acaraho.

Adia and Acaraho were thinking the same thing.

To what depths did Khon'Tor reach into himself that he could speak as he did. It was an unfathomable dichotomy—that one who himself was capable of so much evil and selfishness was also capable of moving others to so much love and compassion.

CHAPTER 9

However, it was not just the five of them left in the room.

Way in the back in the shadows stood someone who had not been moved by Khon'Tor's speech—or at least not in the same way as the others.

Hakani did not want the People to embrace and forgive Adia. She had been thrilled when she heard Adia was with offspring. Finally, the great Healer had fallen like the rest of them. Adia had been brought down, shown to be no better than anyone else, and Hakani had come to the meeting anticipating that the People would turn away from Adia in disappointment. Perhaps, if Hakani were very lucky, even in disgust.

But none of it happened—because of Khon'Tor and his krellshar speech. And to make it worse, he did not even mention I would be the one to raise the offspring. That

Adia's offspring would be taken away from its disgraced mother and given to me to raise instead.

Hakani had come to see Adia shamed, not glorified. Rejected, not embraced. The hatred and the rebellion fired up again within her; against Khon'Tor, against Adia, and against Adia's unborn offspring.

She slipped out of the room amid the shadows, but not unnoticed; the movement caught Acaraho's eye.

❁

As she walked back to her quarters—Khon'Tor's quarters—Hakani developed her plans for revenge. She would make sure they all suffered for this— especially her mate.

She did not yet know how, but she would make him pay most of all.

As she was almost through the door of their quarters, someone grabbed her, pushed her up against a wall, and overpowered her from behind. Pinned and helpless, her hands were bound, and something hard was pressed into her mouth and tied there while another wrapping completely covered her eyes. She could not move; she could not see. She could not make a noise. Then she was dragged roughly inside and pushed down to the floor.

Khon'Tor had been waiting for her.

❁

Acaraho accompanied the females back to the Healer's Quarters. They walked slowly, reverently. Nadiwani had her arm around Adia's waist. Acaraho brought up the rear, keeping an eye on Adia. He could see she was exhausted.

When they were halfway there, Adia stumbled and fell forward. In one swift movement, Acaraho was in front of her, sweeping her up into his arms. She was too tired to resist and surrendered to the sweet comfort of being carried, letting herself lean up against him.

Acaraho was warm, and she could hear his strong, slow heartbeat. She felt safe and protected. And the memory of being carried back from the cold that night when Khon'Tor had attacked her came flooding back. She remembered, in contrast to the pain and the fear and the cold, the same feelings of comfort, warmth, protection. Love.

Awan, the guard at the end of the tunnel, saw them coming and went on ahead to open the door. Acaraho carried Adia to the back of her quarters and gently laid her down on her sleeping mat. He caressed her face, and before he could stand, she reached up and grabbed his hand. Not saying a word, still holding hers, he nodded to her and with his other hand he signed, "I know."

Adia closed her eyes and let out a long deep breath. A feeling came over her—a feeling that everything was going to be alright.

Nadiwani thanked Acaraho as Mapiya and Honovi left for Mapiya's quarters.

Acaraho then stepped out quietly, and with Awan walked back the way they had come.

When he got to the end of the tunnel and Awan's post, he said, "Be extra vigilant for the next few days, Awan. Tomorrow I will explain." Before he returned to his quarters, Acaraho doubled the guard to two additional posts between the Healer's Quarters and the other routes in the area. He was not taking any chances; not ever again.

Knocked to the floor and bruised, Hakani struggled for all she was worth. She knew it had to be Khon'-Tor, but she was terrified just the same. It was him, but it was not him. He was more like a primal beast sprinting from the shadows and attacking her.

He grabbed her by her hair and pulled back hard, exposing her neck. His breath was heavy and hot on her skin. She felt his barred teeth brush her throat and then slowly take part of her flesh between them and bear down, just enough to hurt but not enough to draw blood, a low menacing growl deep in his throat. Her heart was pounding. He had her trapped, barely able to breathe. He was crushing her with his weight, demonstrating how powerless she was against him. His other hand was cutting into her soft flesh, threatening to violate her at any moment.

Then suddenly, as quickly as it had begun, her hands were freed from the lashings and she was released. She lay there terrified, afraid to move, fearing another attack at any second. Finally, realizing Khon'Tor was gone, she broke down, sobbing.

She did not understand the reason for the attack. *Is he just reasserting his power over me, reminding me that he has not forgiven me? Is this the start of more demands?*

Whatever it was, it was the most violent Khon'Tor had ever been with her. She shuddered to think what he would have done had she not behaved at the meeting in accordance with his warning.

His point was made; he could overpower her any time he chose. And there was nothing she could do about it.

She got up and went to her sleeping area, bruised and aching. She tried to sleep but was not able to, wondering if Khon'Tor was coming back or if he was finished for the time being. There was no way to barricade the room against his entry. Nothing she had the strength to move into place would slow him down even a bit. Why had he not announced that she would be taking Adia's offspring after it was born? Surely he was not going to go against the High Council's decree?

Hakani did not sleep well that night. Or the next. Or the one after that.

The following day Adia woke with a feeling of relief, then, finally alert, she remembered yesterday's events and Khon'Tor's eloquent and moving speech on her behalf. She wondered if Honovi had been as moved by his eloquence as had everyone else.

Well, almost everyone, she thought. She knew her small circle would have noticed as she did, that he left out the part where her offspring would be turned over to Hakani after it was born. She knew Hakani had been in the room, and she would certainly have noticed. Adia believed that Khon'Tor did not mention it simply because it would have shifted the reverent mood he was creating. But that was a story for another time. She marveled again at what a skilled strategist he was.

Seeing Khon'Tor at his best underscored her decision to keep his secret. No one could replace Khon'Tor, and certainly not at this time.

Adia then remembered Hakani's miscarriage. Khon'Tor needed to produce an heir—one who could assume his position of Leader one day. One whom he could openly acknowledge, unlike the one she was carrying. Adia felt a twinge of sadness that her offspring, if it were a male, would be cheated of his rightful heritage as Khon'Tor's successor. *He would have the blood of leadership on both sides*, she reflected, thinking of her father, the Leader the People of the Deep Valley.

Of all the communities, the People of the Deep Valley was the second largest, lying many days journey past that in which Kurak'Kahn, the Overseer of the High Council lived. The People there enjoyed a rich and abundant life. As here, the People of the Deep Valley also lived underground. Adia did not know how common this was, because word only traveled so far among the People. But unlike the jagged rocky elevations and swiftly moving waters of Kthama, theirs was set amid a gentler, more rolling and verdant terrain. She missed walking great distances as an offspring without worrying about her footing or having to duck to avoid sudden outcrops of boulders. Here, at Kthama, there were paths where one slip could result in a fatal tumble to the turbulent waters below. The darker cold months made sojourns along the outside rocky elevations even more treacherous, despite the People's low light vision.

Adia had many fond memories of nights spent sleeping under the stars with her Father, cradled in the soft grasses on gently sloping hillsides. She never let herself think of her Mother very often; the loss of never having known her was too painful, and she kept it locked in a part of herself she rarely visited.

She knew too well the painful longing for that one person who would never abandon you, never turn her back on you. Who would always be there—no matter your age—to love and support you and guide you through life. The thought of any of her offspring, Waschini or otherwise, living with that emptiness inside of them was unbearable.

There were other thoughts Adia never let herself dwell on for long. One was Khon'Tor's attack. She did not understand the reason for it. There had long been rumors that Khon'Tor and Hakani were estranged. Sometimes she wondered if his assault on her had sprung from years of frustration, his long-burning anger, and that the opportunity had presented itself. But the fact that Hakani was with offspring belied that. And his rage had been so inflamed, so out of proportion at her leaving Kthama, that it still did not add up. But no circumstances could excuse what he had done.

The other thoughts she did not allow herself to entertain long were those about Acaraho. How much she admired him, how honorable he was, how protective he was of her. And then there was another set—thoughts forbidden to a Healer. Hopeless longings that could never be satisfied and were best kept locked away forever.

It was not much later that one of the watchers delivered a message to Acaraho from the High Council; they had located a Healer to look after Adia and help with her delivery. She was from the community of the People of the Far High Hills and escorted by two assistants. Acaraho immediately began making arrangements for her living space.

The People of the Far High Hills were situated

farther north and east than Adia's people, the People of the Deep Valley. Much of the journey to and from the Far High Hills could be made underground, along the Mother Stream, the large river flowing through the People's cave at the third and lowest level. It was the Mother Stream that made living in the expansive structure of Kthama possible, delivering fresh water, oxygen, and rich nutrients throughout their hidden community. Because the lower levels of Kthama were accessible via the Mother Stream, all access points along its length were restricted. Except for during the Ashwea Awhidi, the pairing ceremonies, only the higher-ranking members of any of the People were allowed to use it as a conduit between their communities.

Receiving word that the Healer was on her way, Acaraho immediately went to tell Adia. He wanted to check on her anyway after her stumble the night before. On the way, he stopped to speak with his First Guard, Awan, who had been on duty and had missed Khon'Tor's speech. Acaraho told him that Adia was with offspring and that Khon'Tor had asked everyone to remember her dedication to the People and requested that they not judge her harshly.

Awan listened intently but said nothing. When he was done, Acaraho left. He would not have walked away so casually had he known what Awan was thinking. The First Guard had concluded that the reason Acaraho was so watchful and so protective of Adia was that he had seeded her offspring.

It was Acaraho who had been stationed outside of the Healer's Quarters after Hakani revealed the presence of the Waschini offspring. It was Acaraho who had found and arranged for Oh'Dar's Whitespeak teacher. It was Acaraho who had made the arrangements for the High Council. It was Acaraho who had stationed the guards for Adia's protection. It was Acaraho who had volunteered to become Oh'Dar's male role model, tying his life to hers for many years to come. And it was Acaraho who had carried Adia in his arms to her quarters the night before.

Had they stepped back and thought about it, Adia and Acaraho themselves would have realized that virtually everyone was thinking the two of them had succumbed to their feelings for each other.

Adia was nonplussed by Acaraho's news of the Healer's arrival. She welcomed the care and was grateful that the Healer, Urilla Wuti, was very skilled and experienced. But she did not look forward to more people coming and going in her life. And Adia had cared for more than her share of seeded females—it was not that she did not know what to expect or look for.

Adia did think having Urilla Wuti here for the birth was a good idea, though. She had toyed with the idea of asking Ithua to attend her, but if there were problems, Ithua would not have the size or strength to be of much help to her or the offspring.

So Adia braced herself for more company, more commotion and even more intrusion into her private life. She wondered at what point they would take her offspring away from her; perhaps that was another reason to bring in a Healer not tied to the High Rocks. Urilla Wuti would perhaps have less difficulty taking the offspring away from Adia than one of her own people or one of the Brothers would.

The Healer arrived pretty much on schedule and Acaraho met her and her two attendants. He had arranged her quarters for her much as he had for Honovi, though Urilla Wuti did not need the fluorescent stones for lighting in the dark. He located her not far from the Healer's Quarters, but not so close as to be privy to every coming and going. He had installed a wooden door as a courtesy, as he often did for visiting females—the People and the Brothers alike.

Urilla Wuti was older than Adia but in no way out of her prime. Acaraho hoped she had the experience she was purported to have.

She had brought with her two large bundles carried on the shoulders of her attendants, presumably filled with medicines she thought Adia might not have in supply. Her attendants helped her get settled, after which Acaraho asked if they wished to be put up for the night before heading back. They declined but did accept Acaraho's offer of partaking of the evening meal before leaving.

○

Acaraho had not met with Khon'Tor since the last assembly, so once Urilla Wuti was settled and her attendants shown to the Great Chamber for the evening meal, he looked for the Leader.

Khon'Tor was also sitting in the Great Chamber, far from the general commotion of the hour. Acaraho sat down beside him, straddling the bench-like seat to face Khon'Tor directly. As he sat, the bench rocked slightly at the addition of his muscular frame.

"Khon'Tor, the Healer from the High Council has arrived. It is Urilla Wuti from the People of the Far High Hills. I do not know much about her, other than that she is said to be very well experienced in all aspects of carrying offspring, as well as the delivery."

"Alright. The sooner this is over, the sooner we can get back to normal. Are you hearing anything to be concerned about from the outposted watchers?" asked Khon'Tor.

"No," replied Acaraho. "Only the usual activity this time of year; animals waking up from their long sleep, migrations. No sign of the Waschini nor any word from other areas either," he answered. It was early spring and the People's land was starting to blossom in beauty, and sweet fragrance filled the air.

Acaraho looked around the room and realized the People were dealing very well with the fact of Adia being with offspring. He knew the credit belonged to Khon'Tor, and despite what else he thought of the Leader, and despite his vow that Khon'Tor would still pay for his actions, he decided to give the Leader due respect for now.

"Your speech to the People has made all the difference in their reactions to Adia's situation. It could easily have gone in the wrong direction. There is no one with your ability to reach them."

"Thank you. There is no benefit in stirring up animosity toward the Healer. It is in the best interests of none of us to have dissension and rife within our community," replied Khon'Tor.

"Anything else you need of me tonight?" asked Acaraho, arising to leave, the bench creaking as if giving a little sigh at its relief from the pressing weight.

"Yes, there is," he replied. "Place an additional guard at the far end of the access to my quarters. Leave him there until I say otherwise. Instruct him as you have the other but let him know I may tell him to leave when I return. Make sure he is far enough away, however, that he cannot overhear anything from my quarters."

"I will take care of it after I have my nightly talk with the watchers and guards," answered Acaraho.

The High Protector speculated that given what might be going on in the Leader's Quarters, Khon'Tor would not want a guard within earshot. But this made a second guard, as Khon'Tor had already assigned one to accompany Hakani at all times. Acaraho did not question the Leader's orders but had his ideas about the reason for them.

Adia was right. Khon'Tor had not mentioned the part about her offspring being turned over to Hakani because he did not want to leave them with consternation and controversy. He would have to address it with them when the time came, but for now there was a respite because the People had responded to his elocution even better than he had hoped.

Khon'Tor was planning on sleeping in the Leader's Quarters tonight and every night until the delivery. He had only so many more opportunities to exert his control over Hakani. After the offspring was placed in her care, the helpmate ordered by the High Council would be put in place. From that point on, he would have no more intimate access to Hakani; at least not within the convenience of his own living space.

On his way down the stone conduit leading to his quarters, Khon'Tor relieved the first guard he had placed, instructing him to come back after first light.

As he opened the door and stepped inside, he heard small stones scattering and clacking about.

Ah, thought Khon'Tor. *Hakani has set up an alarm system hoping to alert herself so I cannot catch her by surprise again.*

This pleased him because it meant Hakani was not going to submit easily. *All the better for my enjoyment*, he thought, and his heart started pounding in anticipation of Hakani putting up a fight.

All the nights during which Hakani had not slept, waiting for another attack, had given her time to put countermeasures in place. She knew from her last experience that the worst part was the element of surprise. If she could eliminate that, it would go a long way toward managing her fear. Hakani did not believe Khon'Tor would do her so much harm that she would require medical care or even die. But he wanted her to think he would, and when she figured out it was just a bluff, she relaxed quite a bit. He wants to scare me, she thought, that's all.

She was able to sleep once she saw his last attack from a different perspective, but she heard the stones scatter across the stone floor and knew Khon'Tor had entered. She opened her eyes to see his huge silhouette standing over her.

"Wake up Hakani," his deep voice boomed. "Wake up now," he continued.

Hakani sat up, but Khon'Tor just continued to stand there. She wondered why he did not just get on with it.

"We need to talk," he said, his voice gruff and demanding.

Hakani doubted they needed to talk; there was nothing to discuss. Khon'Tor just wanted her fully awake. Sleeping prey provided no sport.

Apparently not expecting Hakani to rise to her feet, Khon'Tor instead sat down next to her on her sleeping mat. She looked at him, just inches away, wondering what this was about. She had been expecting an attack, not conversation.

"I have decided not to comply with the High Council's orders that you should raise the Healer's offspring," he said.

"What?" *You cannot do that!* "You cannot go against the orders of the High Council! The offspring belongs to me. I claimed it, and you have no authority to set my claim aside!" she said, sitting up abruptly.

Khon'Tor raised his eyebrows at her as if in disbelief. He had perfected a countenance of smug disdain.

"Do I not? What if I told them the offspring you were carrying was not mine? That you had confessed it to be that of another male? Do you think they would find you fit to raise the Healer's offspring after that?" he taunted her, the sneering smile on his face revealing his long, white canines.

Hakani drew back and slapped Khon'Tor hard, right across the face, then lunged at him, landing across his chest and digging her nails as hard as she could into his neck, then pummeling him with her fists. She tried to bite him, anywhere, trying to inflict any wound she could.

The Leader caught her fists up easily enough and freed himself of her with one powerful shrug, flipping her over and landing her on the sleeping mat a few inches away. The resounding thud indicated that the impact had knocked the wind out of her. With one hand, he pinned and held her there. His other hand went instinctively to the blood dripping from his neck.

He rubbed the warm blood between his fingers, looking over at her, held prisoner beneath his other hand. No matter about the scratches, he had gotten the reaction—and excuse—he wanted.

He shook his head slowly back and forth and said, "Oh, Hakani. You really should not have done that."

After he saw she had recovered, he released his hold on her, and she came at him again with the same result; he just as easily flipped her off and pinned her against the mat.

He chuckled at her, fuming but powerless against him. *Oh, how I wish I had started this with her long ago.*

Seeing Hakani was exhausted and probably not capable of another attack, he started moving purposefully, menacingly toward her, never taking his eyes off hers, which grew in alarm the closer he came. He grabbed her ankles and dragged her toward him as he crawled forward over her, letting his weight rest on her just enough to pin her in the way he wanted. He could smell his lust for her and knew she could too. He moved slowly, hoping she would recover enough to try another attack.

"Is that all you have Hakani? Have I won so easily?" he goaded her. "So be it. But I think you will find —inventive—is the word perhaps, all the pleasures I have planned for you tonight," he smiled.

It was one of the longest and worst nights of Hakani's life, and one of the longest and best of Khon'Tor's.

The next morning, Khon'Tor was still there. Hakani awoke but stayed curled up on her side pretending she had not. She was trying to forget everything from the night before. She was right that Khon'Tor did not mean to cause her injury. But she had learned an important fact—one can inflict a fair amount of pain without inflicting injury.

Hakani wondered what had happened to Khon'-Tor. She could not believe this monster was the Leader and her mate. *Has he always been like this,* she wondered, *with these appetites? Or is this an aberration caused by what I put him through over the Waschini offspring*? Whatever the reason, she did not believe she could bear even one more night like that.

"Hakani, I know you are awake," he said. "Best sit up and listen to me before I go. You may not leave the quarters today. But just so you have something to look forward to, I will be back tonight. And the next night. And the next night, and the night after that. I want to make the most of our time together before Adia's offspring is turned over to you."

Hakani heard him say that she would be getting the offspring. Was he being cruel the night before? Was it just part of some game to torture her and make her suffer mentally before he made her suffer physically?

She did not have answers to any of those questions. And she wanted to ask why she could not leave the quarters today, but she dared not. Hakani looked up and nodded so Khon'Tor could see she had heard him, and she prayed he would leave so she could tend to her bruised and aching body.

"You can spend your time making plans for where the offspring will sleep and be tended to. But after you have the offspring here, do not forget that you are not absolved of your obligation to provide me an heir," he finished.

Khon'Tor left and at the end of the hallway gave the guard instructions that Hakani was not allowed to leave, that no one other than he was allowed in, and that he would be back later.

The next morning, Acaraho introduced Urilla Wuti to Adia and Nadiwani. Urilla Wuti seemed quiet, not very talkative. As a fellow Healer, Adia wondered what the older female thought of her situation. She wondered if Urilla Wuti thought less of her. She did not want to care, but she could not help but feel somewhat ashamed.

Only a few knew her being with offspring was not of her choosing, and that it was not her fault. Khon'Tor had done wonders in presenting it to their people, and she did not feel judgment from them, though she knew there was still an element of shock. But Urilla Wuti did not have the benefit of Khon'Tor's eloquent discourse and his call for forbearance and forgiveness. She only knew what the High Council had told her.

Adia could not help herself. If this female was going to be her nursemaid during all the time leading up to her delivery, she wanted to know the Healer did not look down on her. For some reason, Adia was drawn to this female and wanted to be like by her. The Healer network was small, and relationships between Healers were cherished.

Urilla Wuti, Adia, and Nadiwani compared notes over the next few days. Adia had no complaints other than those experienced by every female. All seemed to be going smoothly, except that she was putting on a bit more weight than might be expected.

Adia was determined to make the other Healer like her, or at least allow the Healer to get to know her enough to give it a fair chance. She tried to strike up conversations, asking mundane questions about where she lived, how she had become a Healer—anything that occurred to her.

Urilla Wuti put up with it for a little while, but after a few days of it, could no longer cope with the chatter any longer. She was a female of few words and preferred to be subjected to as few words as possible in return.

One afternoon, while Adia was trying to draw Urilla Wuti into conversation, the visiting Healer suddenly put down what she was working on and walked up to Adia, took her by the hand, and led her over to the seating area where she motioned for her to sit down.

Adia sat down and Urilla Wuti sat down next to her.

Urilla Wuti took both of Adia's hands in hers and rested them on the stone bench.

"You have questions."

"Yes," replied Adia, swallowing hard.

"Are you willing to have your questions answered, even if the way I answer them may not be conventional?"

"Yes, of course," Adia frowned.

"Are you willing to trade your secrets for mine?"

By now, Adia was becoming a little confused.

"I trust you, Urilla Wuti, if that is what you are asking."

Urilla Wuti nodded, and still holding Adia's hands, looked into her eyes. Within a few seconds, Adia felt as if a window opened—one that had always been there but that she had never noticed before.

The older Healer closed the link almost immediately, and Adia's eyes widened with amazement.

"What just happened? What did you do?"

"I opened a Connection with you. It is a deep secret known only by a few Healers and a small select number of Leaders. Would you be willing to experience it further? Again, I must warn you; the Connection is a conduit between two souls. There are few secrets in the Connection."

Adia thought a moment. *I have nothing to hide. I am what I am, imperfect but dedicated to my calling and my community.*

"Yes. Yes. Please," she finally said.

Urilla Wuti closed her eyes and opened another Connection, this time leaving it open longer than a second or two.

At that moment, time dropped out of existence, and the space separating the two females disappeared. Urilla Wuti became Adia, and Adia became Urilla Wuti. The consciousness of each Healer swirled and mixed with that of the other until there was only one. After a few moments, the process reversed, and they slowly separated. Each came back to her place on the seat and her separate existence.

Adia had never known such an experience was possible; though she had some unique abilities, she had experienced nothing like this. In the brief exchange, Adia had seen into the heart of Urilla Wuti and knew there was no judgment of her there. It had only taken a few moments, but in that brief time, Adia had also experienced the most traumatic and most uplifting moments of Urilla Wuti's life.

Adia wondered if Urilla Wuti had been born with this ability, or had learned it, and the moment she asked herself the question she knew the answer. And if Urilla Wuti had learned how to do this, perhaps she could too.

Adia knew all the moments of Urilla Wuti's life—those that had shaped her, encouraged her, and those that had almost broken her. She knew about those closest to her—most important to her. She knew her abject grief at her brother's passing, probably the closest person to her, and her pain that she was not able to save his life. She experienced Urilla Wuti's great joy when her brother's offspring was delivered after he had passed, and the happiness the young female brought to her life. Adia did not only know of these events; she experienced them just as Urilla Wuti had.

In return, Urilla Wuti now knew about significant, emotionally charged events that had shaped Adia. She knew how deeply Adia loved her father, and how much she still missed him to that day. Urilla Wuti now knew that Adia had feelings for Acaraho, the High Protector of the People, and how wonderful it felt to be carried in his arms; the sense that nothing could ever harm her as long as he was around. And Urilla Wuti lived it as if she were on the path clutching the locket she had retrieved from the Healer's Cove. She felt Adia's confusion at running into Khon'Tor, the fever in her body, the impact of Khon'Tor's first blow, of being knocked down to the hard ground. And through the fog, she felt his crushing weight on her and the piercing pain just before she passed out. Urilla Wuti had learned as much about Adia as Adia had learned about Urilla Wuti.

The two females sat looking at each other, still holding each other's hands. There was nothing to be said. Adia wondered if this was why Urilla Wuti hardly ever spoke. If she was capable of this type of Connection, might she also sense what was going on in each person she encountered without the need for words? After what Adia had just experienced, speech seemed an archaic, clumsy means of communication.

Adia wondered what would happen if the Connection continued for longer. Urilla Wuti had broken it off; Adia would not have been able to because knowing another person like that—experiencing them at their core through their own eyes and own emotions—was intoxicating. While she was connected to Urilla Wuti, she was not a single entity. She was one, and more than one.

Perhaps that is what it is like to return to the Mother —only instead of merging with one other person it would be like being immersed in a sea of others, separate yet not separate, still you, but at the same time everyone else, thought Adia.

Urilla Wuti had her reasons for connecting with Adia. This was not an experience she shared with many. Only a handful knew she had this ability—the Healer who taught her this, her own Helper, her brother before he had passed, the Leader of her people, a small network of other Helpers—and now Adia.

When Urilla Wuti was a Healer's Helper, she had been taught by her Healer how to establish the Connection, just as her Healer had been taught it. Not everyone could develop the gift, and it took years to perfect—to learn how to control the depth and duration of the flow. Adia was renowned throughout the People, and knowing this, Urilla Wuti had suspected that Adia was able to connect to the Mother in ways most Healers were not able to do. She also realized Adia probably did not understand how gifted she was.

This was why, when she was told by her Leader of the need for a Healer urgently to visit the People of the High Rocks, Urilla Wuti knew it was the opportunity she had been asking for. And the minute she met Adia, Urilla Wuti knew her thoughts had been correct, and the younger Healer had this same gift.

Had she maintained the Connection with Adia longer, the transfer would have been deeper, more detailed, more intimate. But Urilla Wuti let it stream only long enough for Adia to experience the exchange of the most significant experiences in each of their lives. She could have taken Adia to a deeper level, but it would have been too invasive. Only with permission and over a significant time would Urilla Wuti connect with another at a deeper level. Once connected so deeply, the two joined were always just a thought away from being in contact, and information could pass instantaneously from one to the other. But not everyone could go to this deepest level of connection. From her experience, they could only go with someone equally gifted.

Urilla Wuti knew the Age of Wrak-Ayya lay ahead. Over the past several years, she had realized part of her life mission was to create a network of connected Healers. Wrak-Ayya presented the greatest ever threat to the People's existence since the Age of Darkness, and when it came, the People everywhere would have to share information about its challenges, and very quickly. The People could not afford to learn through trial and error within their separate communities; they would have to learn from each other simultaneously. And those lessons would have to be communicated far faster across long distances than was currently possible. Travel took too much time, especially to the outlying communities, and it also put the People at risk of discovery by the Waschini.

They would also have to deal with enormous change, and she knew the People were slow to adapt. However, of all the Sasquatch, including the giants only rumored to exist, the People were the most adaptable. And without adaptation to the coming changes, none of the Sasquatch had any hope of surviving.

Urilla Wuti feared that her people underestimated Wrak-Ayya.

Adia sat, still looking at Urilla Wuti who squeezed her hands and said, "We have much to talk about." Then the older Healer got up and added, "I am going to my quarters for a while. Would you be able to join me there later this evening? Will you have the energy?"

Adia said she would be there. It was not far, and she knew Urilla Wuti needed to talk to her alone.

"You should also rest a while now, Adia. Rest and re-ground yourself."

Urilla Wuti needed a little time alone. After making a Connection, it took time to process what had been assimilated. Emotions were emotions, and when those of another were experienced directly, they left a mark.

On reaching her quarters, she lay down and recalled Adia's experiences. When she got to the night on which Khon'Tor had attacked Adia, she lived it as if it had been done to her. She felt physically sick and weak. She saw herself look up at Khon'Tor in confusion, and then the blow to her head and hitting the ground so hard. It was all there, every bit of it.

Urilla Wuti now understood the turmoil the young female was in, and also how very strong she was to bear up under the burden forced on her. Urilla Wuti knew Khon'Tor had taken her Without Her Consent and that he was the father of her offspring. And that Adia would have to give up her offspring to a female who hated her.

She also knew Adia was in love with Acaraho.

As a Healer, there is not much more that can go wrong for Adia, thought Urilla Wuti.

The afternoon dragged on and on. Adia fussed with arranging and rearranging her worktable. Finally, she was on her way. As she passed First Guard Awan he followed her, as were his orders. She paid him no mind knowing it was Acaraho's doing. It was just as well because, though it was not far to the older Healer's Quarters, she was still feeling a little dizziness off and on.

When she entered, Urilla Wuti did not rise but motioned to Adia to sit next to her. Adia wondered if Urilla Wuti was going to make another Connection. She did not. Instead, she said, "I know you have many questions. And I want to answer them all, but it will take some time.

"Let me start at the beginning. What I shared with you is called the Connection. It is a derivative of what we experience when we return to the Great Spirit. As Healers, we often refer to the Great Spirit as the Great Mother, in honor of our special connection with the feminine aspect of love. When we return to the Mother, we are all connected yet separate. Your experiences become mine, and mine become yours, and on and on. That way, we all experience every aspect of life in every possible form and manifestation. The love we show others comes back to us, as does the pain we inflict. Somehow, we remain us, but at the same time we are everyone." Before she continued, she paused to see if Adia understood.

"In the Connection I opened with you I took you to the second level. There are many levels deeper. The deeper you go, the greater the Connection, and the more the one person becomes the other. What of my life did you experience when we merged?"

Adia answered, "I felt the love you had for your family. I felt the closeness between my brother and me—I mean your brother and you. I lived your grief at your brother's passing; the joy your brother's offspring brings you. Those were the experiences that stood out the clearest."

Urilla Wuti nodded. "The deeper we connected, the more intensely you would feel those experiences. Depending on how much trauma the other person has endured, if you connect too deeply before you are prepared, you may damage yourself severely. No matter how difficult, our experiences come to us because we are ready for them, at a time when we are finally strong enough to endure them. Another person who is not walking that path may be permanently overcome with the depth of the pain and suffering of another because it was not their path to walk. They were not prepared by life to go through those experiences, but the experiences were forced on them through the Connection," she continued.

Adia quickly nodded that she understood what Urilla Wuti was saying.

"Someone can learn how to establish the Connection if the raw ability is there. But it is more than just making the Connection; it is learning how to manage the current—the flow of it. How to maintain it, so it does not break and does not allow you or the other to go too deep. This is the most intimate exchange between two people. It is an art, not a science. Even at the shallowest level, the flow can fluctuate if you are not vigilant. For that reason, there can be few secrets in any Connection, and you must never make a Connection with anyone Without Their Consent," she continued.

Without Their Consent. Adia's eyes widened and then changed to a frown. "Urilla Wuti—" she said, formulating a question.

"Yes, I know. I know Khon'Tor seeded your offspring. I know what happened was done Without Your Consent. I also understand your reasons for not revealing the crimes he committed against you. I respect your decision in this regard. Your secret is safe with me, I promise."

Adia let out a huge sigh and fought back her tears.

"We have a little more time before you deliver, Adia. We will make the most of it. Whether it is a vestigial ability from the Ancestors that still manifests in only a few, I do not know. You, I believe, have great aptitude for learning this if you want to. But there are requirements of any who accept it. It is a gift, and it is also a burden," she said.

"If you think I am worthy of your time, Urilla Wuti, I very much want to learn how to do this," said Adia, though concerned that when it came to meeting the requirements, she was not the best example.

The other Healer replied, "Adia, you are definitely worthy. You forget your situation was forced upon you. You bear the blame for it publicly, but you must separate it from the truth. In the distorted perception of yourself that you see reflected in other people's eyes, do not lose sight of who you truly are."

Adia took her leave and lay late into the night hours unable to sleep.

CHAPTER 10

The weeks following passed quickly. Urilla Wuti spent as much time with Adia as possible, teaching her about the Connection. Adia learned how difficult it was to control the flow and could understand how it took years of practice not to get lost in the other person. There were dangers too, as Urilla Wuti had said. Some emotional wounds were so horrific that they were unbearable to assimilate. The effects could linger after the Connection was broken, making a time of cleansing critically important.

As a Healer using this tool, there were also responsibility issues. If the person with whom the Healer connected had unresolved trauma or deep, unrelenting grief, she had an obligation to help them. And there was the fact that in return, the Healer exposed her experiences to the other.

Urilla Wuti shared her fears about Wrak-Ayya,

the Age of Shadows. Adia quickly understood the importance of establishing a network of Healers who could unite the People through this form of communication, unrestricted by the physical constraints of Etera.

Over time, Urilla Wuti established deeper and deeper Connections with Adia, showing her how each level brought their consciousness even closer to that of the other. Adia could see the stronger the Connection, the harder it would be not to lose yourself. And it was enthralling, connecting with another at such a level. No loneliness; the deep awareness that you were not alone—that you were never truly alone because everyone was already united in the Mother, and each would experience it themselves when they returned to the Great Spirit.

The deeper Urilla Wuti connected with Adia, the longer it took her to clear herself of Adia's emotions. During the first Connection Urilla Wuti had learned of Khon'Tor's attack; had lived through it. At deeper levels, she experienced more deeply Adia's feelings for Acaraho. And she experienced the horror of the High Council's ruling that Adia's offspring would be turned over to the Leader's Mate, who hated her. The pain was almost unbearable, the idea of giving her offspring over to an enemy.

It was unfair to have forced Adia to make this

choice, though Urilla Wuti understood why the High Council had not interfered with Hakani's claim. *But choosing not to interfere in something is one thing, and having to live through it is another. I wish I could share the depth of Adia's anguish with the High Council members.*

There was something else Urilla Wuti had learned during their most recent Connection. Something about Adia's condition that led the visiting Healer to cease her lessons until after the delivery. She did not want what she had learned to pass back to Adia, because it was obvious Adia did not know. And Urilla Wuti knew it would be best to deal with at the time—when there was no choice. Facing it earlier was not going to make it any easier or any less painful.

Urilla Wuti worked with Nadiwani on preparing everything they could think of that might be needed for the delivery. Nadiwani was learning a great deal because the older Healer was a storehouse of information. So when Urilla Wuti was not teaching Adia, she was teaching Nadiwani.

Urilla Wuti asked for some unusual items from the storehouse without explaining their purpose.

The delivery room was finished. Urilla Wuti did not want Adia to give birth in the Healer's Quarters because she did not want the memory of the delivery to hang in those rooms for the rest of Adia's life. Urilla Wuti was doing all she could to remove any daily reminders of Adia's offspring after the fact. She asked Acaraho to prepare a place and to pick one not on a common route. She asked him to furnish it with items recognizable to Adia so she would give birth in as relaxing and familiar a place as possible, as was customary.

So Acaraho hung dried flowers and herbs from the roof and placed baskets of grasses around the room. He created a raised sleeping mat to be padded with fresh grass and leaves when Adia went into labor, in case she wished to lie down at any point. Nadiwani gave him one of Adia's favorite wolf skins to place on the bed. Acaraho whitewashed the walls with chalk to give a softer appearance than the greys and browns of the natural rock. Then he set out pretty stones where they would be out of Adia's way when the time came.

He could have asked any of several people to undertake this work, but he completed it all himself.

Time was drawing close. Khon'Tor was notified, as was Hakani.

Acaraho had not forgotten his orders from the High Council to select a Helper for Hakani. He had narrowed the list down to three. He had spoken to each of them and explained the responsibilities— which would primarily be to help with the offspring and to report to him immediately anything that gave any concern for the offspring's welfare. The three were the first outside of the inner circle to know that Hakani would be raising Adia's offspring as her own. Acaraho knew Khon'Tor would have to handle the general announcement but was confident that none of the three candidates would disclose the information ahead of time.

Acaraho had little contact with Adia after the Healer arrived. He knew from Awan that Adia left her quarters regularly to visit Urilla Wuti. He did not like being cut off, but he had his other responsibilities to attend to; however, now he wanted to see first-hand how Adia was doing. He would leave to her the final decision of which of the three candidates he would assign to Hakani.

Acaraho found Adia with Nadiwani and asked permission to join them. He had not seen the Healer for a while and immediately noticed how far along she was. He could not imagine it would be much longer. Adia now had trouble getting around, and his heart went out to her. *All this, and she must give up her offspring—to that female.*

He questioned the High Council's judgment before remembering that they genuinely did not have further jurisdiction in this matter. They had done all they could by putting a Helper in the environment to keep an ongoing eye on the offspring's care.

Adia was lying curled up on her side on her sleeping mat—the only comfortable position available to her at this point. Acaraho crouched down beside her, one hand steadying himself against the floor, so she did not have to sit up.

Urilla Wuti was at the worktable with Nadiwani, gathering up everything that they would take to the delivery room. Urilla Wuti's two large carrying satchels were coming in very handy.

Adia smiled up at Acaraho when she saw him, and he smiled back in return. He tried to think of something light-hearted to say, but nothing came to mind. So instead, he reached out and touched her cheek gently with the back of his hand.

"Adia, I have narrowed the list of potential helpers for Hakani down to Kachina, Awahi, and Amadahy. I wanted to leave the final selection to you, since—" and he stopped, not wanting to say the rest of the sentence lest it be hurtful to her.

"Thank you, Acaraho. I know each of them and you have done well. Any of the three would be a fine choice. My preference, though only because of size and strength, would be Kachina," she answered.

Of the three, Kachina was the largest and most robust of the females. Acaraho did not know if her consideration was for the sake of protecting the offspring, or for some reason having to do with Khon'Tor. But he did not ask.

"I will tell Kachina and the other two, as well as Khon'Tor and Hakani," he said gently.

"When the time comes for the offspring to be born, I will be right outside the door for as long as you need me. I promise."

She took his hand and squeezed it for just a moment.

Acaraho stood up and crossed the room to the other two females. "How long; can you give me any idea?" he asked.

Urilla Wuti replied. "Within days, Commander. I would stay close." Those were the most words Acaraho had heard her say since she arrived.

"Commander," she added before he could leave, "When the time comes, I want only myself and Nadiwani in the room, and no one else unless I choose them. Anything I ask for, everything I say, must be followed exactly, and without hesitation," she said.

"Kachina will serve as a general helper as required because she is close to the situation and her services as observer will not be needed until we give the offspring into Hakani's care."

Acaraho nodded.

"Please send word for my attendants to come as soon as possible," she added. "They will not be long arriving, Commander. They have known for a while that the time was drawing near. One of them is my midwife, and I want her here in time for the delivery. If you send a messenger in the direction we came, he will find them not too far away," she added.

Well, how in Etera would they know that? he wondered. *Unless just from experience.* He nodded again and left the three females.

The moment he could, Acaraho sent a messenger to find the attendants, and had living quarters set up for them. Urilla Wuti was right; they were only a day's journey from Kthama. They had known the time was close because they were expecting the messenger.

A few more days passed, and then the time came when Adia entered early labor.

Urilla Wuti had not yet moved her to the delivery room, wanting to keep Adia in familiar surroundings as long as possible. The delivery room was a dedicated and fully functioning separate living quarters, and all Urilla Wuti's supplies and preparations had been moved there, including her two large satchels and wrappings for the offspring.

Finally, it was time. Nadiwani stepped outside and asked Awan to tell Acaraho that Adia was in labor and they were moving to the delivery room, and to send Kachina.

Acaraho was sitting in his quarters, his head in his hands. He was filled with nervous energy and unable to stay in one position for long. He tried to push away his fears that something might go wrong and that something might happen to Adia, but they still haunted him from the back of his mind. He did not believe he could be more concerned if it were his own offspring being born. He jumped off his seating stone at the sound of a visitor.

It was Awan. "Commander, it is time. Urilla Wuti wants Kachina to come to the delivery room."

For the first time in his life, Acaraho froze.

Awan looked at him blankly, then said a little too loudly, "Commander!"

Acaraho snapped out of his confusion, came to, and left with Awan. He told the guard where to find Kachina and went himself to notify Khon'Tor and Hakani. He wanted to send a messenger but knew it should come from him.

He went down the corridor, past two somewhat nervous guards who exchanged glances as their commander headed for Khon'Tor's door. Acaraho looked back at them, wondering what their cause for concern could be. He slammed the announcement rock against the door and stood back. Then he smashed it again, harder.

No response.

It was evening, but early evening, and before setting out, Acaraho had confirmed both were in the Leader's Quarters.

Finally, though unprecedented, he called out, "Khon'Tor," and the stone door was suddenly jerked open from the inside.

Acaraho had interrupted something. Khon'Tor was agitated and stood blocking the line of sight into the room. He had a firm grip on the stone slab, making sure that no one could open it any wider.

"Yes, Acaraho?" he asked brusquely, out of breath

even. Acaraho could not help but notice scratches on Khon'Tor's neck and arms.

"Urilla Wuti sent me to tell you that it will not be long now. Kachina is being brought to the delivery area and will keep you informed about the birth," he explained. He kept his eyes locked on Khon'Tor, resisting the temptation to try and see past him. The Leader was making it very clear that *whatever* was going on in there was none of Acaraho's business.

"Anything else?"

"I apologize for the intrusion, Khon'Tor. I thought you should know," said Acaraho.

"Yes," Khon'Tor replied, straightening himself a bit before he pulled the huge stone closed behind him, obviously still taking care to block the view of his quarters even as the stone door was sliding back in place.

Acaraho had never mated, but he was not ignorant of the mechanics. He had no doubt that he had interrupted something *personal* between Khon'Tor and Hakani. There were reported to be those whose tastes strayed into grey areas outside commonly practiced behaviors. Acaraho had assumed Khon'-Tor's attack on Adia was the result of a fight and that he had done what he did out of a loss of control. After what he had just seen, he wondered if Khon'Tor *had* been out of his senses when he forced himself on Adia. Perhaps it was the vein in which his tastes ran.

Acaraho sighed. *Hakani has shown she has no*

qualms speaking her mind. She could certainly bring a complaint. What consenting adults participate in is none of my business.

But if true, it was one more piece of information about Khon'Tor that Acaraho wished he did not know.

When he passed the two guards on the way back out, he understood their earlier reactions to his arrival.

They are not far enough out of earshot, after all, he thought.

Acaraho arrived at the Delivery room, and Urilla Wuti admitted him. For now, Adia was lying on the raised bed he had prepared, and he bent to take her hand for a moment.

Adia and Acaraho were both so wrapped up in the drama of what was going on that they still had no thought of how things looked to observers. It was Acaraho who was constantly tending to Adia. It was Acaraho making all the arrangements, and now he was at her side, comforting her as she was about to deliver her offspring. Of course most concluded that he was the father.

"When Kachina arrives, have her wait outside with the others. I will bring in one or both of my two attendants and then the door will be tightly closed," Urilla Wuti told him

246 | LEIGH ROBERTS

He noticed one of the attendants was a female. He knew two males had been accompanying her on her arrival at Kthama.

It was customary among the People for the mother to be as little disturbed as possible, but Urilla Wuti was not leaving things to chance. "Under no circumstances is anyone to enter this room until I say. When I do signal to open the door, everything must be done as I direct," she went on to say.

Urilla Wuti had kind eyes, which helped offset the fact that she had no trouble speaking her mind. Acaraho imagined that if she were angry, she would most resemble a honey badger. He had no intention of doing anything but what she requested, though he thought her orders were overly strict. Acaraho realized he would miss her once she left.

"I understand, Urilla Wuti. You are the one in charge," he said, smiling at her.

Urilla Wuti then surprised Acaraho by placing her hand squarely in the middle of his chest. "I will miss you too, Commander," she said, smiling at him in return.

Acaraho was touched. He thanked the Great Spirit that she was the one the High Council had sent to care for Adia.

Kachina arrived as ordered but was not allowed into the delivery room. Urilla Wuti asked for her female attendant to enter the room, however, and for the male attendant to remain outside. Then Acaraho handed Urilla Wuti an announcement stone and closed the heavy stone door as instructed.

Now it was just a matter of time.

The four females settled in and waited. Adia became more and more uncomfortable, and moved from position to position, alternately pacing the room, leaning against the stone table Acaraho had installed, sometimes sitting on the semi-circular birthing rock, supported by Nadiwani and Urilla Wuti in turns. The rock was padded with soft skins and had a large, soft pile of leaves and skins beneath it for when the offspring would be born. Eventually, it became obvious that Adia was very close to delivering. Urilla Wuti checked the offspring's position and pronounced that everything was as it should be.

Adia was filled with conflicting feelings—happy because everything was going well, and heartbroken because she would have to give up this offspring. Finally, she moved back to the birthing rock. Nadiwani took up position behind to support her as she strained backward, and Urilla Wuti knelt before her, ready to guide the offspring onto the soft bed waiting below. She told Adia to push one last time. Adia pushed as hard as she could and was not able to help crying out. But then it was over, and the offspring was born! Adia was thrilled to hear the healthy wail.

Urilla Wuti brought the offspring around and

placed him in Adia's arms, against her chest. "It's a boy," she announced. Adia felt a tremendous surge of love for the little body nestled against her. The cord would be left intact until all the life had drained from it into the offspring.

Adia knew that the afterbirth must still be delivered, but it would only require a few gentle pushes and was not at all painful.

Unfortunately, Adia was wrong. She did push a few times, and it seemed she had expelled the placenta, but something wasn't right. She looked up at Urilla Wuti with fear in her eyes.

"What is it, Urilla Wuti? I know something is wrong, please tell me."

Urilla Wuti signed for her female attendant to come over. Then she took the offspring from Adia and handed him to the female.

"No, please do not take him away yet! Let me hold him!" cried Adia, reaching out frantically.

"Adia, he is right here. There is nothing wrong. It is just that you are not done yet," she said.

"Not done yet? Not done yet? How can I be not done?" Adia repeated it as if the words had no meaning.

"There is another offspring, Adia. You have been carrying two offspring," Urilla Wuti explained.

Adia leaned back, realizing why Urilla Wuti had taken her offspring and given him to the attendant. She looked up at the roof, her mind reeling. *How could this be? To have to give up two offspring to Hakani? I cannot do it! I cannot!*

Grief overcame her, and she started to weep. "I cannot do it, Urilla Wuti. *I cannot give up a second offspring to Hakani.* One is punishment enough." She clutched at Urilla Wuti's arm.

"How long have you known?" she asked, now almost angry, and lifting her head to look directly at Urilla Wuti.

"Since our last Connection. You were far enough along that I could pick up the consciousness of the offspring you were carrying. Only there was not just one; there were two. The second offspring is a female," she explained.

Adia turned her head to the side, covering her face with her arms, and sobbed. Urilla Wuti placed her arm around Adia's shoulders.

"Adia," she leaned down to make sure Adia could hear.

"You do not have to give the second offspring up to Hakani. If you wish, I will take one of them back with me. No one need know. I will make sure to place the offspring somewhere very safe. It is not ideal, but it is an alternative for you to consider," she finished.

Adia felt like she was in a nightmare. *Two offspring, when I was never supposed to have even one? And I cannot keep either of them to raise myself?*

At that moment, Adia's faith faltered. She felt betrayed by the Great Mother—that she would be punished so, through no fault of her own. *Why do you not help me? Why am I going through this? Am I being tested? Have I not been faithful to you? This is too much!*

Urilla Wuti stood there next to Adia, waiting for her to weather the storm of her emotions.

Finally, Adia collected herself and asked, "How long do I have to decide?"

"If you wish to keep the second offspring a secret, I suggest you decide quickly. They will both have to stay with you for a short while, but I should take one with me when I leave; when you give the other up to Hakani," she explained.

Adia had only minutes to make a life-changing decision. She was drowning in a turbulent sea of emotions.

"*Why did you not tell me*, Urilla Wuti? Why did you not tell me there was a second offspring?" she asked.

"Adia, your emotions were already affecting the offspring. Had you known there was a second, yes, you would have had more time to consider your decision, but the additional turmoil would have put even more stress on them. I did not want you to risk them both. Usually, when there is more than one offspring, they do not go to full term," she explained.

Adia calmed herself down. If anyone knew Urilla Wuti's heart and motivations, she did. They had connected enough times for her to know there was no malice or manipulation in the other Healer. She had only the purest intentions. Adia knew in her heart that if this was how Urilla Wuti felt it should be handled, then it must be the best way. And she knew Urilla Wuti was right about the risks in carrying two offspring to full term.

Suddenly, the contractions started up again. Adia winced in pain. From the back of the room, Nadiwani left the attendant holding Adia's first offspring and ran over to Adia.

"What is going on? *What's wrong*?" Nadiwani asked.

"Nothing is wrong. There is a second offspring coming," said Urilla Wuti.

Nadiwani's eyes flew wide open.

"Are we prepared for this? Two offspring? Of all the twins I have known about, the second one usually did not survive. Oh, and Adia's mother *died in delivery!* Should we not have another Healer in here with us?"

"Nadiwani, you are here. And my attendant is as well-versed in birthing as you or I. Trust me that we are as prepared as we can be. As long as the second offspring is in the proper position, everything should be fine."

"Well *is* it?" blurted out Nadiwani.

Urilla Wuti moved around to where she could check the offspring's position. After a moment and some discomfort for Adia, she announced that everything was fine. The offspring's head was down, and it's back against Adia's belly. The Healer could not feel any problem with the position of the umbilical cord, and the second placenta was in no way blocking the offspring's movement down the birth canal. She explained all of this to the others in the room, making sure most of all that Adia heard it.

Time passed by. Finally, the second offspring decided she was ready to be born. And before long, she made her entrance and Urilla Wuti placed her on Adia's chest as she had the male before her. The second placenta was delivered shortly after.

Adia moved to the bed with her tiny daughter, and the midwife brought the little male over to her, laying him in her arms as well. Adia had two offspring, one cradled in each arm. Her heart was full but also breaking more than she thought she could bear.

Acaraho was following Urilla Wuti's instructions. No one had interrupted, and since no one knew anything of what was going on inside, Adia had a little bit of time to make her decision.

But she did not have forever, and Urilla Wuti broached the subject again.

"Adia, you can decide to give either to Hakani to raise, and I will take the other to safety if you wish, but you will need to decide soon because we have to tell Khon'Tor if it is a boy or a girl."

Adia searched her heart. She knew no matter how hard it was, it was a wise decision to let the existence of one of her offspring remain a secret and be taken away by Urilla Wuti. Only those in the room knew there was a second offspring. That decision made, she considered which to send with Urilla Wuti. She had to think *strategically.*

The boy would have a better chance here. Though Khon'Tor will never acknowledge him, he would still have a legal claim to Khon'Tor's leadership. Perhaps in time that would bring him favor with Khon'Tor. A female offspring would be of no use to him in any regard. And because Hakani hates me so vehemently, I can see her taking out her hatred of me on a female offspring more readily than a male.

And what if she grows up to resemble me? Who knows what animosity Khon'Tor and Hakani might also transfer to her. If she is raised in another community, she will be safe, and at least one of my offspring will not bear the shame of their conception, should Khon'Tor's crime against me ever be revealed. At least she would grow up feeling loved instead of being shamed for having a fallen Healer as her mother.

There was so much to consider, and Adia needed more time—but time was something she did not have. She let out a huge sigh. She had made her choice.

"Urilla Wuti, I want you to take the female with you. Her brother will be the one to be raised by Hakani and Khon'Tor. I feel that she would somehow be at more risk with them than her brother would." Though Adia had reasoned out her decision, her heart was breaking and tears rolled down her face.

Urilla Wuti spoke gently, "I will announce to the others that the offspring is a male. Kachina will be dismissed to inform Khon'Tor. It will leave only those of us here, my other attendant, and Acaraho to help us move back to the Healer's Quarters.

"You must make another decision now. Do you wish to keep the second birth a secret from Acaraho? I must know before we leave this room."

Adia had no secrets from Acaraho. She had never told him that Khon'Tor was the father, but she knew he knew and that he understood why she would not say the words. She trusted Acaraho with her life. It was a non-decision, really. Urilla Wuti looked as if she knew the answer before she asked but had to ask anyway.

"I could not bear to keep anything from Acaraho. Please let him know, however you think it best to present it to him," answered Adia.

With that, Urilla Wuti went to the door and slammed the rock against it to alert Acaraho outside. He opened the door just a bit.

"Acaraho. Please send Kachina to let Khon'Tor and Hakani know the offspring is a male. He will have to stay with Adia for a while. I will decide when he is ready to be transferred to their care."

Acaraho turned to Kachina and relayed the message, telling her that when she got to Khon'Tor's corridor, she should have one of the guards go to the door and give Khon'Tor the message. Acaraho did not want Kachina witnessing the same disheveled and agitated Khon'Tor that he had. Though whatever had been going on in there was surely over by now. When she had done so, he told her, she could return to her quarters until further notice.

Kachina did as Acaraho said and had one of the guards deliver the message. It seemed to take the guard an extraordinarily long time to come back. When he did, Kachina took her leave and returned to her quarters as instructed.

Khon'Tor closed the heavy door and turned back to Hakani who was lying bound on his sleeping mat. He had her gagged and well secured, so there was little she could do except listen to what he had to tell her.

"It appears you will be raising a son," he said. "Congratulations, Hakani."

He crossed the room and sat down next to her. Mockingly, he gently caressed her face and said, "The good news is that the offspring no doubt has to stay with Adia for a while. So our special nightly time together is not quite coming to an end. I thought you would be pleased to hear it. I know I am." He patted her dismissively on the cheek and then leaned over to pick up where he had left off before answering the door. Though gagged, she could not keep from moaning. She tried to move away from him, but he held her securely with his other hand.

Khon'Tor stopped for a moment, letting her catch her breath. It was hard to breathe when bound and gagged, and he did not want her to pass out and escape any of what he was doing to her.

"I can see from the look in your eyes that you are blaming me for all this. But this is not my fault, Hakani. This is all your doing. If you were half the mate to me you should have been, none of this would have happened. But from the beginning, you seemed determined to defy me.

"And then, instead of coming to me about the Waschini offspring, you planned as damaging a spectacle as possible. How many times when I came to you did you deny me? It seems you enjoyed refusing me. Then you teased me and tormented me, hoping to drive me to take you Without Your Consent."

With each pause he resumed his intimate attention.

"Well, you see how that eventually turned out for you, do you not?" he said, taunting her further with a smug smile on his lips.

"Then you betrayed me by lying with another, forcing me to claim and raise an offspring which was not mine. The list goes on and on. You can lie there and hate me all you want, but the truth is, this is your fault and yours alone.

"I will thank you for one thing. It turns out I was never much into mating, but now I have to admit, thanks to the recent turn of events, I know just how delicious it can be. When executed properly," he sneered.

He let up, giving her a moment of relief and time for his words to sink in.

Khon'Tor believed everything he said; she had brought this on herself and had only herself to blame.

Hakani knew this session was far from over, and that he would finish with her only after he had drawn out her suffering to his satisfaction. She wished he was dead—or that she was. Either way, she could not endure night after night of his punishment much longer.

CHAPTER 11

Having dispatched Kachina to inform Khon'Tor and Hakani that the offspring was a boy, Acaraho turned back to Urilla Wuti, a pained expression on his face.

"Come on in Acaraho, but please close the door tightly behind you," she instructed him.

Acaraho opened the stone door and entered the room, closing it tightly behind him as she had instructed. He could see the bed and could tell Adia was there, partially sitting up.

Before going to her, he turned back to Urilla Wuti and asked, "Is she alright? Did everything go well?"

"Yes. Everything is fine. It all went very well," and Urilla Wuti took Acaraho's hand and led him over to Adia.

Acaraho came around to the side of the bed to face Adia and then stopped, staring. She was holding not one offspring but two, wrapped up snug and warm, one cradled in each arm.

Acaraho rubbed his hand over his mouth as he often did when he was buying time to think. He was not sure what the appropriate expression was. He did not know how Adia was feeling about this. He wondered if she'd had any idea she was carrying twins.

Adia freed one hand and reached out to take his hand in hers.

"Adia, are you alright? How are you feeling? This is a surprise; did you know?" he asked, not giving her time to respond in between each question.

"I am fine, really. I am exhausted, and right now I am doing my best to deal with everything. No, I did not know ahead of time that there were two. They are not identical twins; this is a boy, and this is his sister," she said, lifting each one a little bit so he would know which was which.

Acaraho could not tell them apart; they looked exactly alike to him.

He turned to Urilla Wuti, "You had me send word through Kachina that the offspring was a boy. What are the plans for the girl?" he asked.

"I will take her back with me and find her a suitable family. She will be safe, I promise," she replied.

Acaraho turned back to Adia and asked, "Do you agree with this?" Though even as he asked it, he believed it was the best possible way.

"Yes, Acaraho. It breaks my heart to give her up,

but there is no better solution for her. The High Council was clear that I could not raise a second offspring, let alone a third. And if she stays here, Hakani might have a claim on her as well. I do not want to risk it," she answered.

Acaraho could see she was holding back tears.

"Very well. So, where do we go from here?" he asked Urilla Wuti.

"Has everyone been dismissed from the corridor except for my other attendant?" she asked.

"No, there are two guards still stationed not far off. I did not want to take any chances and I knew I would be distracted," he replied. "I will dismiss them and be back shortly."

He returned within a few moments.

Urilla Wuti told him, "I have wrapped both offspring identically, and I suggest you, Adia, and one of my attendants go on ahead to the Healer's Quarters. When she is situated and comfortable, come back to get the rest of us, and escort us back," she said.

Acaraho understood immediately. "Yes, that is a good precaution. Anyone happening to notice will not realize there are two, one taken on each trip. And though there should be no one around at this time, it is better to be safe than sorry."

He went to the door and told the attendant outside to be sure no one came near. He did not like to leave anything to chance. Acaraho liked having contingency plans, but he was not thinking as clearly as he normally would, so he was glad Urilla Wuti had thought this through beforehand.

Adia handed the offspring over to Nadiwani and the midwife, and Acaraho helped her down from the raised bed. It was clear she was worn out, so without asking, he picked her up in his arms to carry her back to her quarters, as he had done before.

Nadiwani handed the little male back over to her, and now Acaraho was cradling Adia, who was, in turn, cradling the offspring.

He effortlessly carried them both the short distance and when Awan saw them approaching, he opened the door immediately.

Acaraho carried them in carefully and laid Adia gently down on her sleeping mat. She immediately curled around her offspring and arranged the wrapping so she could see his face. She counted all the little fingers and toes and then, satisfied, sat up and cradled him, seeing if he would latch on and begin feeding.

Acaraho went back to Awan and told him he was relieved for the night and should come back in the morning. He then turned to Urilla Wuti's male attendant, a sizeable fellow, and asked him to stand watch at the door.

Making sure Awan had left, Acaraho went back for the others, returning with Urilla Wuti, her midwife, and Nadiwani who was carrying the other bundle. At Urilla Wuti's request, Acaraho took the two satchels with him. He then asked the Healer if there was anything else she needed from the delivery room, and she said no; everything else could be retrieved later.

Nadiwani brought the second bundle in and sat down next to Adia until she was ready to take her tiny daughter. Even Adia would not have known which was which if she did not already know it was the little male who was nursing. Even though they were not identical twins, they certainly looked it.

Everyone was exhausted. Urilla Wuti stayed with Adia and the offspring until she was confident both were latched and nursing. Finally, happy that everyone would be alright for a few hours, Urilla Wuti announced she was going back to her quarters. Acaraho had arranged living quarters for her attendants, but the male attendant offered to stay and help him keep watch, for which Acaraho thanked him.

With that, Nadiwani lay down on her sleeping mat, and Acaraho stretched out in front of the stone door. Nadiwani knew no one could get through with Acaraho inside and Urilla Wuti's attendant outside.

Before she drifted off, she remembered watching Adia and Acaraho in the delivery room. They were becoming so comfortable with physical contact that her concerns took another giant step forward.

Acaraho woke first and sat up, propping himself against the cold stone wall. He did not want to disturb the others, and especially not Adia. He could not imagine how she was feeling, having to give up two offspring when she was not supposed to have even one. However she had decided which to keep, he supported it.

No one was happy about Hakani claiming the offspring. And it was unclear what the protocol would be if there were two offspring. That had never happened before. It was uncomfortable enough that Hakani was getting one.

Acaraho had no intention of letting the situation go on forever, though. He, as well as Kachina, would be vigilant in keeping watch for the first sign of danger or concern, and he would do anything he could to void Hakani's claim on the offspring.

Nadiwani stirred next, getting up to check on Adia and the offspring before she did anything else. All three were asleep.

After checking on Adia, she came over and sat down next to Acaraho. She used Handspeak, so as not to disturb Adia and the offspring. "This is a twist, is it not?" she asked, knowing it was a rhetorical question.

"It never occurred to me," he replied, but then thought it should have, because Adia was carrying a lot of weight toward the end. Acaraho realized he was losing his objectivity toward her. He was letting his feelings cloud his thinking, and that was dangerous—for both of them.

"I do not know how she is bearing up through this. Her heart must be breaking. She has suffered so much already," said Nadiwani quietly, looking over at her sleeping friend.

"She is very strong, Nadiwani. I have never met anyone like her," he said, dropping his guard with the Helper. She and Adia were becoming the family he did not have.

"I do not want to see her hurt any more than she already has been," said Nadiwani, and looked up at Acaraho before continuing.

Taking a deep breath, she said, "The path you are on, the path you two are on, leads to nowhere but heartache. You must know that. Are you prepared to live a lifetime of denial, constantly fighting your feelings for each other? Leading half-lives, satisfied alone with your dreams at night?"

Acaraho looked down at Nadiwani as she sat next to him. What she said was no surprise to him, and he was relieved to have someone to talk to about it. He was not sure what to say, though. He had the same self-recriminations and struggled with them daily.

"I do not know what to tell you, Nadiwani. I am not sure how this all really happened. But I struggle with it daily, just as you have said. I do not know what the solution is. I know we can never be together, but I do not know how to be apart, either.

Somehow, we will both have to find the line between what we can live with and what we can live without. To pull out of her life now, out of your lives, is not an option for me. I would rather suffer by not having everything I want than suffer by having none of it," he added gently.

"I do promise you this, though, Nadiwani. If the time ever comes that Adia wants me out of her life, I do not know how, but I will find the strength to do it. The last thing I want is to cause her any more pain."

Nadiwani nodded. *It has gone too far. They are in too deep.* She knew it had not been intentional; they had not set out to find themselves in this position. *At least they are not alone any longer. And perhaps having a limited place in each other's lives* is *better than having no place at all, as Acaraho says.*

She could see Acaraho's feelings for Adia were genuine. She did not know what she would do in their position. She did not know if she would have the strength to keep to that line; to deny their longing for each other for the rest of their lives.

Healers had ways to deal with their physical needs, but this was far past that. There were no herbs or tinctures able to help once the heart was involved.

Their conversation was interrupted by a soft knock on the door. Acaraho and Nadiwani both rose, and

Acaraho opened the door as slowly and quietly as possible. He stepped into the corridor.

Within a few moments, he came back in. The attendant had gone to check on Urilla Wuti and then to rest for a while himself.

"Nadiwani, how long will it be before Urilla Wuti leaves with the girl?"

He knew it would be unspeakably hard on Adia, but he also knew the longer her daughter was there, the greater was the chance of detection. They were lucky that the two offspring looked identical. And with the same wrappings, it made it impossible to tell them apart. Acaraho considered that for a moment. *How had Urilla Wuti known to prepare two sets of identical wrappings? Or two at all?*

"It will be several weeks, because they should both be feeding from their mother as long as possible," explained Nadiwani.

Acaraho was confident that Urilla Wuti had a plan and had already thought this through. She had said the offspring would be raised with someone in another community. As hard as it would be, Acaraho had to convince Adia that once she handed the female offspring over to Urilla Wuti, she must do her best to put her daughter out of her mind. To continue to ask about her would be to risk exposing her existence.

Eventually, Adia awoke and immediately reached out to check on her offspring. They were beautiful lying there, seemingly content in their warm wrappings. Seeing that she was awake, Acaraho moved swiftly to her side and asked if she was alright. Adia signed back that she was. He told her he was going to go and check on the guard duties and would be back later in the day, and if she needed anything to send word through Awan, who should be back at his post by now.

What Acaraho needed was sleep, but that was not going to happen for a while. And he needed time to think without all the emotions clouding his thought processes. He wondered how Khon'Tor and Hakani had received the news. He knew the longer Adia had the boy, the harder it would be to give him up. To give up either of them.

🜨

Acaraho went to the general eating area, realizing only a few of them knew Adia had delivered her offspring. He also remembered Khon'Tor had never announced that Hakani would be raising the offspring. He assumed the Leader was going through with it, though he believed Khon'Tor wanted no part of it. And Khon'Tor really had no choice—there was no jurisdiction to overrule Hakani's claim on the offspring. Like Adia, Acaraho feared this was the worst solution possible, and as hard as change was for the People, he believed this was one of the protocols that must be re-examined.

Khon'Tor was sitting at one of the far tables when

Acaraho arrived. Knowing it would be expected, he went across to greet the Leader who was finishing up.

"Congratulations on the birth of a son," said Acaraho as he sat down next to Khon'Tor, straddling the bench to face him.

Khon'Tor caught his breath. His heart stopped cold.

"Well, you know what I mean. Figuratively speaking that is, as the offspring will be yours to raise," Acaraho clarified.

He had been waiting for just the reaction Khon'Tor had given him. He did not care that he was tormenting the Leader. Considering what Adia was being put through, Acaraho felt he deserved a jolt at the very least.

Khon'Tor shook it off. "Yes, thank you. Hakani is certainly pleased," he said. "How did the delivery go?"

"I was not in the room, obviously, but there were no complications. The offspring is doing well," answered Acaraho. "Mostly he and Adia need quiet for the time being," he added, paving the way for what he was going to say next.

"Khon'Tor, I know you can understand this is a terrible time for Adia. As males, I do not think that either of us can comprehend the extent of it. And Hakani and Adia have had their share of problems between them. That makes it doubly difficult," he explained.

"Believe me, Acaraho. If I could set aside her claim to the offspring, I would," said Khon'Tor in a rare moment of self-disclosure.

"I am saying I believe it would be best if you held off announcing the transfer until it is time for it to happen. From what I understand, it will be a few weeks. And I'm also asking that you give Adia as much privacy as possible in the meantime," he said.

"I understand. I have no problem with that," Khon'Tor replied.

"I do not know precisely how long Urilla Wuti will be staying, either. When I know something, I will tell you," Acaraho said as he got up to leave.

As he was about to walk away, Khon'Tor interrupted him. "Acaraho," he said, "I need you to return to your regular duties, but I understand you have become protective of the Healer and probably wish to maintain as much contact with her as possible," he said.

It was more of an acknowledgment than a question. Acaraho nodded and left. Khon'Tor's charity toward Adia and her circle told him that the Leader felt he had won on every front and was interested in keeping the peace.

What Acaraho did not know was that Khon'Tor was very happy to have him continue his close involvement with Adia. The Leader knew that members of the community had noticed the unusual relationship and were concluding that Acaraho was the unnamed father of Adia's offspring. Khon'Tor's jealousy of Acaraho was growing, and he was glad to support anything that could besmirch Acaraho's character.

The Leader knew there would be a backlash of emotion, so there was no rush on his part to let the People know that Adia would have to surrender her offspring.

However, he would soon have to allow Hakani some freedom during the day. She had to prepare the room and gather supplies for the offspring. For now, meals were being brought to her under the auspices that she was too depressed after her miscarriage to rejoin the community.

A few weeks passed. Both offspring flourished. Access to Adia's quarters was restricted to Nadiwani, Urilla Wuti, the midwife, and Acaraho. Even Mapiya, who was caring for Oh'Dar throughout this, was not allowed to visit. They could not take a chance on anyone else knowing there were two offspring.

Urilla Wuti had kept her two attendants at Kthama; the midwife was still helping with the care of the offspring, and the second attendant was doing guard duty with Acaraho.

Nadiwani had selected Keeping Stones for each of Adia's offspring and she set them back down in their secret place in the Healer's Quarters. She had started the Keeping Stones when the twins were born—the record of the number of days and significant events that each of the People kept. To avoid anyone discovering that there were two of everything, she had picked identical stones. The female would be going with Urilla Wuti, and until that point, the markings would be the same for each. She took care to make each strike identical to the one on the other stone, feeling that somehow this honored the tie between them of which neither would ever know.

Though she was currently recording each day, after the first full year larger stones would be selected and the marks would decrease in frequency. It was not proper to use the mother's line, but she went ahead and put Adia's family mark on the male's stone anyway. However, she did not know what to put for the female offspring's mark. She could not use Adia's, as that could trace her back to her birth mother. So the mark of the bloodline would be conspicuously absent on her stone.

Urilla Wuti urged Adia to refrain from naming the girl, cautioning her that it would be hard enough to give her up as it was. Adia had named the boy Nootau. Even though she would have to give him up, as his mother she still had the right to name him. And despite Urilla Wuti's warning, she had secretly named the girl Nimida.

Urilla Wuti continued to work with Adia. She connected with her at deeper and deeper levels, stretching her capacity to withstand the Connection. Since they knew they would soon be separated, they experimented with communicating images of symbols between them, each of which represented agreed-upon messages or questions.

Urilla Wuti taught Adia about the different types of Connection. For example, how one could push visual and emotional messages without touching the recipient.

As time got close to when the offspring would be taken from Adia, Urilla Wuti knew she needed to help ease Adia's fears. She decided to do something she had never done before. She would establish a Connection between the mother and her offspring, with herself as the conduit.

One morning when she thought the time was right, Urilla Wuti approached Adia. She opened every important conversation or Connection with Adia by sitting across from her, holding her hands and sustaining eye contact. This was the signal for both to clear their minds of everything but what was happening between them at that moment.

Adia was curious because this was not a scheduled session.

Looking at her with kind eyes, the older Healer explained. "The time is close. You know it is. No one knows better than I, even without our Connection, how difficult this is for you. If I could make it easier, or make it go away, I would. But I have an idea that I think will ease your mind to some extent as time increases the distance between you and Nootau and Nimida."

Adia looked away briefly, ashamed that Urilla Wuti knew she had named her daughter; but, of course, she would know, through their Connection sessions. At the deepening levels of Connection they were making, it would be extremely difficult to hold back any corner of their minds from one another.

"I would like to establish a Connection between you and your offspring," said Urilla Wuti.

"But you told me I must never attempt that because an offspring's consciousness cannot tolerate the experiences adults have endured."

"That is true. I would never advise a student to attempt such a thing. But I will maintain and control the Connection, making only the lightest lock. It will not be enough for them to share your experiences, but it will be enough to let you know of their general well-being despite the distance between you," explained Urilla Wuti.

"But what if I learn something is wrong and I do not know what?"

"For myself, I will create a deeper one-way Connection with them. Trust me; if at any point either offspring is in serious trouble, I will know before you do. And I will be able to arrange for help and let you know what is going on."

Adia was relieved beyond words. As usual, Urilla Wuti had thought of everything.

Once Adia understood, they began. Adia had thought they would have to touch the offspring, but again, she was still learning. Urilla Wuti explained that at her side of the portal, Adia would have to close her eyes and remain passive, moving her consciousness neither toward nor away from the other Healer.

Adia felt the Connection opening. It was a shallow Connection, unlike any other she had experienced. She was receiving from Urilla Wuti, but she could feel that nothing was flowing back from herself. She realized the Healer was acting as a one-way conduit between her and her offspring, allowing information from Urilla Wuti to pass to her while allowing nothing to flow back in return.

Within a few moments, Adia was aware of another Connection opening; this one small and narrow and opaque. Again, information was coming to her, but nothing was flowing back out. She recognized it as Nootau. She felt how relaxed he was; warm and comfortable. He was content. That Connection faded and then another opened, this time to Nimida. Her daughter was also lying comfortably, on the verge of sleep. She could feel how content Nimida was—neither too warm nor too cold nor hungry. Then, as the other had, the conduit closed and Adia instinctively opened her eyes.

She was enormously relieved. She was so grateful

to Urilla Wuti for thinking of this. Adia knew she would drive herself mad if she checked on the offspring constantly, but at least she had some reassurance that she would know if they were sick, cold, frightened, or being harmed in some way.

Urilla Wuti read Adia's mind, as usual.

"You are right; do not open a conduit with the offspring very often. You will always be connected to them, and they need to move on to their own destinies. If the girl develops a higher seventh sense, in time, she will begin to recognize the touch of the Connection, even though they are one-way."

Adia nodded her agreement and hugged Urilla Wuti impulsively while thanking her profusely.

Khon'Tor had been forced to let up on Hakani and give her latitude to prepare for the offspring's arrival. Kachina was helping her with the task.

Hakani knew Khon'Tor had no fear that she would report what she had suffered at his hand. She would do nothing to confirm the High Council suspicions that this was not a fit home for the offspring. As long as Hakani had the offspring, public opinion would not allow Khon'Tor to set her aside. She had put up with his torture this long, and she was not going to quit so close to regaining control over her life. She was still mate to Khon'Tor, Leader of the People of the High Rocks.

That afternoon, Acaraho brought word that Hakani had completed her preparations and was asking for the boy.

Adia could see the wear on Nadiwani was starting to show. She had been handling all the Healer requests as well as helping Mapiya with Oh'Dar. The offspring were robust enough, and there were no more excuses to keep Nootau from Hakani, other than that Adia's heart was going to break.

After he brought the news, Acaraho had stood watching Adia. Urilla Wuti was there, and she went over to the new mother and stood behind her, placing her hands on Adia's shoulders to help her find strength.

Adia just nodded her agreement, then bent forward and hid her hands in her face.

Urilla Wuti broke the silence. "I think it best that I leave too, with Nimida. I will send my two attendants to bring back a wet nurse, so there will be no risk to her on the days of journeying back. Ours is a large community, and I know of several candidates."

No one was surprised that Urilla Wuti also had this part of the plan covered.

That settled, Acaraho and Urilla Wuti left, each to attend to their own business, leaving Nadiwani and Adia alone.

Nadiwani put her arms around her friend and tried to comfort her. It was all so wrong, and Nadiwani wondered what the Great Spirit could be thinking, to allow everything to come to this.

And what of these innocent offspring—are they never to know how much their mother loves them and will grieve over them for years to come? At least Nootau will still be here among our people. But the female—what will become of her and how can Adia ever have any peace not knowing?

Of course, the Helper had no idea that thanks to Urilla Wuti, Adia would at least have some general idea of how they were doing.

Nadiwani offered to help pack up Urilla Wuti's supplies, but the Healer said that she would take only the few items she needed for the journey and that Adia and Nadiwani could keep the rest.

The females prepared for Urilla Wuti's trip with Nimida back to her people. They packed one of the two large satchels with items the Healer was taking with her. They prepared the other as a carrier for the little female. Urilla Wuti had strengthened the sides so it would keep its form but not be obviously modified. They were so close; the secret of the second offspring had been kept safely for months. A misstep now would be a tragedy.

Though it seemed on the surface to be more hurtful, Adia agreed that both the offspring should be taken from her at the same time. "A clean-edged cut always heals faster than a torn and jagged one," she said.

Acaraho notified Kachina that the transfer was almost underway. She was still to be his communication link to how Nootau was being treated. While most of the People's customs had stood the test of time, Acaraho felt even more strongly that this one should be revisited. *It was meant to be a means for an orphaned offspring to be placed with loving parents—but these offspring are not orphaned; their mother lives. The High Council has made a grievous error in this case.*

It was not long before Urilla Wuti's wet nurse arrived, passing as yet another of her helpers.

Nadiwani packed the last of the Healer's things, leaving the most perishable items for last. Just before everything was ready to go, she asked for time alone with the offspring to say her goodbyes. Adia agreed, and they did as she asked.

The Helper tucked Nimida's Keeping Stone into the satchel with the other items. It would not add much weight, and it was the offspring's only tie to her real home. But before she did so, she made a special mark on Nimida's stone indicating the day she was taken from Adia. She put Nootau's in the pile of the things to go with him, with the identical mark that signified the date of their separation.

The time had come. Nadiwani told the others everything was ready, and they came back into the room. Adia hugged Urilla Wuti and looked into her face for what would be the last time in quite a while. An attendant picked up one satchel and stood waiting by the door.

Adia took a few moments to hold Nimida, tears running down her face, before she placed the tiny offspring carefully into the carrying case. It comforted her to see that Nimida would be completely safe, comfortable, and protected. The other attendant lifted the satchel with Nimida in it, making sure she could not shift position inside.

Adia knew her daughter was in good hands. *I wonder if I will ever see her again, the daughter I was never supposed to have; the daughter I will think about every day for the rest of my life.*

Nadiwani put her arm around Adia, knowing nothing could make this bearable.

Acaraho stepped forward into the hallway and waited for Urilla Wuti's group to file past. He gave Adia one last look and then closed the door behind them. Adia's sobs carried down the hall as he led the group to the Mother Stream, where they would travel safely underground back home.

He bid farewell to Urilla Wuti and her party and then returned to the Healer's Quarters to find Nootau wrapped up and ready to go. Nadiwani had already sent word for Kachina to come, but when she arrived to take Nootau, Adia refused.

"No. This I have to do myself. I have to see where Nootau will be kept; I have to know first-hand that everything has been properly prepared for him. I cannot simply hand him over. I will not," Adia said, standing tall with Nootau held protectively in her arms.

There was no one to tell her she could not, but Acaraho said, "Alright, Adia. I will go with you."

"No. I have to do this alone. You said they are waiting; I will take Nootau there. If you are worried, you can follow in a while, but give me time to do this myself," she said firmly.

Acaraho hated letting Adia go alone, but it was not his place to dissuade her. She was turning over her son, and he supported whatever she needed to do to help her get through it. It made him almost more uncomfortable than he could bear, but he also knew Khon'Tor would not let any harm come to Adia at Hakani's hand. The last thing the Leader wanted was for the High Council to have any more involvement with High Rocks.

Adia picked up Nootau's things and left with him. Acaraho, Nadiwani, and Kachina stood there, looking at each other. Then, having unexpected time available, Kachina returned to her quarters briefly.

The only comfort for Acaraho was that there were still two guards stationed a short way from Khon'Tor's quarters, and he knew for a fact they could overhear what went on in there.

Unlike the special meeting rooms that had been

soundproofed, there had never been a reason to soundproof any of the living quarters. Especially the Leader's, which were situated at the end of a long tunnel and where, short of dire emergencies, no one ever entered. So he knew that if there were any altercations, he could count on the guards to be at Adia's side in a few seconds.

Adia kept putting one foot in front of the other and tried not to think. She did not want to upset Nootau, who so far was sleeping peacefully.

As Adia approached the guards, they parted for her to pass. Then they turned and watched her travel the rest of the stone hallway to Khon'Tor's quarters. The door was open, but the People did not enter others' quarters without making their presence known and receiving permission. It felt inappropriate to follow proper courtesies under these circumstances. But, instead of walking in, Adia stood in the doorway waiting for them to acknowledge her. She was not prepared to risk antagonizing Hakani, to whom she was about to surrender her precious offspring.

Khon'Tor and Hakani stood there, not saying a word when they saw it was Adia who was bringing the offspring. Finally, the Healer spoke up.

"I need to see where he will sleep," was all she said.

Khon'Tor motioned to the other side of the room to a small alcove that had been converted into a nursery. She walked over and looked at the warm, cozy place prepared for him to sleep. It was very welcoming, a fact Adia attributed wholly to Kachina's doing. She looked around the rest of the room and saw appropriate wrappings and supplies had been assembled.

Convinced that Kachina had done an excellent job, Adia laid Nootau down in the little nest. She bent over him, taking a long, last look. Her tears fell gently down upon her son, soaking into his wrap. He lay there looking up at her with his big brown eyes. She placed her hand on his little chest and said a blessing and a prayer of protection over him. It took her a while to break away.

No Mother should have to go through this, she thought. *And neither should any offspring. This is barbaric. Unfair. Cruel. This custom is for situations where the mother has died or abandoned her offspring. When, ever, has a mother been forced to give up her offspring? And to someone who is only using the offspring as a weapon.*

Under normal circumstances, there are few true victims in life, but in this case, Adia was one. None of this was her fault, none of this was her doing, and yet she was paying for Khon'Tor's crimes. She had gotten through the scars of the attack and made peace with it as best she could, but this— This was beyond what should ever be asked of anyone. And especially not an innocent person of Adia's caliber who had put herself last. She was protecting the monster who had caused her to be in this position—all in an effort to prevent the destruction of her culture and community with the truth.

Adia turned and faced Khon'Tor and Hakani again. Her eyes were steely cold; her face still wet with tears. If she ever hated anyone, she hated these two now. And she did not try to hide it—from herself or from them.

"I would like to check on him regularly."

Hakani spoke. "That will not be necessary. You forget, he is not your offspring any longer, Healer. He is *mine* now. A wet nurse has been arranged, which means he has no need for you anymore. I suggest you go tend to your Waschini child, the one you chose over this one," she taunted.

Adia stood frozen, shocked at the cruelty of what Hakani was saying. It took all her self-control not to attack her. Instead, not trusting herself a second longer in the female's presence, she turned to leave.

Khon'Tor heard Hakani take a breath as if she were going to say something else to cut Adia more. He turned, raised his hand to her with his index finger up, and narrowed his gaze to glare at his mate. He snarled at her, "Tend to your offspring, female." He then stepped into the hallway and closed the heavy stone door behind him.

Adia was most of the way down the corridor by the time Khon'Tor caught up with her. What made him go after her? It was not that he was concerned for her, because it was not within Khon'Tor's ability to care for anyone but himself. Whatever the reason, his following her had disastrous consequences.

CHAPTER 12

Adia had reached the two guards by the time Khon'Tor got to her. He grabbed her arm and turned her around to face him. Adia looked at his hand and sank her nails into it as hard as she could, drawing blood.

Khon'Tor released her immediately and caught up his bleeding hand. He turned to the two guards who were standing there aghast and snarled at them, "Leave here. *Now*! *Qa!*" The two males turned and left, running directly to find Acaraho.

When he turned to face her again, Adia took a step back and open-handed Khon'Tor as hard as she could across his face, her eyes wild with anger.

"*PetaQ!* How *dare* you touch me!" She leaned toward him and snarled. "Do not ever lay a hand on me again! *Ever*! Have you not done enough to ruin my life?"

It was over; her last thread of self-control had snapped.

"Why? Khon'Tor? *Why*? What did I ever do to you that I deserved this? How could you hate me so much to do what you did? I am a Healer. I was a *maiden,* and you knew it when you took me Without My Consent. You had no right! And as I lay there helpless and barely conscious, at your mercy? *Just how heartless are you?*"

She was oblivious to their surroundings, oblivious to anything but Khon'Tor standing in front of her—the cause of her heartbreak, humiliation, and disgrace in front of the High Council and her people.

"And then you left me there to die. And now this? Having to give up my offspring—an offspring I was never supposed to have—to stand by and watch a female who hates me raise my son. *Your son.* A son you will never claim, but who rightfully should take your place as Leader?"

It all came pouring out.

"You made your deal, Adia," said Khon'Tor through gritted teeth, his face still stinging from her slap.

"If you are talking about the Rah-hora, my silence about what you did to me has *nothing* to do with that, Khon'Tor. I decided to keep my silence long before you struck that bargain. I have kept my silence because of what it would do to our people, and for no other reason. As sad as it is, they need you. They need a Leader with your will and drive. If it were not for them, you would have paid long ago for what you did to me," she hissed at him, her teeth bared and her face inches from his.

She turned to leave and then looked back to fire one last insult before she went.

Looking Khon'Tor up and down with disgust, she said,

"By the Mother! What kind of male has to take an unconscious maiden to satisfy himself? Tell me that! What does that say about the *magnificent* and virile Khon'Tor, Leader of the People of the High Rocks?" she asked, throwing at his manhood the worst insult she could think of.

Khon'Tor stood still and let her leave. He closed his eyes to focus his thoughts. He was sure Hakani could not hear, as far away as they were, but he was not sure if anyone else might have entered the passage. He gave Adia a brief head start, then went up the corridor and looked both ways down the connecting tunnels. He saw no one. *Well, if anyone did hear, I will know soon enough. And if so, somehow, while I am still able, even if it is the last thing I do, I will make her pay for what she said,* avowed the Leader.

He retraced his steps to where he could see back down the corridor to his quarters. The door was still tightly closed. He knew Hakani, and he knew if she had overhead any of the argument, she would have flown out of there and come after him in a furious rage.

Needing a private place to think, he went to his

meeting room and sat down to figure out what to do next.

Khon'Tor was very wrong about two things. One was that he knew everything there was to know about Hakani. The other was that sound did not travel down the corridor into his quarters.

Hakani had heard it all. Because of the precise place where Adia and Khon'Tor had stood and argued, every word was conducted down the tunnel and into the Leader's Quarters.

Hakani flew around, her fists in her hair.

His offspring? This is his offspring? Through Adia? The female who has been his First Choice all along? Her mind was reeling. It was not possible.

All this time, he was laughing at me behind my back, realizing that, unawares, I would be raising his offspring after all? And I thought it was I who had tricked him by claiming the offspring. And all those times he took me by force; he was using me to relive his enjoyment of what he did to Adia?

It was truly more than any mind could bear, and especially one that had systematically been broken and tortured over months and months. Hakani had one thought only. To make them all pay. In whatever way she could strike the hardest at both Khon'Tor and Adia was what she would do now—or she would die trying.

Nootau let out a little cry from the safety of his bed in the alcove. That was it. She knew just how to strike them both a fatal blow and end her pain at the same time.

Hakani dragged the door open. Then she snatched up Nootau and hurried down the corridor.

Having given Adia time to hand Nootau over to Hakani, Kachina was making her way to check on how he was settling in. When she got to the door of Khon'Tor's quarters and saw it was open, she went in and looked around for Hakani and the offspring.

The room was in disarray.

She spotted Nootau's wrappings on the table and went over to the alcove to see if he was there sleeping —though if he had been left unattended by Hakani that was certainly a serious strike against her. Nootau was not there. She quickly checked around the rest of the quarters, even the personal care area.

Hakani was never to take Nootau anywhere without one of the guards or me as an escort. Speaking of the guards, where are they? They were not at their post when I came by! Maybe they are escorting her somewhere?

Kachina flew out in panicked pursuit of anyone who could tell her what was going on.

Adia had turned into the tunnel leading to her quarters when she stopped. She crumpled to the ground in an emotional heap. The two guards saw her and raced to her side.

Acaraho was still in the Healer's Quarters with Nadiwani, having given Adia the space for which she had asked. As the minutes ticked by, he was growing more and more alarmed. Finally, not being able to wait any longer, he stood up.

"I am going after her. I have a terrible feeling about this," he said. Just as he stepped into the hallway, he saw Adia slide down the wall and collapse near the guards.

"Adia!" he bellowed, and left in a dead run down the corridor, reaching her just seconds after the two guards. Nadiwani came bolting out of the Healer's Quarters after him.

Acaraho was at Adia's side, bending down to her. She was in tears, sobbing uncontrollably. He circled his arms around her. Just then, the two guards from Khon'Tor's area came barreling around the corner in search of Acaraho, followed close behind by First Guard Awan who had seen them running through the corridors.

"Acaraho!" shouted the front guard the minute he saw Acaraho on the floor holding Adia.

"*What happened*?" Acaraho belted out. The males stepped backward.

"Adia and Khon'Tor," gasped one while trying to catch his breath.

Just then Kachina tore around the corner and came to an abrupt stop when she saw them.

"Hakani is gone, and so is the offspring!" she shouted.

Acaraho looked at Adia whose eyes were wide with terror. He looked up at the two guards and ordered one, "Take her back to her quarters and tend to her. Nadiwani—" he said, and Nadiwani nodded that she would also go.

He turned to Awan, "Stay here. *No one* comes down this corridor to her quarters until I return, understood?"

The First Guard nodded. "Yes, Commander."

Then Awan quickly put his hand on Acaraho's shoulder in the People's demonstration of brotherhood. Acaraho took the seconds needed to place his hand on the other male's shoulder in the return gesture. It was the same gesture that Kurak'Kahn of the High Council had made to Acaraho at the end of the hearing.

Acaraho took off at breakneck speed, traversing the tunnels and corridors toward the Great Chamber. As he entered, he shouted—just as he had the night Is'Taqa found Adia lying hurt in the cold outside.

"*Guards!*" Within seconds bodies came pouring into the room from all directions.

"Spread out. Search everywhere. Even the female's bathing area. All protocols are suspended on my authority. Hakani has taken the Healer's offspring. If you find her, use whatever force is necessary to ensure the offspring's safety.

"Does anyone know where Khon'Tor is right now?" he shouted. "Search for Khon'Tor, too, and if you find him let him know what has happened. But the offspring's safety is your priority."

The guards had sworn to allegiance to both Khon'Tor and Acaraho. They looked at each other, unsure of what to do.

"Commander," one of them asked. "What if Khon'Tor has—" and his voice trailed off.

"Secure the offspring, whatever it takes. Leave Khon'Tor to me," snarled Acaraho.

Any doubt in the guards' minds that Acaraho was the father of Adia's offspring was now completely dispelled. Every male with a family knew that in Acaraho's situation, he would react the same way.

They disbanded in all directions.

It did not take them long to find Khon'Tor in his satellite post. A guard came to the door and knocked abruptly.

"Adik'Tar. Your mate is nowhere to be found, and neither is the Healer's offspring."

No, Khon'Tor said to himself. *There is no way she could have overheard Adia shouting in the corridor.* But as the thought formed, he knew he had to be wrong. And if so, he knew in his gut that there were no limits to what Hakani would do.

"Acaraho has dispatched the guards in all directions to look for them," the guard told Khon'Tor.

But if Khon'Tor's thoughts were correct, he was certain Hakani and the offspring were no longer within the walls of Kthama.

Back in her quarters, Adia was still shaking. Her worst fears had been realized. She had been afraid all along that Hakani might hurt Nootau and she was now filled with regret at having confronted Khon'Tor, and so close to his quarters. She knew that if Hakani had heard anything of what they had said, it was the reason for her disappearance with Nootau.

As she sat trying to think, a window opened up in her mind. It was Urilla Wuti. Then she remembered that if either of the offspring were in danger, Urilla Wuti would know it before Adia did.

It took all of Adia's will to slow her breathing and calm herself down. She did as Urilla Wuti had taught her to open the Connection slightly deeper. As she succeeded, she knew Nootau was somewhere outside. She could hear birds and feel the cool air.

And dampness. And something else—the sound of a waterfall.

Adia's eyes flew open. "I know where she has taken him!" She scrambled to her feet and flew out of the door as fast as she could move. Awan saw her coming. "Healer, where are you going?" he shouted.

"I know where Hakani has taken my offspring," she shouted back as she ran past him. Awan quickly followed Adia, shouting to the other guard to take over his post and let no one enter the Healer's Quarters.

On her way to Kthama's exit, Adia passed Khon'-Tor, also on his way outside. He took off after her.

She turned just enough to see Khon'Tor following her but could do nothing to stop him. She prayed to the Great Mother that when she found Hakani and Nootau, Khon'Tor would have the decency to help her rescue the offspring. If he did not, there was no way she could prevail against both of them.

Adia exited Kthama and took the first path to the right. She knew exactly where she was going.

Khon'Tor could have overtaken her but to what avail. He followed her.

Akule was coming in from his watch when he saw Adia, Awan, and Khon'Tor racing up the Eastern path. This time the watcher was not going to keep silent. Because Awan was already there with Adia, he ran inside to find Acaraho.

When she found Hakani, the female was

standing right where Adia expected her to be. She was holding Nootau in her arms and Adia was relieved to see that so far, he appeared unharmed.

Khon'Tor and Awan arrived just seconds behind Adia.

Hakani was glad they had found her. It made what she was about to do all that much sweeter. This way, they would know exactly what had happened to the offspring—*their* offspring.

"Do not come any closer," she warned. She was within several yards of the edge of the path. Behind her was a considerable drop down to the waters below. Whether an adult could survive such a fall, Hakani was not sure, but she was certain an offspring would not.

"What are you doing, Hakani?" asked Khon'Tor.

"What am I doing? *What am I doing*? Asks the *great Leader*—a male who raped his Healer and left her to die?" she said, raising her voice.

Khon'Tor and Adia had their answer—she had indeed heard everything said in the corridor.

"Hakani," Khon'Tor said, trying to calm her down.

"*Shut up,* Khon'Tor. You have told me your last lie. And to think how much I wanted you. And then later, year after year, I put up with you, thinking that it was somehow all worth it—to be the mate of the revered Avik'Tar Khon'Tor!" she spat out.

"I have known almost from the beginning it was she you wanted. I knew almost from the first day of our pairing that she was your First Choice. You did not want to lose face, to have others suspect the one you wanted was forever out of your reach, so you selected me at the last minute after *she* was named Healer," Hakani continued.

"But you always win, do you not Khon'Tor? You could not have her, but you found a way to anyway, Without Her Consent."

"The esteemed Khon'Tor, the revered Leader whose mate I was proud to be, does now not even leave me that. When they find out what a monster you are—" her voice trailed off and took up again.

"And you wanted a second mate, Khon'Tor? Good luck with ever finding anyone else once they realize how your sick appetites run. And do not count on whoever your next victim is to keep quiet, as I have," she continued.

She turned to look at Adia.

"You are lucky. What the great Khon'Tor did to you happened once. It was nothing compared to what he has been doing to me nearly every night since," she said.

Adia stood transfixed, frozen. She had been Khon'Tor's First Choice? That was what it was about? Hakani's jealousy? And what Khon'Tor did to her was not a fluke? If Hakani was telling the truth, Khon'Tor *was* a monster, and he was twisted in more ways than she realized.

What had she been protecting all this time? Not a great Leader whom the People needed. Had she suffered all this for nothing? And now her offspring might die because of a misplaced belief that some horrible circumstances or pressures made Khon'Tor snap and do what he did? But then, again, with Hakani, who knew what the truth was?

"Hakani. Hakani, please. The offspring is innocent. However much you are hurting, please do not take your anger out on him." Adia was desperately trying to reach any corner of the female's mind that might not be consumed by hate.

"Anger? You think this is anger? Oh, I am not angry. Not anymore. I *have* been. I have been consumed by anger. Rage. Night after night, I planned my revenge. But now I am not angry. I am past anger. I see that there is nowhere for me to go from here. I have no place except at the side of a male who is about to be disgraced for all history. When word gets out about this, it will spread like wildfire," she said.

Hakani turned to face Khon'Tor.

"You have left me with nothing. And so I will leave you with the same. No mate to torture and humiliate every night. No offspring born of the female you love. And no heir to your precious leadership, either."

She moved the hand that was not holding Nootau, down to rest on her belly.

She saw Khon'Tor's eyes follow her motion.

"That's right, Khon'Tor. All those nights of taking me Without My Consent, you finally achieved your objective. I am at last bearing your offspring, your seed forced within me, an offspring conceived in hatred and bile. I have finally met the demand you made of me, to produce an heir for you. So you have two offspring. One by the female you wanted and one by the female who wanted you."

"*Too bad neither offspring will live past today.*"

As Hakani was addressing Khon'Tor, her eyes locked on his, Adia was slowly and carefully inching toward the path's edge. From the other side, next to Khon'-Tor, Awan was also watching and listening. As Hakani spat out her threat, Awan took a noticeable step forward. Hakani's head snapped in Awan's direction.

At the exact moment Hakani turned her attention to Awan, Adia threw herself forward, grabbing the bundle of Nootau as she knocked them both to the ground. She curled around the offspring, making a cage of her body to protect him, and rolled as far away from Hakani as she could.

Hakani dragged herself to her feet and started toward Adia, who was lying just a few feet away, holding a screaming Nootau.

Even better! thought Hakani. *It will take nothing to roll them over the edge together*!

Awan started to move toward them, but before he could reach Hakani, or Hakani could reach Adia, a giant figure flew out of nowhere and landed squarely between Hakani and Adia. The ground seemed to shake from the impact, and dust filled the air.

A snarling Acaraho stood towering over Hakani, arms outstretched, muscles rippling, teeth bared.

"*If you have caused harm to the offspring,*" Acaraho growled, in the lowest register possible, "*your life will not be worth living.*"

"My life is not worth living now, Commander," said Hakani calmly.

And with that, she quickly closed the few steps between herself and the edge of the path. Locking eyes with Khon'Tor for a second, she took a last step backward and disappeared over the edge to the roiling waters below.

Everyone froze, their minds not accepting what they had just witnessed.

Acaraho snapped himself out of it and rushed to Adia. He helped her sit up, cradling her in his arms while she checked the hysterical Nootau. Seeing that they were all right, if visibly upset, Acaraho slowly turned his head to look at Khon'Tor, who the whole time had been standing, frozen, to the side. He had not attempted either to help Adia or to stop Hakani.

Acaraho rose up and crept menacingly toward the Leader, a spine-chilling growl coming from his throat. Awan moved to join Acaraho, who put his hand out.

"No, Awan. Khon'Tor is mine," he ordered.

Awan moved slowly to Adia's side to ensure her safety in the bloodbath about to take place.

Khon'Tor was no match for Acaraho. Perhaps they would have been equals in regular hand-to-hand combat, but not with Acaraho like this. Not in this state of adrenaline-fueled rage.

Acaraho took another measured step toward Khon'Tor. Khon'Tor crouched, ready for Acaraho's attack, and the two giants circled each other slowly. Acaraho ached to sink his canines into Khon'Tor's neck. He imagined the satisfying feel of pulling the flesh away in strips and tasting Khon'Tor's warm blood pumping out from the gash. He clenched and unclenched his fists, ready for the satisfaction of Khon'Tor's neck snapping under his grasp. His glare looked as if it could burn holes in the Leader.

They continued to face each other, still circling. Acaraho's rage showed in every aspect of his being. "You had no right. Maybe Adia will not hold you accountable for what you did. But I will. You are going to pay for your crimes. And do not expect any more mercy from me than you showed her."

Khon'Tor had only seconds to live.

"You can kill me, Acaraho. But then what? Is this the legacy you will leave Adia? The father of her offspring eviscerated in front of her? Is that what you want to leave Adia to explain when her offspring is old enough to ask what happened to his father?" he shouted, hoping his words could penetrate the storm blazing in front of him.

Acaraho knew Khon'Tor was saying something, and some of it seemed to be making sense.

Adia was watching wide-eyed, holding Nootau close. "Acaraho, no, please *stop!*" she called out. Then, using all her willpower to tear herself away from the scene in front of her, she closed her eyes.

All of a sudden, Acaraho was overcome with what could only be described as a glowing current of warmth seeping through some opening inside him. The warmth increased, and suddenly he was aware of the deep and abiding love Adia had for him.

He had known she cared for him, but this was different. This was an experience of her love. It was physical, it was real, and it was unmistakable. It spread through him like a warm silvery liquid carried through his veins to every cell. It was beyond description.

He glanced over to see her staring at him. Adia was willing him to hear her message.

Acaraho turned his attention back to Khon'Tor. He closed the distance in seconds. Khon'Tor was prepared for his attack, but before he could defend himself, Acaraho drew back and hit him on the jaw as hard as he could, knocking the Leader several lengths to the ground.

He followed, and Khon'Tor scrambled a few feet farther away. Acaraho closed the distance easily and straddled the disoriented Leader as with one hand he grabbed him by the neck and dragged Khon'Tor's face up to his own, wrapping the other around Khon'Tor's throat. His face inches from Khon'Tor's, Acaraho released the bone-chilling Sasquatch roar that declared his right to kill his defeated opponent. Khon'Tor tried to cover his face with his arms and turned away from the ear-splitting howl.

The sound echoed across the hills and down to the moving waters below as they followed the river channel along the winding length of the Great River.

Then Acaraho growled at Khon'Tor. "I should take my rage out on you as you lie there defenseless —just as you did to Adia. But you are not worth it, Khon'Tor. I refuse to become the monster you are." Acaraho released the Leader's neck, shoving him back to the ground.

And he stepped over Khon'Tor and returned to Adia and her offspring.

Just then, Akule appeared around the bend, running blindly. He came to an abrupt stop, scattering dust and stones everywhere.

He looked down at Khon'Tor crumpled on the ground, still recovering, one hand to his aching jaw. Then Akule looked over at Adia rocking a shrieking offspring, Acaraho crouched protectively behind them both, and First Guard Awan standing guard in front of them.

"Where is Hakani? Did she take the offspring after all?" he asked.

Awan answered, "Yes, Hakani took Adia's

offspring. But he is safe now, as you can see," nodding over in Adia's direction.

"But where is Hakani?" Akule asked again, looking around.

"Hakani is gone. She stepped over the edge to the Great River below, of her own volition," said Awan.

Akule looked from Awan to Acaraho, incredulous.

"It is true; it is as he said," confirmed Acaraho. Adia nodded in assent.

"I doubt she could have survived; I doubt anyone could have. But to be sure, we will send a complement out to search for her," said Acaraho.

Khon'Tor stumbled to his feet. Acaraho stood and helped Adia up. She was shaken up and dirty but appeared to be uninjured. She had shielded Nootau from harm, taking all the impact herself.

"Do you need me to carry you?" Acaraho offered. Adia declined, saying she preferred to go home under her own steam if at all possible. Acaraho walked beside her, steadying her along the way.

When they arrived at Kthama, Acaraho called off the original search for Hakani and started a new one along the riverbank below. If she had fallen into the waters, her body would have been carried far downstream in a matter of moments. As Acaraho had said, he doubted she had survived, but on the off chance that she had, despite her crimes, he would not leave her to die, injured, as Khon'Tor had Adia. And no matter what their standing, each one of the People deserved to have their return to the Great Spirit honored appropriately in the crossing-over ritual.

As the guards dispersed, Acaraho turned to address Khon'Tor, who was sitting slumped to the side on one of the seating benches in the Great Entrance.

'What happens to you from this point on lies in Adia's hands. As it always has. If it had been up to me, I would have fought you to the death long ago, Khon'Tor. It is only her protection that has kept you alive. Whether you live to take another breath rests with her. You would do well to pray for her mercy."

"Regardless of whether Hakani is found alive or not, Khon'Tor—" said Adia, moving forward and looking him squarely in the eye, "—her claim on my offspring is forfeit. And no matter what you, or the High Council, or *anyone* says, I will never relinquish his care to someone else.

"If you do not agree, I will be happy to change my mind and let Acaraho have his way with you right here and now," she said, intentionally creating a play on words for Khon'Tor's benefit.

"Very well," said Khon'Tor.

"The offspring is yours. For what it's worth. I certainly stake no claim on it," he added.

Only a handful knew the High Council had

ordered that Adia could not keep the offspring and raise him herself.

Adia continued, "And as for the Rah-hora? It has always been an unbreakable vow of honor. But I see now that a vow with a male of no honor such as yourself is not binding. I declare the Rah-hora vacated, just as is Hakani's claim on my offspring. As of this moment forward, you have no claim against me either, Khon'Tor."

His one hand still nursing his jaw, Khon'Tor raised his right hand, palm facing outward. Adia approached him and as she had done before, brought her open palm up against his as hard and fast as she could. The resounding *crack* echoed off the high ceilings and bounced along the walls of the Great Chamber.

"It is done," said Khon'Tor.

Then Adia backed away slightly and slapped Khon'Tor again, as hard as she could right across the face, before walking off.

Adia was free. Nootau was returned to her. She was released from the Rah-hora. Even though she believed what she had said, that it was not binding on her, she still felt relieved that it had been sealed. And her decision to defy the High Council was immovable.

Change came hard to the People, and as far as the

High Council was concerned, she would deal with them when the time came. But there was no power on Etera that would make her give up her Nootau —ever.

Change came hard to the People, but not always.

CHAPTER 13

Acaraho helped Adia and a slightly calmer Nootau back to her quarters. Nadiwani ran to meet them the moment they came through the door. Adia handed the offspring over to her care, and the Helper quickly whisked him away and began checking him over for injuries.

This time Acaraho was not asking; he swooped Adia up in his arms as he had wanted to do back on the path. He carried her over to the mat as he had done so many times before, but this time after he laid her down, Acaraho stretched out next to her, drawing her to him and wrapping his arms around her.

Adia did not protest nor resist. She melted into him, and he held her as she cried.

When she calmed down, she looked up at him. This was where, for the longest time, she had wanted to be. With him, like this, only more. She did not want it to end. She wished she could stop time and have this moment last forever.

"How did you find us?" She had to know. It was as if he appeared out of nowhere.

"It was the oddest thing, Adia. I was looking for you, not sure where to go, really panicked, I will admit. And then all of a sudden, the clearest picture of you flashed into my mind. I could see it all. I could see where Hakani was standing with Nootau, I could see you to one side, Khon'Tor to the other. I could see Awan. I knew where you were exactly, and I have no way to explain it." he replied softly.

Adia knew it had to be a message from Urilla Wuti.

"And then, when I was seconds away from killing Khon'Tor, another strange thing happened. Only it was not a vision; it was a feeling of intense love that spread through me. And this time I knew where it was coming from—it was coming from you," he said.

"It was. I was trying to tell you how much I love you. I was trying to reach you before you killed Khon'Tor. Not for his sake, but for yours. Because I knew what he was saying was true—you would regret it later, and it would haunt you for the rest of your life. And I could not bear to have you live with that burden," she said.

Acaraho tucked her head down under his chin, and he pulled her close to him again. However Adia had done that, there was time to talk about it later. Adia surrendered to his embrace, curling her fingers in his thick chest hair and soaking in the warmth of his body pressed against hers.

The High Protector's reserves were depleted. Allowing Khon'Tor to live had taken his last act of self-control. Feeling Adia next to him, his heart began pounding. His breathing slowed and deepened. She looked up into his eyes and placed her hand on his cheek, then ran her fingers gently over his lips. For a moment, time stopped. He became lost in the scent of her in his arms at last. Then Acaraho realized that his body had quickened in response to her attentions and her body pressing against his. He released her and rolled away. He knew there was no way she could not have noticed his bursting desire for her.

Nadiwani's words of warning came back to him, and he had to admit she was right.

Adia put her hand on his shoulder, his back now partially facing her, as he tried to cut off his reaction to her.

"I am sorry, Adia. I thought I could control this. This desire to be with you. But I am not sure now that I can, knowing you feel the same. I do not know how to stop wanting to be with you. I know I must not, but I love you, Adia."

"Acaraho, please. Please do not pull away from me. I do not know what we will do, but I know I cannot live without you. I need you, and I love you too. I do not have the answers, but perhaps we can figure it out, one day at a time. *Together,*" she pleaded with him softly.

Acaraho breathed deep, then finally turned back to her having regained control. He placed his hand on her cheek and lay back down to stay with her a while longer. Within a few moments, her breathing had changed, and she had fallen asleep. Not caring what Nadiwani must be thinking, he let himself relax and fell asleep next to the female he loved, but would never be able to claim.

CHAPTER 14

There were still the matters of Khon'Tor, and Hakani's death. Adia broached the subject with Acaraho the next morning.

"What about Khon'Tor?" she asked, standing next to him in her quarters.

"What happens to Khon'Tor is entirely in your hands, Adia. It is your decision and yours alone," he replied.

Adia had thought long and hard on the subject. As it stood, Khon'Tor's power over her was neutralized. Short of harming her physically, there was nothing he could do any longer. For all intents and purposes, Khon'Tor was Leader only as long as she allowed him to be.

Hakani was gone, no longer a threat to her or Nootau.

As a result, Nootau had come back home to Adia's care. She had the help of Nadiwani and

Kachina, as well as Mapiya and many of the other females.

There was only one thing to be concerned about. The High Council. If they found out she had Nootau back, she would deal with them at that time. Only the High Council members and a few of the People knew about the decision that she might not raise both Nootau and Oh'Dar.

Adia was tired of battles and fighting and strategy and looking over her shoulder. She rubbed her forehead, thinking. She did not want Acaraho to think her weak. She was back where she started in her thoughts about Khon'Tor.

"Acaraho, I am not sure what you will think, but I am inclined to let things be for now," she said. "I learned from my Father that the height of turmoil is not a wise time to make far-reaching decisions. There is time to consider the next course of action. Khon'Tor is unlikely to step out of line any time soon. I expect he will be on his best behavior for quite some time now. At least, he had better be."

"The only ones who know the truth are you and I, and Awan who overhead Hakani before she died. But I trust Awan with my life. He will not speak a word of it. This I know," Acaraho assured her.

"And what I think? What I think, Adia, is that you are the strongest person I have ever known," he said, looking down at her, his eyes crinkled up with kindness.

"Then it is settled. I suppose I should let

Khon'Tor know. And he needs to tell the People about Hakani," she said.

Oh'Dar, playing on the floor with his stacking rocks, caught Adia's attention.

"Acaraho?" she started to ask, watching Oh'Dar playing on the floor and then turning to look at Nootau sleeping in his sling, "Do you think you could manage to mentor two little offspring instead of one?"

"I would be honored to do my best, Adia. If you are asking me, the answer is yes," he said, smiling.

On the other side of the vast expanse of Kthama, Khon'Tor was in a different world; one certainly devoid of either peace or contentment.

As far as the offspring was concerned, it was nothing to him if Adia wanted to go against the High Council and raise it herself. He had never wanted the offspring anyway. And the last thing he wanted was any further involvement of the High Council in the affairs at High Rocks.

But as to where everything else stood, Khon'Tor was not sure what to do. Acaraho now also knew what he had done to Adia and that he had seeded the offspring she bore. Someone was going to have to let the People know Hakani was dead. They could not let it go much longer. And somehow, he had to find out what Adia and Acaraho were going to do about his crimes against Adia—if anything had changed from what she had said before. All the power rested with them now. The strain was nearly unbearable.

He did not have to wait long, as shortly after that, Adia and Acaraho tracked him down to his satellite meeting room.

Acaraho did not deign to knock. He opened the door, and they walked right in. Khon'Tor noticed the lapse in protocol and knew it was intentional; as far as Acaraho was concerned, Khon'Tor was in charge in name only.

Khon'Tor was beyond pretense at the moment. "Say what you have come to say and make it quick," he said, cutting to the chase.

Adia spoke to Khon'Tor directly. "For the sake of the People, until I decide otherwise, I will protect your secrets, Khon'Tor."

"*All* of them," she added, narrowing her eyes slightly. Khon'Tor recognized that she was alluding to his treatment of Hakani.

"You need to make an announcement to the People about your mate. But other than that, if you agree to leave us in peace—Acaraho, Oh'Dar, Nadi-wani, the new offspring, and me—then we will do the same for you. Hopefully, we can all move forward, and peace and calm can return to our people," she finished.

Khon'Tor did not readily admit defeat. But in this case, he had little choice. He had no platform of power left. At this point, he was the Leader in name only. *I am lucky Adia is leaving me that.*

He told them he would call a meeting, and the three of them could address the People together. He said he would let them know when he had arranged it.

Khon'Tor called the assembly for the next morning. As he walked to the Great Chamber, he reflected on the gut instinct which had kept him from announcing that Adia's offspring was to be turned over to Hakani. It was now a detail no one needed to know—and one that would not have brought him favor with the People.

Everyone was in place well ahead of the sounding of the announcement horn. Mapiya was carrying Oh'Dar. Nadiwani had Nootau, who had since returned to his contented self.

As agreed, the three of them, Khon'Tor, Adia, and Acaraho approached the front of the Great Chamber together.

As they walked up to the front, many of the members exchanged smiles. To all appearances, the three Leaders were in harmony with each other.

Khon'Tor stepped to the front and raised his hand as was his usual signal that he was about to speak. An immediate hush fell over the crowd. Only Nootau could be heard cooing softly in Nadiwani's arms.

"Thank you for coming. The last time I addressed you was to announce that Adia was with offspring. Since then, she has delivered a healthy male whom she has named Nootau."

Khon'Tor motioned back to where Nadiwani was holding him. As if on cue, he gave another burble, and the People laughed.

"A new offspring has joined our people, and we have cause for celebration."

Khon'Tor paused before continuing, waiting for heads to turn back his way.

"Unfortunately, on a more serious note, I am sorry to report that my mate, Hakani, has returned to the Great Spirit. Hakani fell to her death near the Falls two days past. I delayed telling you in the hopes that she might be found alive somewhere. But she has not. There was little hope, considering the height of the fall and the depth and speed of the waters below. Hakani was a complicated female; I do not think it unfair to say that. But I hope when you remember her, you will do so kindly. We all have our battles to wage, and sometimes the hardest ones to win are those we wage with ourselves.

"Thank you, that is all," and Khon'Tor raised his

hand again to signal that he was done, then dropped his arm and stepped down.

As Acaraho and Adia started to follow Khon'Tor off the platform at the front of the room, an unidentified voice cried out from the crowd.

"Acaraho. Adia. Please. We have all been through so much. We respect and look up to you both, regardless of what has happened. We have no judgment of you or Adia; we only ask to know. Acaraho, is the offspring yours?"

Adia's jaw dropped. She started to speak, but Acaraho raised his hand, stopping her.

He took a step forward as if shielding Adia and protecting her.

"If you are asking if I claim the offspring named Nootau," he said, then paused to make sure the room was silent, looking across the crowd to be certain he had everyone's attention—though there was little doubt he had.

"I do," he said.

The room burst into immediate chaos. Khon'Tor stopped in his movement through the room and turned and stared incredulously at Acaraho, his eyebrows pressed tightly together in confusion.

Adia's eyes widened and she, too, looked at Acaraho in disbelief.

Then, taking Khon'Tor's cue as his own, Acaraho raised his hand to quiet the crowd, which instantly became dead silent.

"And I claim the Waschini offspring, Oh'Dar, as

well," he stated, looking out over the crowd, letting his even gaze rest on all of them.

Then he lowered his hand, continued walking, and ushered Adia out through the back of the room, on the way gathering Mapiya with Oh'Dar, Kachina, Nadiwani with Nootau, and the rest of their little circle.

The members of the crowd looked at each other in confusion. At first, they thought Acaraho was claiming to be the father of Adia's offspring. Then, when he said he claimed the Waschini offspring as well, they knew that was not what he was saying. In the end, they still did not know with any certainty who the father was; only that Acaraho was officially claiming the father's role in raising the two young males.

Khon'Tor shook his head at Acaraho's strategic genius. If he had to be beaten by someone, he could not have picked a more worthy adversary.

But as for Adia, that was another story. As soon as they were clear of the crowd, she laughed out loud. "By the Great Mother above, Acaraho. I thought you had lost your mind!" she said playfully.

Acaraho just smiled back at her and replied teasingly, "I am glad I can still surprise you from time to time, Healer."

As she had before, Adia found herself walking back to her quarters with her makeshift family. Once again, she had weathered innumerable storms and survived intact. Adia glanced around at Nadiwani, Mapiya, Honovi, Oh'Dar, and little Nootau. Her family was growing.

Adia's faith was slowly seeping back. The Great Mother never promised a life without struggle, but Adia thought she could see her hand in the provision of Urilla Wuti and the Healer's foresight in helping to arrange for Nimida's safety. Any other Healer without Urilla Wuti's special abilities would never have known there was a second offspring. And it could just as easily have been a Healer who would not help her, who would not have protected the secret that there were two. And Acaraho would never have known where to find her and Nootau at the path's edge with the Great River below.

As far as the High Council knew, Hakani and Khon'Tor were raising her offspring. She would cross that bridge if she had to. Her heart was in turmoil because Nimida had been taken away for her own safety. But even with Hakani out of the way, Adia feared for Nimida. Khon'Tor was subdued now—but it could change. And should they find out, the High Council members would never let her keep a third offspring. Her daughter was lost to her either way, and Adia knew it was the most precious gift she could give Nimida—to grow up loved and secure, never at risk of learning the soul-scarring facts of her conception. In anonymity, she would live a normal life.

Adia wondered if she would ever see her daughter again. And if she did, how could she explain sending her away, without having to tell her she had been conceived by an act of hatred from a male who would never claim her as his offspring?

Her thoughts turned to Acaraho, walking beside her. Acaraho had committed to being in her life and those of her two male offspring. The People seemed to have accepted her back into their good graces, and their respect and admiration for Acaraho seemed to be intact, even if they did all suspect he had seeded Adia's offspring.

Like Acaraho, she knew there was a line they could not cross. But could they be strong enough? She and Acaraho had to find a way to be in each other's lives but deny themselves the physical expression of their love for each other. She knew she was asking too much. How could she expect him to be less than a male?

Though silenced for a while, Adia knew the conflict between her and Khon'Tor was not over. But for now, she could focus her attention elsewhere.

As for Oh'Dar, all the hardest challenges still lay ahead for him. What would become of him? He would never be the strongest or the fastest. He would never be able to compete with the other males as a provider. And none of the females would have him, neither those of the People, or the Waschini; she had sentenced him to a life as an Outsider, never to belong to either world. Adia feared Khon'Tor had been right on that count. He was just an offspring now, and his needs were few. He lived protected within a small circle of love. But when he became an adult and struggled to find his place in the world, would he curse her for having saved him?

Only time would tell.

PLEASE READ

Thank you for your interest in my writing. If you enjoyed this book, I would very much appreciate your leaving a review.

Reviews give potential readers an idea of what to expect, and they also provide useful feedback for authors. The feedback you give me, whether positive or not so positive, helps me to work even harder to provide the content you want to read.

If you would like to be notified when the other books in this series are available, or if you would like to join the mailing list, please subscribe to my monthly newsletter on my website at https:// leighrobertsauthor.com/contact

Wrak-Ayya: The Age of Shadows is the first of three series in The Etera Chronicles. The next book in this series is:
Book Three: *Oh'Dar's Quest*

ACKNOWLEDGMENTS

Once again, to my dear husband who managed unwavering support for me in this process.

A special thank you to my beloved brother Richard who has never stopped believing I could accomplish my goals.

To all those of my dogs who did *not* bark incessantly while I was trying to write. (And to those who did— it's okay, I love you all dearly regardless.)

Once again, my incredibly talented (and patient) right hand, Joy Sephton. She is an editor-extraordinaire and, on the entire globe, I could not have found anyone as good.

Made in the USA
Las Vegas, NV
25 September 2023